# HUNTER'S MARK

WENDY SMITH

Edited by LAUREN CLARKE

Cover Design BOOKISH GRAPHICS

Photography by GOLDEN CZERMAK / FURIOUSFOTOG

Cover Model NICK PULOS

*ISBN-13*: 978-1-991303-06-6

❀ Created with Vellum

# DEDICATION

*To the Ops team at VNGS. Miss you guys, and I hope you don't have too much fun without me. <3*

# GLOSSARY

*Moko* - The Māori word for grandchild
Jandals - Flip-flops (thongs in Australia)
Ute - Utility vehicle
Chilly Bin - Insulated box. Designed to keep food cold.
Box of fluffies - Phrase that means 'everything's good'

# 1

## COREY

HE HAS BLUE EYES. They both do. Just like their mother.

I cradle my nephew in my arms, and those big blue eyes stare up at me. Not blinking, just staring. Like my face is the most fascinating thing he's ever seen.

He's six months old. It probably is.

Him and his sister are already permanent fixtures inside my heart. Hooking his fingers into my beard, the little fella pulls my face closer.

The living room in my brother Adam's house might be full of family celebrating the christening of the twins, but for my nephew, I'm the only person in the room.

"What are you doing?" Drew asks.

"Ask your son. He's taking a closer look at Uncle Corey."

Drew shakes his head. "Why on earth would you want to do that, Logan? Daddy's so much better to look at."

I chuckle. "He likes my beard."

Drew sighs. "Well, I don't know if your mum would like me growing a beard, little man."

Logan's eyes widen as he grips me tight.

"I can because I'm not pussy-whipped."

Drew slaps me on the arm. "Don't say that shit around my son."

"What on earth are you two doing?" Hayley walks toward us, Logan's sister, Amelia, in her arms.

"Drew's swearing in front of the baby."

One of her eyebrows rises, and I smirk.

"Just to tell Corey off. Logan will never pick it up," Drew hedges, looking sheepish.

She nods, sighing. "You two are so naughty."

I chuckle. "Say that again? But just me this time."

Shaking her head, she turns away and heads toward the couch and Ginny. Ginny's eyes widen, and I smile at the look of pure joy on her face as she takes Amelia in her arms.

"Well, that's the christening over. I guess there's nothing more to worry about until their twenty-firsts."

I laugh. "That's if they're good." Shifting my focus back to my nephew, I shake my head. "Don't you be like Uncle Corey when you're a teenager. Be good to your mother."

"What about his father?" Drew laughs.

"Oh, you can be naughty for him."

He laughs. "Oh well, give him here. I'm going to take him to see Mum."

"Good thinking." I hand over the baby, but not before pressing a kiss to Logan's forehead and disentangling his fingers from my beard. "See you later, bud."

Mum's face lights up as Drew walks toward her with the

baby. She's so frail now, and even being out at Adam and Lily's is a lot of effort.

When she meets my gaze, I give her a smile. Once she started going downhill, there was no stopping it. I don't know how much longer she's got.

It makes moments like this more precious.

A hand lands on my arm, and I turn. "Have you got a minute? I want to show you something."

I smile. Lily's been my best friend for so long, and if it's something that makes her as happy as her smile would indicate, I want to see. "Of course."

"Come into my bedroom in about five minutes."

I place my hand on my heart. "Are you propositioning me? We're surrounded by family."

She punches my bicep. "No, you dick. Seeing as you're giving me away for the wedding, I want you to see the dress."

"Don't you want to show Hayley and Ginny?"

"They saw it last night. I'm just so proud of it. Made it myself."

I grin. "Did you now? This I have to see. Make sure Adam knows that's why I'm disappearing into your bedroom."

"I already told him. He thinks it's weird that I want to show you, but he loves me so he's fine."

Laughing, I cock my head. "Go on, then. See you in a few minutes."

As soon as she's gone, Adam walks over to me. "Is she going to show you her dress?"

I nod.

"Everyone's seen it but me."

"You're not supposed to see it until the day."

He sighs. "I know, but I can't wait."

I slap him on the back. "Dude, it'll be awesome. You two have waited long enough."

Nodding, he grins. "You're not wrong." The wistful look on his face is so good to see. If anyone deserves to have their happy ending, it's Lily and Adam.

"Anyway, I'm off to your bedroom to hang out with your fiancée. Suffer, little brother."

He laughs. "Go on, then."

Max sits out in the hallway, his dog, Lucky, at his feet. "Hey, bud. What are you doing out here?"

"It's too noisy in there. And everyone just wants to see the babies."

I squat in front of him. "Do you know when I come here, it's to see you?"

"Really?" From the unimpressed expression on his face, I'm not sure if he believes me.

"Every time." I hold out my hand, and he fist-bumps me. "How about next time I'm here, you and me take Lucky for a walk in the bush?"

His eyes widen. "Dad said I'm not allowed back there. Now the fence is up, we have to keep the gate closed in case Rose goes through."

I nod. "Your dad's making sure you guys are safe. But I'm sure he'll be fine if I take you."

Max grins. "That'd be awesome. Thanks, Corey."

"Any time. Give me a few minutes with your mum, and I bet anything I can beat you in *Mario Kart*."

He laughs. "I'll go and set the Switch up in my room."

"You do that."

I watch him run toward his room, Lucky right behind him.

Now to check on Lily.

REACHING Adam and Lily's bedroom door, I knock. "Are you decent?"

"Come in," she calls.

I push open the door, closing it behind me.

What I see takes my breath away.

I have been in love with Lily Parker since I was fifteen years old.

Not that I could ever tell her, or anyone else.

She's only ever had eyes for Adam, and even when he wasn't here, her heart belonged to him.

Even if she didn't know it.

*I did.*

Max was four when I offered her my world. It would have been platonic, but I'd been prepared to give her and Max everything they needed—a roof over their heads, food on the table, and love. I was stupid enough to imagine that one day she'd love me back.

Maybe I should be thankful that she said no.

It doesn't mean she no longer has any effect on me.

Especially when she's standing there in her wedding dress.

My mouth is dry, my palms are sweaty, and she's got this wistful look on her face that I know has got nothing to do with me.

"Well? What do you think?"

I nod. "You look amazing, Lily."

Her mother was a seamstress, and Lily inherited her

skills. I know she's poured hours into this, finding the cream fabric she wanted, stitching it into a figure-hugging, low-cut thing that Adam's going to love.

Her blonde brows knit as she frowns. "Are you sure? You don't seem sure."

I lick my lips. "You'll be the most beautiful bride that's ever been in Copper Creek." My lips twitch as I rethink my words. "Just don't ever tell Hayley I said that."

She laughs. "I don't know why I asked you. I'm never going to know if you're being honest, or just being nice."

"I can't remember ever being dishonest with you." I grasp her arms. "Seriously, just you being there will make Adam the happiest man on the planet."

*Shit.*

I sigh. "I didn't mean that the way it came out."

Last time they were scheduled to be married, Lily never showed up. We didn't know at the time, but her mother had locked her in the basement. Everything fell apart for Adam and Lily after that, and they weren't reunited for a further twelve years.

"It's okay. I know what you mean. It's just … I've waited so long for this, and it's finally here. I don't want to let him down when it comes to any aspect of this wedding."

"There's literally no way you can let him down. You two have been to hell and back, and seriously, doll, all you need is each other."

They've been back together for more than three years now, and it still breaks my heart a little thinking of her getting married to him. I let go of the hope she'd see me a long time ago, and yet it hurts.

At the same time, I'm truly happy for both of them.

I'll be happy to give her away.

---

AFTER DINNER WITH THE FAMILY, I drive home.

I scowl as I pass my neighbours'. That fenced-off community makes me angry every time I see it, and there's no way for me to avoid it on my way home.

Graham Taylor, the senior sergeant at the local community police station, is on my doorstep when I pull up to the house. I jump out of the ute.

"Graham," I say, extending my hand. He's here so often that I view him as a friend now "Always a pleasure."

He smiles. I gave him and the rest of the police department permission to use my property to keep an eye on the community next door ages ago. While I know undercover investigations take a long time, this seems to have gone on forever. They have two guys living in the community, and others who monitor the property basically living in my back yard.

"I thought I'd pop in and give you an update."

Nodding, I unlock my front door and open it. "Come in. I think I can make a coffee."

"You think?"

"Depends on how you take it. If it's black with no sugar, you'll probably be fine."

He follows me through to the living room. "I'd almost given up waiting. I popped down to see how things were going and take the guys some food."

I reach the kitchen and check the jug for water. Filling it,

I set it down and flick the switch. "I just had dinner at Adam's."

"How are they all?"

"Good. It was the twins' christening today. And Adam and Lily are preparing for their wedding. It's still a few months away, but they've waited so long for it. Everything needs to be perfect."

He chuckles. "I'm sure it does. They deserve every happiness."

"It's a bit surreal, you know? It wasn't that long ago that I couldn't imagine Adam being back. Now they're finally getting what they both wanted all those years ago. Max is so excited."

"I doubt it takes much to get Max excited." He grins.

I grab the cups from the cupboard and spoon the coffee into them. "Not really. It'll be eventful, that's for sure."

I pour the water, then give the coffee a quick stir before passing him a mug. "Let's go and sit in the living room."

He nods, following me into the room at the front of the house.

I place my cup on the coffee table and sit. "So, what updates do you have for me? Have you got enough on that bastard yet?"

He sighs, sitting on a chair opposite. "All I can tell you is that we haven't got to the bottom of what's going on, but it's all leading somewhere."

I sigh. "Well, you know you have use of my land for however long it takes."

"We know, and we're grateful. I'm just sorry it's taken so long." He takes a sip of his coffee. "How's Hayley doing?"

I nod. "Yeah, she's good. The twins are on the verge of crawling, so she's about to get really busy."

Graham grimaces. "One child was bad enough."

I laugh. "She loves it. The plan was for her to go back to work, but I think she's enjoying herself too much."

He nods. "It is a shame she left. She was a huge asset to the community."

"Well, nothing and no one can hurt her now." I'll never forget the day one of Graham's guys turned up on my doorstep. He carried my now sister-in-law in his arms— she'd been drugged by the maniac next door. What else goes on behind those walls?

"I just want the guy caught for whatever it is he's doing and put away for a long time where he can't hurt anyone else."

Graham nods. "Me too, Corey. Me too."

## 2

### OWEN

THIS ISN'T the life I signed up for.

It's not the life either Ginny or I planned.

When we decided not to worry about contraception, and to let nature take its course, we thought getting pregnant would be the hard part.

That turned out to be easy.

But after two miscarriages in six months, Ginny's shattered.

The second one happened last night.

There was no work for Ginny or me today, no day care for Ava.

Instead, Ginny, Ava and I are in bed, and I'm facing Ginny, who has Ava snuggled in tight against her. Ava who won't move because even though she doesn't know what's wrong, she knows something bad has happened.

Ginny's eyes flicker open.

"Hey," I say softly.

She gives me a wistful smile. "Hey."

"Are you hungry? I could kill a bacon and egg panini."

"That sounds so good right now."

I reach for her hand. "Let's go and get some alone time before the munchkin wakes up."

Ginny's smile grows, and my heart lights up. I never knew what love was until I had her and Ava in my life. Now, I'm overwhelmed by the feelings I have for both of them.

I tug on my jeans while Ginny puts on a dress. She heads to the kitchen to get out the bacon and eggs while I go through to the bakery to grab some fresh paninis.

"Oh, so his lordship decided to get out of bed, did he?" Mel winks at me.

"Yep. When the stomach grumbles, you can't ignore it."

I reach for the bread. The rolls are still warm, and I take a deep breath. All these years as a baker and I'll never get enough of that smell.

"How's Ginny?"

I shrug. "Alright. We're just going to have breakfast while Ava's still asleep."

"Does she even know what's going on?" I sent Mel a text last night to tell her that I wouldn't be in the kitchen first thing and why. She's one of the few people who knows.

I shake my head. "She just knows Ginny's sad. That's enough for her."

"There's a gingerbread woman over there for her." Mel points to a bench.

I laugh. "You think of everything."

Mel places her hand on her heart. "I live vicariously through you guys. You've shown me what true love is."

Shaking my head, I throw a panini at her, hitting her on the arm.

"What a waste of food. I'm telling my boss on you."

"You do that." I pick up the cookie and another panini, and go back through to the house, chuckling.

Ginny turns as I enter the kitchen. "Everything okay?"

"Everything's fine. Mel made Ava a present."

Ginny laughs. She doesn't even look at what I've got in my hand. "I'm just surprised that girl isn't made of gingerbread. She eats enough of it."

I peck the woman I love on the cheek, and she leans against me. "Go and sit down. I'll cook this up and bring it to you."

"Are you sure?"

"Today is Take Care of Ginny Day."

Her green eyes are so full of love, it takes my breath away. "That seems to be every day with you."

"Always."

---

AFTER BREAKFAST, we take Ava to the park. We're the only people there, though that's hardly surprising since it's the middle of the day.

"What do you want to do first?" I ask.

"The slide." Ava jumps up and down, excited.

"Go on, then."

Ava runs to the slide, and I plant myself on a wooden bench nearby, pulling Ginny down onto my lap.

"What are you doing?" She laughs.

"Loving you. It's the easiest thing to do in the world."

She hooks her arms around my shoulders. "I like it when you say things like that."

I bury my face in her neck. "Then I'll say them every day."

Ginny sighs. "I just wish things had worked out this time."

"So what do we do now?"

She shrugs. "Take a break for a few months? I don't know."

"It might be a good idea. Not permanently. Just while we all recover."

She pushes off my lap and sits next to me. "I don't know if I will recover."

I slip my arm around her. "I'm so sorry, baby."

"If you want someone else, I'll understand."

Squeezing her shoulders, I bury my face in her hair. "There'll never be anyone else for me, Ginny. You know that. It's only ever going to be you, whether we have more children or not."

"Mummyyyyyy!" a child screams.

Ginny's head shoots up. "That's Ava's voice."

She takes off, running toward the playground. Ava limps around the slide, and I see the problem straight away. Her knee's all bloody and raw.

Ginny runs, and Ava walks toward her, wailing and holding her arms out. "Mummyyyy," she calls again.

My heart stops. Ginny drops to her knees in front of Ava and pulls her into her embrace.

I run up behind them, squatting to see my daughter.

"Did you fall, sweet pea?" I ask.

Ava nods, letting out a cry that breaks my heart. "Mummy," she whimpers.

Ginny digs into her pocket, and pulls out a tissue, then wipes Ava's eyes.

"Let's get you home," she says. Ava wraps her arms around Ginny's neck.

"Here, I'll carry you." I open my arms to Ava, but she shakes her head.

"It's okay, Owen. We don't have to walk far."

"Are you sure you're okay?"

"I just want to get Ava home and cleaned up."

I walk behind them back to the car. Ava's resting her head on Ginny's shoulder, her face covered in tears and snot.

When we draw close, I come to a stop. Maybe we didn't start out as a family, but all the breath is sucked from my lungs as I realise I'm watching my daughter and her mother. Biology be damned. In the absence of Ava's real mother, Ginny is it.

Ava knows it too.

It sends a shiver through me.

"Owen?" Ginny reaches the car, and turns, her eyebrows dipping in confusion.

I shake myself out of my stupor. "Sorry."

I reach for the door, stepping out of the way to let Ginny place Ava in the car seat.

"Let's just go home."

---

I SPEND the rest of the afternoon watching.

Watching as Ginny washes Ava's knee and gently places a Band-Aid on it. Watching as they snuggle together on the couch.

I excuse myself to make dinner, and then I wash the dishes while Ginny takes Ava for her bath.

It's after Ava's asleep, when Ginny's in my arms, that I finally bring up what I witnessed. "You didn't even notice, did you?"

Ginny raises her eyes to meet mine. "Notice what?"

"What Ava called you."

For a moment, her face goes blank, and I know the moment it hits her because her lower lip wobbles. "I was so worried about her that I didn't even hear it," she whispers.

Wrapping my arms around her, I close my eyes as she buries her face in my chest. "You're her mother, Gin."

"But, I—"

"Don't fight it. She'll never forget Cara; we'll make sure of it. But *you* are her mother now."

I don't realise she's crying until hot tears soak through my shirt. "Hey, no more tears."

"I never thought that'd she'd … I mean, I guess we have that kind of relationship." She looks up, and I raise my hand, pushing her hair back behind her ear.

"You're the one who makes her breakfast in the morning, takes her to day care, tucks her in at night. You sing to her; you buy her clothing and toys. You're everything to her, Ginny. Just as you're everything to me."

I take a deep breath. "Let's talk to Drew."

She nods. "I thought he might have said something last time we saw them."

"I didn't tell him about the miscarriage. Either of them."

Her eyebrows twitch. "I thought you would have. You two are so close."

I shrug. "I don't tell him everything. And this has been for us to deal with together."

Tears well in her eyes again. I can't bear to see her so up and down. It's hard on those days when she struggles with pain and spends the day in bed being miserable. When she does, I bake for her, bring Ava into bed with her. Anything to bring a smile to her face.

"How'd I ever get lucky enough to find you?"

I smile. "Well, I blame Max."

She chuckles. "He did bring us together."

"That kid has the best timing. It was a pretty difficult period after seeing that accident. You made everything better."

Ginny palms my cheek, and I turn my face to kiss her hand.

"I never thought I'd be settled with one woman and have a family. But here we are: you, me, and Ava." I move my face closer to hers. She gives me a shy smile that sends a shock through me. It's funny how things have changed. A couple of years ago if anyone had asked me if I had plans to settle down, I would have told them they were mad. I liked my lifestyle. It was rare that anyone got hurt.

Cara's death woke me up.

Ginny's arrival gave me life.

"Now, how about we get some sleep? Tomorrow is another day, and it'll be a little better than today."

Ginny nods. "Sounds good. I'm so tired."

"I'll give Drew a call in the morning if you want me to."

"Please," she whispers.

"Anything for you."

I WAIT until Ginny's at work and Ava's at day care the next day.

Drew answers on the first ring.

"What's up?" He sounds so cheerful, and I'm about to bring him down.

I let out a breath. I'm not sure if Ginny's told Hayley about her medical issues, and maybe Drew already knows, but I still feel awkward telling him, even with my woman's permission.

"Well, I need to ask for some medical help."

"Owen?" He switches to a serious tone.

"For Ginny."

"Anything. Tell me what you need."

"She has endometriosis." I'm glad she's not here because the emotion of the past few weeks catches up, and I've got tears in my eyes. It's not that I'm concerned about her seeing me cry, but I'd rather she not deal with the guilt I know she'll feel. "Dude, she's had two miscarriages, and I don't know if she can take anymore."

"When?"

"The first one was a little while after she moved in. We decided to let whatever happened happen, and she got pregnant pretty quickly. She miscarried at six weeks. Then she lost a second one the night before last at seven weeks."

"Shit. How's she holding up?"

*How do you think?* I want to scream at him, but it's not his fault. Ginny's family, and of course he cares about how she's coping.

"Well, we all spent yesterday morning in bed. I convinced

her to take Ava to the park in the afternoon, and we had a family day together."

"Good. She needs all the support she can get. So do you."

"Can you help her?"

He catches his breath. "I would if I could. But you guys are family. I can refer you to a friend of mine, though. He'll do what he can."

"Is he good?"

"Almost as good as me." That smartarse tone is in Drew's voice, and I roll my eyes.

"I think we both know there are no guarantees, and she's been to doctors before we got together, but the difference is that she's got me now, and I'll be there for her no matter what."

"Mate, that's such an important part of this. If you two want to try for a baby, there'll be ups and downs. You have to be a team."

"Ava started calling her Mummy," I blurt out.

"That's wonderful. At least, I'm assuming it is. It goes to show how stable she feels with you two."

"I'm not sure if her timing is good or bad with what's going on."

Drew laughs. "Probably both. When are you guys coming to visit? Taking a break might help."

"I'll talk to Ginny. It'd be good to get away before Ava starts school."

"You know, I'm so proud of you. It's like you grew up. But I guess you had to with the insta-family."

I chuckle. "I could say the same for you. You always were an over-achiever, but twins?"

"They're amazing. I look at them, and I see both Hayley

and me. They're just perfect." He sighs. "Anyway, I need to get some work done. Thanks for letting me know what's been going on. I'll talk to Dion and get you an appointment with him."

"He's the best, right?" When there's silence on the other end, I laugh. "After you, of course."

"I was really wondering where that brotherly love had gone for a moment. He's good. You can trust him to be honest with you."

"Thanks, Drew."

"Anytime, bro. Talk to you again soon."

As I hang up the phone, I think about Ginny again. The pain in her eyes lately has been too much to bear, but I'll be by her side whatever happens.

I can only pray we get the result she needs.

That night, we're about to climb into bed when my phone buzzes on the bedside cabinet. It's a text from Drew.

He's given me the name of a doctor, and a date and time. I guess he's gone ahead and made us an appointment.

"What's that?" Ginny asks.

I show her the phone.

"Is that …?"

"I'm hoping that's our future."

**3**

———————

CONSTANCE

I RAISE my face to greet the sun. It's supposed to rain tonight, but it's nice to enjoy the heat while it's here.

The warmth makes me smile, and I sigh at the unfairness of having to wear a long dress on a day like today. What I wouldn't give to put on a short skirt and let the breeze cool me down. Not to mention getting rid of my socks and boots.

I don't know what the founders of our community were thinking, adopting this garb when the community was formed. It's supposed to make us look uniform because everyone's equal.

As if.

The one man who's far from equal is Ash.

My teenage crush, and now the head of our community, he summoned me about half an hour ago. But like I always did when I was younger, I'm keeping him waiting.

"Constance?"

I turn my head at the sound of Michael's voice. Ash has

two groups that surround him. There's the larger group which Michael belongs to, and Ash's much smaller inner circle. The latter are the ones I try and avoid. Smiling, I say, "Michael."

"What are you doing? Ash is waiting for you."

"I'm enjoying the sun. I don't get out much while looking after Mum."

A smile crosses his lips. "I guess not. But we'd better go."

I sigh. "Okay. Any idea what he wants?"

He shrugs. "Your guess is as good as mine."

"Maybe he's decided to make an honest woman out of me." I grin, knowing that I'm the last person Ash would ever want to marry.

"You? Honest?" He laughs.

"Oi!" I slap him on the arm.

"Seriously, I hope he's not going to be too much of a dick to you." He lowers his voice. "I'm getting worried, Constance. Something's not right with him."

I nod. "Why do you think I've tried to stay off his radar for so long?"

Michael frowns. "That's a really good plan. Be careful."

"Why are you still so close with him? You know what he's like."

He sighs. "I feel safe keeping an eye on him." Flicking a glance to the house and back, an indecisive look crosses his face, like he wants to say something but doesn't know if he should.

"What's going on?"

Michael shakes his head. "Nothing. You'd better get in there."

I stand on my tiptoes and plant a kiss on his cheek. "Yes, boss."

"That's the kind of attitude that's just going to annoy him." Amusement plays on his lips.

"I know. That's why I do it."

---

ASH SITS BEHIND HIS DESK. There's no hint of a smile, like I get from my other friends.

He used to have a sense of humour.

Increasingly, there is nothing.

"Constance, you decided to show up." His tone is dry, but that's nothing new when it comes to me.

I smirk. "You summoned me, oh great leader."

Ash sighs loudly. "I've made a decision about your marriage."

My heart sinks. For so long I thought I've tried to avoid this day, but I knew it couldn't be put off forever. While I've helped nurse my ill mother, I've kept off Ash's radar. But I'm twenty-two, and I'm too old now for his little harem group.

Who will it be? The men who have joined us most recently, Jared and Kane, are probably the closest to my age. It'd be unusual to be married to someone so soon after their arrival, but Ash is unpredictable.

"But first, there's something you need to do for me."

My mouth goes dry. There's always something Ash wants. He was always like that growing up, even before his father died. Ash was the one who got dirt on as many people as he could, so when he took over there were no questions about him taking control so young.

"I've got an associate coming to discuss business in a few days. I need you to entertain him for the night."

My heart sinks. "Me?"

Ash turns on that charming smile that just makes my stomach ache. I know what's behind it, and I don't want to know what's coming.

"Anderson's already had a couple of my girls, but he's intrigued by the idea of someone with no experience. You were the obvious choice."

I swallow hard. He wants me to prostitute myself for him. "Ash, I can't—"

"You can, and you will. He's a very important man who will fund this community for a long time to come. You'll be married to John Parsons the following day when my associate is gone."

*John Parsons.*

Panic grips me, and I hold onto the arms of the chair I'm in so tightly that my knuckles turn white. "He's as old as my father."

"I thought someone with a lot of experience would be a good match for you. Besides, he's happy to accept you after you do my little job for me."

This is payback. I'm sure of it. When we were teenagers, Ash urged me to speak to my father about a future match between us. He was eighteen to my thirteen at the time, and although I was young and impressionable, I knew I wasn't ready for anything serious. I refused, and his father laughed him off when he suggested it. Ash stopped speaking to me after that. He blamed me.

"I won't do it. Any of it."

He leans across the table. "You always were argumentative. I haven't known what to do with you until now, but it seems like I solve a whole lot of problems this way."

I narrow my eyes. "What kind of problems?"

"You, mostly." He smiles. "John's known for keeping tight control of his women, and you're way too mouthy. You always have been."

"There was a time when you didn't think that."

His expression straightens. I'm grasping at straws, but if I can take him back to when he had feelings for me, maybe …

"You ruined that," he says softly. "We could have been married with children, but you didn't choose me."

"I was a child. I'm a woman now. And maybe I made a mistake."

His blue eyes flash with … is it regret? "Things are different now, Constance."

"But why do they have to be?" I have to think fast. "I always thought you'd come for me when your father died."

He steels his gaze. "We both know *that* would never have happened. Why would I want you when I could have anyone?"

Despite my fear, the slight irritates me. "I don't know what I ever saw in you."

His eyebrows rise.

"You were everything to me, and then you were nothing. You walked away from us. It was never the other way around." My tone is hurt. Even though I haven't wanted him for years, his words still sting.

For a moment, I hold my breath as he seems to take in what I'm saying. His expression turns thoughtful and sad. "Don't try and rewrite our history. You made the choice that stopped us from being together."

I let out a sigh. "I'm sorry, Ash. I hope one day you'll forgive me."

He gets up from behind his desk, and my skin crawls at the thought of him touching me. I take a deep breath and wait.

But he goes past me and hangs his head out the door. "Scott, can you get Doctor Jackson in here?"

My heart seizes. Doctor Jackson is not known for having any real medical knowledge. After Julia's issues giving birth, Ash brought someone in to live here who doubles as the community doctor. But I doubt he has any real qualifications. He knew nothing of my mother's illness.

And multiple sclerosis isn't exactly rare.

"All my girls have the contraceptive injection until I decide it's time for them to become pregnant. It's your turn. I don't want you having a kid to Anderson."

I roll my eyes. "Really? I thought it would give you a huge ego boost to have a bunch of little Ashes running around."

The words are out of my mouth before I can stop them.

Pain races through my scalp and down my neck as he grips my hair. "You just can't help it, can you?"

There's no point in backing down now. "You always did bring out my sarcastic side." Tears prick my eyes. I don't want him anymore, but I still mourn the love that could never be. "And you used to laugh at it. You know, back when you weren't the egotistical control freak you are now."

Behind me, the door opens.

Ash holds me in place while his 'doctor' tries to roll up the long sleeve of my dress. I slap him, but Ash uses his free hand to grab hold of my arm. He's too strong, and I try to fight, but my sleeve goes up anyway.

"She needs to stay still."

"No," I cry out. This isn't even about contraception. It's about Ash proving he's more powerful than I am.

The needle slides into my arm, and tears roll down my cheeks as Ash finally loosens his grip.

"What the hell is wrong with you?" I glare at Ash.

"It's time you realised who's in charge. I kept you out of my way for a long time, but now it's time to repay me for what you did. You can tell people about your match, but our other business is between you and me. Tell anyone, and you put your parents at risk."

I swallow down more tears. "I didn't do anything to deserve this."

His tone softens. "That is the problem, Constance. You didn't do anything."

———

WHEN HE LETS ME GO, I storm out of the house, slamming the door on my way out.

"Constance?" Scott Abernathy gives me a curious look. He's another one of Ash's hangers on, one of his inner circle, and someone I've known since childhood. He stands in front of me, blocking my path.

"Get out of my way."

"Woah. What's going on? You look upset."

I swallow. "You've got your beautiful young wife at home that Ash picked out for you. Right?"

He nods, confusion clouding his eyes.

"I'm being given to a violent old man. Please, tell me why I wouldn't be upset."

I can see the internal fight going on inside him. He's so far up Ash's arse that Ash could burn this whole place to the ground and Scott would swear it caught fire by itself.

"Who?"

"John Parsons."

He blanches. We've all seen the damage that man has inflicted on his previous partners. "Ash must have had a reason."

"You mean apart from being vindictive and cruel?" I push past him, marching toward my parents' small house.

"Constance."

I roll my eyes.

"What's wrong?" Michael runs after me, grabbing me by the arm, the arm that was just injected. *Ouch.* I tug it away, wincing. "What the fuck did he do to you?"

"He's chosen my partner." I sniff. "And worse. So much worse."

His dark eyes search mine, and we both know there's nothing either of us can do about it. Something happened about two years ago that left this place on a tighter lockdown than ever before.

People used to come and go at one point. If they chose not to be here, they went with everyone's blessing. If they returned, they were welcomed back with open arms.

Now, no one leaves.

The only person who's left this place in the past couple of years was Julia when she had Andrew. And even that was a frantic rush in the night.

I was sad when she came back.

This is no place for a child.

Michael grabs my arm again, disrupting my thoughts. "Worse? Con, tell me what's going on."

I close my eyes, the urge to cry overwhelming. My tears ignore my wishes and roll down my cheeks anyway. "I can't tell you."

"Why not?"

I open my eyes again and look upon the face of a man I've known all my life. I still can't trust that he won't run back to Ash if I tell. "He'll hurt my family if I do."

A look of agony crosses Michael's face. "He threatened them?"

I nod. "I shouldn't even have told you that."

Wiping my cheeks with my sleeve, I turn. "I have to go home."

"Constance, who did he pick?"

"John Parsons." The words are a whisper on my lips. I can't look at Michael for fear of seeing the pity I'm sure is in his eyes.

"I'll talk to him."

"And put yourself at risk?" I turn back. "Ash is a dangerous man."

"So is John Parsons."

I nod.

"Somehow, we need to get you out of here. Go home. I'll do what I can."

I swallow. "Be careful."

He nods. "We all need to be careful."

"Don't say anything to Scott, either. He says Ash must have a reason for picking John."

"Scott's a fool." He licks his lips. "So is Ash."

"You shouldn't say that too loudly."

He shrugs. "I'll do what I can to help."

That's all I can ask for.

---

IT'S JUST Mum at home when I get there.

Dad will be out somewhere on the farm or tending plants in the greenhouse. He might be sixty-five, but he's still physically active every day. Even more so than I am.

I flop on the couch beside my mother, rubbing my arm.

"What's wrong?" she asks.

"Ash made a decision about who to match me with."

She smiles. "It's about time." Her smile falters. "As long as it's not in that house with all those other women."

"It's worse than that."

She scans my expression. "Who?"

"John Parsons."

She raises her hand to her mouth. "No."

Tears well in my mother's eyes. This isn't the future she wanted for me. She and Dad were barely out of their teens when they moved here together, and just when they thought that they'd never have children, I was a menopause baby.

It means I spend my days taking care of my mother who's not only elderly but has a chronic illness. And I do it gladly because I know how much my parents love me.

"He can't," Mum says.

"He has."

Her expression tightens. "Wait till your father hears about this."

"What's he going to do, Mum? He's no match for Ash."

"I know, but—"

"John Parsons will kill me."

His first wife was my mother's friend. Over time John seemed to care less about the bruises she sported. In the end she appeared to take her own life, but my parents never believed that.

What goes on behind closed doors stays behind closed doors in this community. It wasn't until I was an adult that I realised that. Ash isn't the only monster here.

She swallows hard, and nods. "It won't happen quickly, but I agree. He will."

"I think that's why Ash chose him. To make me suffer."

"Oh, Constance. Ash cared so much for you."

"Cared, Mum. Past tense. That was a long time ago."

She sighs. "I still thought …"

We both turn at the click of the door, and my heart swells at the sight of my father. He'll know what to do. Won't he?

"Hi, love." Dad bends to kiss Mum's cheek and smiles at me. "What an afternoon. We got all the seedlings transplanted into the field, and they'll get a good drink of that rain when it comes tonight."

I love these two with all of my heart. My life has been dedicated to looking after my mother, and now I can't even make her proud of my future.

"Constance has some news," she says quietly.

"Yes?" He looks up at me with so much hope in his eyes that it makes me want to cry. No doubt he'll know I was summoned to see Ash, but he clearly has no idea about the outcome of that visit.

"Ash made a decision about who to match me with."

A worried expression crosses his face. He knows now

that something is wrong. I can see it, and I don't want to hurt him by telling him. But I have to. "It's John Parsons, Dad."

His worry turns to fury, and he stares at me. "That can't be."

"It is."

"He shouldn't even be living in this community. That man is not one of us—hasn't been for years. I'll talk to Ash. Tell him how stupid he's being. He can't expect my little girl to go through with this."

I swallow. "Well, he does." I can't even bring myself to tell him anything else. Dad doesn't need the stress.

"Constance, I'll take care of it."

"It's too late."

He sits on the couch beside me and pulls me into his arms. God, how I used to feel safe being with my father. Ash's father and mine knew each other since they were children. This used to be a happy community, but now it feels fractured and weary. How can I tell my dad that I don't feel safe here anymore?

"We need to work out what to do. That man is not getting his hands on you."

Tears roll down my cheeks as my father rocks me.

I hate this life.

I hate Ash Harris.

***

I COOK DINNER, but my stomach is so wound up I can't eat a bite of it. I put my plate in the fridge and sit on the chair in the living room.

When Mum and Dad have finished, they join me. Dad frowns. "You have to eat *something*, Constance."

A knock sounds at the door. I look up, my heart in my throat as my father stands up from the couch and opens it.

"Julia?" I say as she steps into the room.

She gives me a strained smile. "Michael sent me. He's so worried about you."

I shake my head. "What's there to worry about?"

Julia takes my hands in hers. "Did you tell your parents?"

I nod.

"You might be good at putting up a front, but no one in their right mind would want to be John's wife."

I squeeze her hands. "Let's talk in the dining room."

I don't want Mum and Dad to hear this.

Swallowing hard, I meet her gaze. "There's something else he wants me to do."

"What?"

I shoot a glance at Dad and lower my voice. "Entertain one of his business associates for the night."

Her jaw drops; she releases my hands. My hands drop to my sides. "I thought …" She stops before she finishes the sentence.

"You thought what?"

"There's this guy who Ash is doing some business with. I'm not sure who he is or what that business is. But he's already had two of Ash's girls spend the night with him." She grimaces. "I was hoping that was all he wanted."

I take a deep breath. "Well, it's my turn. And if I don't do everything he wants me to do, he'll hurt my parents."

She shakes her head. "He'd never hurt your parents. He might be a sociopath, but he loved you once."

"He has a funny way of showing it."

She nods. "He's nuts."

"I don't know what to do."

"Run."

Dad steps up behind her and nods. "She's right, Constance."

"What do you mean?" I ask.

"I mean, there's a gap in the fence about halfway down the maize field. Get out, Constance. Save yourself from whatever Ash has planned for you," Julia says.

I sit up, but my heart beats so fast I feel as if I'm going to pass out. "Where am I going to go?"

"If you get through that fence, someone will help you. I can't tell you anything other than that."

Dad licks his lips. "You need to get out of here."

"Dad—"

He shakes his head. "Don't argue. Ash is trying to show he can control all of us with this latest move, but I won't let him. John's not a nice man. I'm not going to let you be hurt by him."

Tears prick my eyes. I want to run, but terror fills my heart. "What if I get caught?"

Dad's face drops. "You have to take the risk. I know you can do it. You were always the tough one."

I stand, wrapping my arms around his waist. "Can't we just leave together?"

"Your mum and I … Starting again is a lot to ask of us, and I think we need to leave too, but I need time to plan." He holds me back, scanning my expression. "Knowing you're safe is what's important to me right now."

"But you two …"

"We can't go out the same way as you. We'll never get your mother's wheelchair through that field. And we're fine."

"There's no way of knowing how fine you'll be when Ash finds out I'm gone."

He gives me a small smile. "That's a risk I'm willing to take."

I look over at Mum, and she nods. "Your father's right."

The last time I left our community was when I used to visit the cove as a child. It's been so long since then.

I swallow down my fear.

It's the least I can do for my parents.

"Michael will be here soon. It'll be dark by then, and most people will be in the food hall. Someone will help you on the other side," Julia says. "Don't worry about taking anything with you, it'll just slow you down. We haven't got a message out yet, but I promise you, you won't be alone."

That doesn't help the butterflies in my stomach.

MICHAEL'S there on the dot of eight, just as Julia promised he would be. On the worst day of my life, I've found support in so many places. I'll never be able to express my gratitude.

"I can't stay out long, but I'll take you to the edge of the maize field. All you'll need to do is walk down the fence line until you find where it's broken."

I nod. "Thank you."

"No. Thank you. I've been concerned for a while now, but I wasn't sure what to think. Today has opened my eyes."

"It's done that for all of us," Dad says. "Thank you, Michael. It can't be easy. I know you're close with Ash."

"Not as close as I used to be. I don't know what's going through his head."

"Nothing good." Dad gives me a small smile, and I wrap my arms around his waist. He strokes my hair. "Be safe, sweetheart."

He plants a kiss on my hair and lets go of me. I turn back to Mum. Crossing the room, I lean over and hug her tight.

"Love you, Constance. I'm sure we'll all be together again soon," she whispers.

"I hope so."

Michael clears his throat. "We need to get going. There's a movie on in the hall, and Ash is in there so we'll have to be quick."

I nod.

Leaving is the hardest thing I've ever done. I spent my life in this house, and I always thought when I left it would be to join my husband in our own home or the communal living area.

Instead, I'm running away to save my life.

Michael leads me across the property. We pass the big house where Ash lives. It's dark and silent. No doubt his little harem is with him in the common room.

It's a long walk to the maize field. It's on the right-hand side of the property and there are fields between the house and it.

"Have you been through this gap?" I ask.

Michael shakes his head. "No. I didn't know about it until today. Julia knows I've doubted Ash for a while." He chuckles. "She's turned into quite the little spy."

"I'm grateful to you for doing this."

He lets out a loud breath. It's dark, but there's enough

moonlight for me to see, and the air rises from his lips. "I'm not about to let anything bad happen to you."

We reach the edge of the field. "Here's where I have to leave you. I need to get back quickly so no one misses me," Michael says.

I grasp one of his hands, tears welling in my eyes. "Please take good care of my parents."

"I'll do everything in my power to protect them." He takes a breath. "Ash is up to something, and I don't know what it is. But I'm going to find out. Then you can come home."

I throw my arms around his shoulders, brushing my lips on his cheek. "Thank you. Please stay safe. If anything happened to you and Ingrid …"

"My wife comes first. I'll do what it takes to protect her."

Nodding, I let go of him, patting him on the chest.

He smiles. "Go."

I follow the fence, feeling my way down it. I don't know how far halfway is, but it seems like I walk for a long time.

The heavens open, and the rain we've been expecting all day buckets down.

It doesn't take long for my boots to be weighed down by mud, the soil full of water. I hoist my dress up, but it's no use.

Something lands on my face, and I drop my dress to brush it off. I hate insects, especially flying ones, and I'm almost glad for the dark. At least I can't see what it was.

*I want to go home to Mum and Dad.*

I can't.

Tears roll down my cheeks. I feel like I've been walking forever, but the fence gives no sign of the promised gap.

I jump when a loud crack of thunder sounds overhead.

This is just what I need. I'm so torn about whether to turn around or not, but I can't give up. I must be so close.

Reaching to feel the fence, my hand falls into nothing, and I catch my breath. There's just enough room to squeeze through. I slip to the other side before bending, my hands on my knees.

I did it.

I'm safe.

I look up. Where to now? I guess I follow the fence line back the other way until I find the road. And then what?

I have no money. No food. Nothing but the clothing I'm wearing.

Ash will find me. He'll find me and he'll kill me.

*What have I done?*

**4**

———————

COREY

I SHAKE my head when the thunder claps.

The air's had that heaviness about it all day, and the smell of rain has been hanging around for hours. But I was beginning to think it would clear.

The sun set about an hour ago, and it's time for me to head home.

Working away from here, I tend to neglect my own back yard. And I love just walking through the bush, seeing what's appeared since I last looked. I wouldn't have things any other way.

I hear her before I see her—the quickened breathing, the gasps that come as the rain hits. They give her away.

One of the reasons I'm so good at what I do is that I have such a keen sense of hearing. She's near the little hideout the cops put on my property, but I catch them unawares every time I come out here. She could walk right next to them and they'd miss her.

Not me.

Enough moonlight peeps through the trees for me to see her. She's standing beside the fence, looking around.

From the look of that long, grey, drab dress, she's from next door. And from her position along the fence, she's come through the gap the police made to give their guys an easy escape route.

She shivers.

"Are you okay?" I ask.

A clap of thunder sounds overhead, and she jumps, placing her hand over her heart as if calming herself.

"I don't know." She gasps again. The rain is so cold, and if I wasn't wearing a heavy jacket, I'd be doing the same thing.

"Let's get you out of the rain. You must be freezing." I slip out of my jacket, and wrap it around her.

She fixes her gaze on me. "Thank you." She speaks so quietly, I barely hear her. I need to get her in the house so I can make sure she's really okay.

"This way." I set off, turning after a few steps.

She hasn't moved.

"Come on." I beckon her forward, but she just stares.

"I don't … I don't know you."

"Does that matter right now?"

Another clap of thunder sounds, and I walk back to take hold of her hand to try and pull her toward the house. She curls her fingers before I can grab her hand, presumably to stop me.

"We need to get inside. Come on."

Her eyes widen. "You want me to go inside your house with you?"

"It's better than being struck by lightning."

She scrunches up her nose. "The odds of that are astro-nomical."

I huff. "Look. They might be a million to one, but—"

"About two hundred and eighty thousand to one, actually."

*Is she for real?*

Shrugging, I laugh. "What's a few hundred thousand between friends?"

I take a deep breath. "I'm assuming that you came through that fence for a reason, and I don't see you going back. You're safe now, and I don't know about you, but I'm over being out in this rain."

She takes a tentative step forward. If we move this slowly, we might reach my house by morning.

"Oh, screw it."

She shrieks as I grab her by the legs, throwing her over my shoulder.

"Put me down!"

"If you won't walk, I'll carry you."

She hammers on my back with her fists, and I roll my eyes.

"Put me down," she says again.

"I will when we're out of this rain."

My long strides make short work of the walk. The rain lashes the trees, but I know the path well enough to keep some shelter above us.

Reaching the back deck, I walk up the steps and to the back door. She stops wriggling as I turn the handle, and push, stepping into the kitchen.

She glares at me as I drop her to her feet, and her hands go straight to her hips. "You didn't need to do that."

"If I wanted to get inside tonight, I did. I wasn't about to leave you there."

"I'm fine."

I sigh. "You came through that fence in the pouring rain, and then just stood there. Where were you going? This is the only place you'll get shelter for miles unless you want to go back."

She shakes her head. "I'm not going back."

I run my gaze over her. She's soaked and must be frozen to the bone. It's autumn and while the days are still pretty warm, the nights are cold.

Her dress drips on the floor, leaving a puddle where she's standing.

"I'll light the fire. You can have a shower and warm up. We just need to get you out of those wet clothes."

Her grey eyes widen, and I give her what I hope is a kind smile.

"I'll find you something to wear in the meantime. That dress is soaked, and you'll end up with pneumonia or something."

"I'm sure I'll be fine." She straightens up, and I take a good, long look at her.

Her hair is the colour of honey, tied up into a neat bun. Her eyes are the colour of her dress, and despite her shivering, there's a sense of pride coming off her. She doesn't like that I've brought her here.

"Don't be stupid. You need to get dry. I'll throw that dress of yours in the dryer, or you can dry it in front of the fire, but it's too wet for you to stay in."

Her chest rises and falls as her indignation fills the room. "Do you have any suitable clothes for me to wear?"

I shrug. "I don't have any women's clothing, if that's what you're asking. But I do have shirts that'll be more like a dress on you."

Indecision crosses her face. For all she knows, she could have leapt from the frying pan into the fire. "Look. If you were trying to get away from Ash, you're safe."

Her eyes grow wide. "You know Ash?"

"Unfortunately."

Her shoulders slump, and tears form in her eyes. "Thank you," she whispers.

"It's no problem. Let's get you changed and then we can settle in for the night. The weather's only going to get worse out there."

A clap of thunder overhead leaves us both looking toward the ceiling. I'm the one who looks back down first. She's quite tall, probably at least five-foot nine, and she has the most incredibly graceful neck. I can't help but look. I'm a bit of a neck man.

*No. You can't do that. Not with her.*

Her gaze drops back to meet mine. "I couldn't wait."

"I understand."

"No. You really don't."

I nod. "I guess I don't. I'll go and find some shirts and you can pick one. Take off your shoes and leave them by the door. Bathroom's through to the living room and up the hallway. First on the left."

"Thank you."

I lick my lips. "I mean it when I say you're safe here. If Ash ever came onto my property, he'd be biting off more than he could chew."

Her expression becomes a mix of relief and fear. It's like she's not sure which to feel.

Turning, I get halfway up the hallway before I realise I don't even know her name. Does it matter right now?

I pull open my drawers and pull out a few shirts. There are a couple of button-down flannel shirts I usually wear when I'm hunting. They're soft and warm, and she might be tall, but these will probably be down to her knees.

I also grab a couple of T-shirts. They'll be a similar length, and the flannel's probably better, but at least this way she has a choice. I need to make sure she's comfortable while I work out what to do with her.

The bathroom door's open, and she's standing in the centre of the room, looking around. When I built the house, the one thing I wanted was a decent bathroom. There's nothing better after a few days of sleeping rough than to have a hot bath. The tub is huge. So is the shower.

"Here you go. Hopefully there's something there that suits for the night. Have a shower if you want. There's plenty of hot water. The towels are in the cupboard, and I'll grab your dress when you've finished and dry it."

She licks her lips. "It needs a wash first. I'll take care of it."

I look down when she raises a foot. The hem of her skirt is caked with mud.

I nod. "That's fine. I can throw it in the washing machine. I'll leave you to it."

With a stiff nod, she turns away. I take that as my cue to leave, closing the door behind me.

It won't take long for the fire to heat the room—it never does. When this place was built, I made sure it had all of the creature comforts, given how isolated it is. It's fully insulated, and cosy in the winter when the fire's lit.

I'm lost in thought as I stare into the flames. Who is she, and why did she run? What could Ash have done for her to be so desperate to leave that she was out there in the rain?

As much as I want to know the answers, she needs to feel comfortable sharing them with me first. I'm not about to interrogate her.

"I didn't know where to put my dress, so it's hung over the towel rail."

Turning at the sound of her voice, I'm greeted by the sight of this very attractive woman dressed in my shirt. She's chosen one of the flannel ones. It's soft and long, and it comes to around halfway down her thighs. Without thinking about it, my eyebrows creep up. "I'll grab it in a minute and put it in the washing machine."

She nods. "Thank you."

"Come over here and get warm." I point to the big chair near the fireplace.

She lets out a little sigh as she sits. "Thank you."

"You're welcome. I'm Corey, by the way."

I'm rewarded with a smile. "Constance."

"That's uhh, kind of an old-fashioned name."

One of her eyebrows creeps up. "My parents are pretty old-fashioned."

"Nothing to do with you coming from some weirdo cult?" I chuckle.

The smile disappears.

"Sorry. That wasn't very nice."

She shrugs. "It probably seems that way since Ash took over."

"To be honest, it was pretty weird before that happened too. But that fence doesn't help, and he hurt someone close to me a while ago. So, I'm not an Ash fan."

She lets out a sigh. "Believe me, neither am I. Most of the people there are good, but not him."

"Are you hurt? Injured?" I ask.

Shaking her head, she gives me a tight smile. "I'm fine, thanks to you."

"I'm sorry for carrying you in. It was very caveman-ish of me."

"Is caveman-ish a word?" She laughs.

"It is now."

Her grey eyes show her amusement. It's better than the hands-on-hips annoyed woman from earlier.

"Are you hungry? I need to make myself something to eat, and a big cup of coffee."

"Coffee sounds good."

"I hope you don't mind not having milk and sugar. I'm out."

She nods. "I usually take them, but I'm fine. The coffee will warm me up."

"I'll be right back."

By the time I return with her coffee, she's lying across the chair, her head on the arm. Her eyes are closed, and her breathing's slow. I have a vague idea of where the buildings are next door from before the fence went up, and it's a decent hike for her. I don't know how far she had to run, and by the looks of her dress and boots, she had to walk in the mud. It would have been a long journey just to reach my place, and she must be exhausted.

For a moment, I watch her sleep. I don't know her, but I

want desperately to protect her. Maybe it's because I'm still so frustrated over the crap Ash tried to pull on Hayley. Since the day that cop turned up on my doorstep with her drugged out of her brain, I've been so angry.

I've been told patience is a virtue, but I'm all out of patience.

There's no way Ash is getting near Constance again.

I'll do whatever it takes to keep her safe.

Picking up a blanket from the back of the couch, I drape it over her. She'll be warm out here as the fire dies down, and I can move her into the spare room tomorrow if she needs to stay.

And she can stay as long as she needs.

I won't let Ash get hold of her.

# 5

## CONSTANCE

I RAISE my hand to my neck and groan.

I've obviously slept with my head on a funny angle. When I raise my head, my neck cramps, and I …

*Wait.*

The blur of last night comes back to me in a rush. *Running, my feet sticking in the mud, the rain drenching me.*

And *that* man.

It's early. There's a morning chill in the air, and I pull the blanket tight around me. I'm in a big chair near a fireplace that's long since burned out.

Relief floods through me. I got away.

I train my gaze around the room. There's a dining table in one corner, and the kitchen is on the other side of the benchtop next to the table. A large leather couch faces the biggest television I've ever seen. Not that that'd be hard.

Ash had all the fancy things in the main house. My parents' needs were basic. I spent so much time with my nose buried in books while growing up, only seeing the odd movie when spending time with other children.

I blush at the memory of what happened last night and look down at my attire. I'm dressed in a long, checked flannel shirt. It's soft and warm but knowing it's Corey's brings a warmth to my cheeks.

Corey. That is his name.

"Good morning."

I look up to see him walking toward me.

The man's beautiful. There's no other way for me to describe him. He's tall, at least six-foot six, and solidly built. His eyes are dark and warm, and even with his thick beard, there's no hiding how genuine his smile is.

"Morning."

"I hope you were comfortable last night. When you fell asleep, I didn't want to move you. Is there anyone you need to call? I can take you wherever you need to go."

I swallow hard, shaking my head. "No one. I was told there would be someone on the other side of the fence who could help me."

His eyebrows rise. "No one was waiting. If I hadn't been out there …"

"I'm glad you were. I don't know what I would have done if you hadn't shown up."

He smiles. "Well, if you need to stay here for a while, there's a spare room you can use. I'm around a lot of the time. I don't have a regular job, and I work at night here and there."

His kindness makes me want to cry. "I'd appreciate having somewhere to stay. Until I work out what to do next. It seems things weren't as planned as I thought they were."

Corey nods. "Of course. Stay as long as you need."

"Thanks."

"Want some breakfast?"

My stomach grumbles as if on cue.

His lips twist. "I'll take that as a yes. Toast? Or do you want a cooked breakfast?"

"Whatever you're making. And coffee. I think you were making one last night when I fell asleep."

He laughs. "You were out like a light. I came back to find you passed out in the chair."

I rub my neck and yawn. "I can't even remember falling asleep."

"I went to make coffee and you were asleep by the time I got back. You must have been exhausted."

I pinch my forehead. "I was. I just had to get out of there."

He nods. "I figured, given the weather. Like I said, take as long as you need. It'll be good to have some company for a while."

As he walks toward the kitchen, I stretch and take in more of my surroundings. There's a large bookcase by the dining table, and I smile at the sight of its full shelves. When I was a child, I read everything I could get my hands on. But the supply of books dried up over the years.

"Help yourself to anything you need," Corey calls.

I make my way to the bookcase, running my finger across the spines of the books.

"There are more books in the spare room where you'll be sleeping."

"Really? I think I could get lost for weeks in these."

He chuckles. "There are some boxes in the garage, too. I

got as far as putting up the two bookcases and then ran out of steam."

"I think I died and went to heaven."

The smell of bacon fills the air, and I take a deep breath. "That smells so good."

"Hope you're hungry. There's plenty of food."

"Starved. I felt like I was walking forever last night."

He turns to look at me and nods. "I bet. Breakfast's ready. Want it in the living room, or up at the table?"

"I can sit at the table." I smile.

He nods. "I'll have this done in a minute. I'm pretty hopeless when it comes to groceries, but you caught me at a good time."

"Thank you."

He smiles. "You're welcome."

My heart skips as I sit at the table. Last night was awful, but I seem to have landed on my feet.

Corey places a plate in front of me full of scrambled eggs, bacon, and toast. My stomach grumbles at the sight of it.

"I haven't eaten since lunch yesterday," I say. "I was a bit wound up last night."

He looks up from the bench he's returned to. "I'm sure it was all a bit crazy."

*You don't know the half of it.*

"Pretty crazy."

Corey nods toward my plate. "Don't wait for me. Dig in. I'll just make this coffee and I'll be there."

"Thank you."

I close my eyes at the first bite. This is so relaxing, and I feel a little guilty that I'm not doing more to help.

"Good?"

"Amazing."

He grins as he sits down, sliding a cup of coffee in front of me. I take a sip.

"Also amazing." I place it back down and pick up my knife and fork.

Corey cuts a piece of toast and piles scrambled eggs on it. "So, tell me about where you came from."

I shrug. "I think you probably know a lot of it. We live mostly off the land and keep to ourselves. Although it's become increasingly isolated the past few years."

He nods. "Since the fence went up."

"I still don't know how Ash talked people into that. It scared the hell out of me."

"Why didn't you leave, then?"

I meet his curious stare. "My parents. They can't leave."

He reaches across the table and places his hand on mine. The contact doesn't scare me like I thought it might, but is he going to want something in exchange for me staying here? "I'm sorry. It must be hard being without them now."

I nod, lifting my hand to cut a slice of bacon. "My dad works in the greenhouses, but my mum is chronically ill. I help care for her."

I'm not sure what I've said, but something seems to have struck a nerve. Corey puts down his fork.

"Did I say something wrong?"

He shakes his head. "No. My mother's terminally ill. My dad cares for her, but I go and see them at least once a week and take them meat if I've been hunting."

"I'm so sorry."

He shrugs. "Sometimes you can't help the shitty things

life throws at you." Picking up his fork, he takes another bite of his food. "So, what made you decide to leave them now?"

Should I tell him? I don't even know this man.

But something about him—those caring dark eyes, the calm and gentle way he moves—makes me trust him. Feel I can open up to him.

"I think my parents will leave if I can find a way. But I had to get out now. Ash chose someone about the same age as my father to be my husband."

Corey sucks in a breath, coughing as his food seems to catch in his throat. I leap up, rounding the table.

*Thud.*

I smack him between the shoulder blades, just the way my father taught me.

He laughs. *Laughs.*

"What's so funny?"

"It wasn't that bad. Just a bit of food that went down the wrong way."

My cheeks burn. "Sorry."

Corey pats my arm. "It's okay. I appreciate you looking out for me." He frowns as I take my seat again. "I guess that whole 'arranged marriage' thing was why you left?"

"Mostly."

"And nothing was planned, so you had nowhere to go."

I nod.

"I guessed that before you told me because you showed up with nothing but the clothes you were wearing. Really awful clothes too, by the way. And you're still here."

I sigh. "I hate that dress."

"Why wear it?"

"Because that's literally all there is to wear. It's like an unofficial uniform that all the women wear. Back when the community was formed, they decided everyone was equal, and to reflect that everyone should dress the same."

He stares at me. "Equal."

"Obviously everyone but Ash these days."

I look up at the sound of a car engine outside.

"Ash." My breathing accelerates.

"Ash knows better than to come here. Besides, even if it is him, he can't do anything. You're a grown woman."

I can't breathe. My lungs won't expel air, and my chest aches.

"Constance."

"I … can't … breathe."

"You're having a panic attack."

Heavy footsteps outside leave me sucking in air with no release.

"Sit." Corey points toward the bedroom. "Go and sit in there and I'll get rid of them. I don't care who it is."

"But …"

He wipes tears from my cheeks with his fingers. "Go."

For a moment, I hesitate.

"Go." His tone is so gentle. I nod, and head to the bedroom.

I sit on the bed and listen to conversation at the front door. It seems to go on forever. But at the end, the man at the door asks Corey if he knows about anyone coming through the fence.

My heart seizes.

"No."

I stare at the closed door.

What I hear next makes my heart sink.

"If I saw one of those happy-clappy weirdos, you would be the first to know."

Is that really what he thinks of me?

I don't hear anything else after that. It's so confusing.

I wasn't prepared for any of this.

Closing my eyes, I try and calm myself, and soon I'm breathing normally again.

"Constance."

I look up to see Corey in the doorway.

He walks to the bed and sits beside me. "That was Graham Taylor. He's the senior sergeant from our local police station." Corey runs his fingers through his beard. "They're investigating Ash."

I stare at him. "Really?"

He nods. "One of his guys on the inside got word to him that you'd come through the fence."

"On the inside? Did you tell him I was here?"

Corey shakes his head. "Not after the way you reacted. I'll tell him in a few days once you're not so on edge."

"Is that the right thing to do?"

He shrugs. "I have no idea, but I'm not about to throw you to the wolves. They're good people, and they're really keen to nail Ash. I am too, but right now I need to put you first." With a smile, he reaches up and brushes a lock of hair off my face. My heart leaps to my throat. "I know I've said it before, but you're safe here with me. You don't have to do anything you don't want to, and you can do things in your own time. When you're ready to talk to Graham, tell me."

I nod. "Thank you."

"Are you okay now?"

"I think so." Licking my lips, I gaze into his eyes. His

expression is so caring. How do I reconcile that with him insulting the life I've always had? First the cult comment, and now this?

I'm so confused.

I SHOULD DO SOMETHING.

Maybe look for a job. At least go into town and try and get my head around the idea of building a life out here.

But Corey tells me to relax, take my time, and so I lose myself in his books.

Corey's in and out of the house. He chops wood and makes lunch. But instead of us sitting and talking again, I curl back up with a book and eat as he sets up the fire.

"Your dress is clean and dry." I look up to see him with a handful of grey fabric.

"I don't know if I want to wear it."

"The alternative right now is one of my shirts. Want another one?"

I shake my head. "I'm fine for now. I'll have another shower tonight and get changed."

He looks down at the dress in his hand. "Want me to throw this out?"

I shrug. "When I do leave the house, I might need it."

"I'll put it in your room. You can decide what to do with it."

"Thanks."

Corey frowns. "You okay?"

I nod. "Fine."

He pauses for a moment as if he's about to say something

else but smiles instead. "I'll put dinner on. Lamb chops okay? I make a mean mashed potato."

I look back up. "Sounds good. Want some help?"

He shakes his head. "No. You look comfortable. I'll sort it out."

"Whatever you need me to do, I'm happy to."

Corey scans my expression. "I know. But you're my house guest, so I'm going to take care of you. Besides, I think you've been through enough next door."

I smile. "My life wasn't that bad until yesterday. I think you're mistaken about what my home represents."

He shrugs. "Whatever floats your boat. Though apparently it doesn't anymore, otherwise you wouldn't be here."

"I told you why I'm here."

"Sure you did, and if he'd arranged a marriage to someone you found more likeable, you'd still be there. With that dodgy prick running the show."

He's right.

It sucks, but he's right.

I can't think of anyone I'd want to marry there, but I would have made it work with a number of men. But Ash didn't choose me a partner based on who was best for me; he chose based on some sick sense of revenge.

There's nothing more I can say, and Corey turns and walks away before I can come back with some smart retort.

My mood darkens, and not because he's in the wrong.

Because he's right.

BY DINNERTIME, whatever ease was between us seems to have reappeared, but I'm still thinking about his words from this morning and our earlier conversation.

My whole life, I never thought about how the outside world thought of us. Maybe it was something other people thought about, but no one ever said anything.

It's depressing.

"Food alright?" Corey interrupts my train of thought, and I look up to see him smiling at me.

I nod. "It's lovely. You're a good cook."

He shrugs. "I'm pretty good at meat and veg. Anything else is a bit beyond me."

"I'm good at mac and cheese. It's my dad's favourite."

Corey grins. "I haven't had that in forever. Though it's my own fault. I'm terrible at buying groceries. But I always have a freezer full of meat, and it's a bit wild, but there's a bit of a garden out the back. The potatoes are fresh out of it."

"You can tell." I lower my gaze, and then flick it up again. "We always have fresh food. There are gardens both outside and in the green houses. And there are cows for fresh milk. And there are animals, but we also get meat delivered."

"I always wondered about that. I'd imagine it's almost self-sufficient."

"We could live on the vegetables we grow, but variety is good."

A smile spreads across his face. "I wanted to be like that here. But I think I'd die without coffee, and the Copper Creek fish and chip shop makes the best fried fish. My brother, Owen, owns the bakery, so I usually grab something from there if I feel like bread."

"I can bake bread too."

"Maybe I should tell Owen he has competition."

"I doubt it's as good as his." I laugh. "If he's a baker."

"Just the thought of that hot bread smell makes my mouth water."

I laugh. "Is that a hint?"

"Maybe a trip to the supermarket is in order."

Hot prickles run up and down my body. I could deal with the vague thought of leaving the house, but the thought of actually being out leaves my heart racing.

"I'll go by myself. You can stay here. I'm not going to drag you out of the house."

"Could you blame me for thinking that? You did drag me in."

Corey chuckles. "I guess I did."

I push the mashed potatoes around on my plate. "Can I ask you something?"

"Anything."

"Do you really think we're weirdos?"

Confusion crosses his face, and then it's like a lightbulb's gone off. "What I said to Graham earlier? I didn't want him to be suspicious."

"Is that it?"

Corey puts down his fork. "Honestly? Yeah. The whole thing's weird. But I have to admit, I barely paid attention until that damn wall went up. It's such a huge area to do that to, so what's hiding behind there?"

I shrug. "Just a bunch of people wanting to live a quiet life."

"Ash is up to something dodgy. And whatever it is has hurt people, and he will keep on doing that unless he's taken down."

My chest aches.

"So, yeah. I'm sorry if it upsets you that I'm not a fan of the cult next door."

I don't know what hurts more: my naivety where Ash was concerned, or the way Corey references my home.

We eat the rest of dinner in silence. Corey says he'll clean up and rejects my help, so I take my book and hide in the bedroom.

Not that I read.

Our brief conversation's hit me hard.

The room grows dark. The bed is hard, and it makes me want to sleep in the chair even though my neck still aches.

My bed back home wasn't anything flash, but the mattress was soft. I miss it.

This bed is like sleeping on rocks. I hate it.

*Maybe Corey's asleep.*

Maybe I could make myself a cup of tea and lie down on the couch.

I push myself up to sit and rub my neck. Tiptoeing to the door, I slowly pull it open.

Corey's tall.

I'm pretty tall for a woman—about the same height as Ash. I think that's one of the reasons he never came near me —If I know Ash at all, he likes the feeling of superiority towering over his women.

It's refreshing to find a man who towers over me.

And he's standing right in front of me half-naked.

It's hard not to look. He's in the middle of his living room, with no shirt, and wearing grey tracksuit pants that hang really low on his hips. I don't mean to, but my gaze travels down his chiseled chest, over those defined abs and to the deep *V* just below his waist line.

In my confused state over him, I'm actually angry that he looks so good.

"My eyes are up here," he says.

I glare at his smirk.

"The bed's ridiculously hard."

"Well, sweetness, I don't know if you can complain when the accommodation's free." He leans toward me. "You're welcome to leave."

"You know I don't have anywhere else to go."

He nods. "True. My bed's much more comfortable. And it's not really my fault you've gone all 'princess and the pea' on me."

Tears prick my eyes as I stare at him, but I'm not giving in. I'll be damned if he'll make me cry.

My nostrils flare as I hold everything inside of me. I don't even know why I'm acting this way. I don't know why he's acting this way. At least he's not kicking me out.

"Good night," I finally manage to say.

"Sweet dreams." His tone softens.

I just catch his soft laugh as the door clicks shut. Tears prick my eyes. I'm so grateful to Corey for letting me stay here. Why can't I just say it?

I curl up on the uncomfortable bed and close my eyes.

The thought of his softer mattress leaves me yearning for Corey Campbell's bed. But it's not just that. It's him.

Everything about him screams of masculinity. He's not like any of the men in the world I left behind.

And he thinks I'm a joke.

I DON'T KNOW what time it is when I wake.

It's still dark outside, and I hear the noise again that woke me.

Someone's walking around. The wooden floor creaks in the still of the night, and fear runs through my body.

*Has Ash found me?*

Corey said he'd protect me, but I don't know him. I've been so trusting, but is that the right thing to do?

Can I trust him?

I can't help it. My curiosity gets the better of me, and I slip out of bed. Padding across the floor in bare feet, I slowly pull open the door.

The fire's low, and it illuminates enough of the living room that I can look around. I take a step back as the front door opens.

Corey steps inside. He's oblivious to my presence. His expression is serious, and part of me mourns that he's now wearing a T-shirt.

"Is anything wrong?" I whisper.

His head shoots up, and the first thing I see is concern in his eyes, swiftly followed by the relief that sweeps his face. "No. I heard something, but I think it was a possum. Damn thing. I circled around the house to make sure no one was here."

My lower lip wobbles. I can't help it. "Do you think they'll come after me?"

His eyebrows knit as he frowns. "Not if they're smart. Ash knows he's not welcome on my property. I made that clear back when he put the fence up."

I blink to hold back tears. "I'm frightened."

His expression softens, and next thing I know, I'm in his arms. He pulls me into his solid chest, and for the first time since I left home, I feel truly safe. I don't know what it is about him, and I'm not sure if my attraction to him is because he's someone new, or because he's so contradictory. But I don't care because it feels so right.

When I first saw him, his size and the way he held himself scared the crap out of me. In twenty-four hours, I've seen his gentleness. As he plants a kiss on my head, I'm so grateful for him.

We might snipe at each other, but I do trust this man. Right now, I'm trusting him with my life, and there is nowhere else I'd rather be. Even if I haven't gone that far from home.

I raise my face to look at him, and his gaze bores through me. He lifts a hand to my face, running his thumb along my cheekbone. "You're safe here. I'll never let them hurt you. For as long as you're staying with me, you have my word."

My heart thuds. I have zero experience with men, bar boys who stole kisses when I was growing up. But Corey stirs something in me. It's something I know I never would have felt with John.

Flickers of desire shoot through me. But it's so confusing. Do I want him because I'm in his arms, and he makes me feel safe? Are my feelings real?

Until I know for sure, I can't do anything about it. The last thing I want is to humiliate myself, and right now, I need Corey.

He put a roof over my head, no questions asked. My heart

leaps. I left home with no plan, no idea of where I was going. All I knew was that I had to get out of there.

"Go and get some sleep, sweetness," he says softly.

I nod.

"I'm going to bed now too. If you need anything in the night, you know where everything is. Help yourself to whatever food you want." He smiles. "Are you warm enough in that room?"

"It's fine."

"It's just the uncomfortable bed."

I give him a small smile. "That's fine, too. I'm sorry if I complained earlier."

He shakes his head. "You just left behind what's been your life since the day you were born. I'm pretty sure it's normal to have trouble adjusting." His lips curl into a smile. "You can use me as your punching bag any time."

I have no idea what he means, but I laugh.

He loops a lock of my hair around his fingers. "You should wear your hair down. It looks nice." With a kiss on my forehead, he lets me go. I can't help but smile at him. The way he behaves with me is so familiar, and it makes me feel protected. "Good night again, Constance."

I nod. "Good night, Corey."

My smile grows as I climb back into bed. Corey will protect me.

I'm safe.

# 6

## COREY

I HELD her in my arms.

I'm not sure how to feel since I only just met her, but there's an unmistakable spark between Constance and me.

I kissed her on the forehead.

I felt her silky-soft hair.

My brain won't turn off.

I stare at the ceiling with my mind on the woman in the room next door. All I want is to protect her. I'll be damned if Ash Harris ever has his hands on her again.

For the first time in my life, I'm truly stumped over what to do.

My path has been clear since I became an adult. I have a job I love, my own property, and I can just be myself. I can't imagine what it's like for those women next door who have their husbands selected for them. I can't imagine not being able to choose a woman for myself.

The only time I've ever thought about settling down was

when I invited Lily and Max to live with me. I've had women in my life, but I can take or leave sex. I'm not usually one for one-night stands, but I'm also not one for a long-term relationship.

It's been months since I was last with a woman. Or was nearly with a woman.

The memory still makes me laugh.

This gorgeous, leggy blonde threw herself at me during Drew's wedding. I wasn't about to say no to that. But right when I thought I might score, she fell asleep. That motel couch is the most uncomfortable thing I think I've ever slept on.

We didn't keep in touch.

When I was a kid, I ran with the wrong crowd. And I'm so glad that I did because that led me to the life I have now. The life I love.

And now, Constance.

I roll over. She's not here permanently. She needs to get back on her feet and work out where she fits in this world.

And I need to tell Graham the truth. If she didn't look at me with so much fear over what was going to happen, I would have told him she was with me.

Maybe she just needs a little time.

All I know is that I need to protect her.

---

I GET up in the morning to what looks like a different house.

It's usually clean because I don't have a huge amount of stuff. I like living pretty basic. But today my living room is spotless.

I've clearly slept through the vacuuming, and where the living room carpet meets the dining room, the polished wooden floor is freshly mopped. I washed the dishes last night and stacked them to dry, but the benches are clear of them.

Constance sits at the table, the aroma of her coffee reaching me. She looks up and smiles. "Morning."

"You had an early start."

She nods. "I didn't sleep that well. It'll take a while to get used to being somewhere else."

"With a bed that's not that comfy."

Shrugging, she takes a sip of coffee. "I can live with it. Sorry for being cranky last night. The last couple of days have been really tiring."

"I bet. I'll grab a coffee and join you."

As the jug boils, I close my eyes. I could get used to this. While I don't expect her to do anything, it's sweet that she's done so much.

"I wasn't sure where everything went, but I think I worked it out." Her voice shakes me out of my thoughts, and I turn and smile at her.

"It doesn't matter. Wherever you've put things is probably better than my efforts."

She laughs. "I just hope you can find it all."

"I'm sure I'll be fine." Wherever she's put things it's probably better than my haphazard system of sticking things in the cupboard where there's a space.

Presuming she stays, I can always ask her.

Although, after the way she reacted when I was dismissive of that cult, maybe she doesn't want to stick around. Maybe staying with me is at the bottom of her list.

I mix the coffee with hot water. Giving it a quick stir, I head to the table. "I think I need to tell you why I feel the way I do about next door."

She nods.

Sitting opposite her, I take a sip of coffee and sigh. "Ash tried to hurt someone I care about. My sister-in-law, Hayley."

Her eyes widen. "I'm so sorry."

"He didn't get away with it thanks to some help she got within his little group, but I'm doing what I can to bring him down."

Her face is so full of emotion, but I am betting that's for her parents and not for Ash.

"When I was growing up, it was just a group of people who wanted to get away from the stresses of life. People came and went, and things were good." She sighs. "Things started going downhill not long before Ash's father died. He was sick, and my parents and I talked about leaving at that point. We should have, but we had nowhere to go."

I nod. "I understand that. It must be a big change being here."

"It is, and I haven't even left your house yet."

Taking a sip of coffee, I smile at her. "We'll have to fix that."

The colour drains from her face. "Do we have to? Can't I just stay here for a little while?"

"Of course." I nod. "I'm not expecting miracles. You have to feel ready."

"Thank you."

"You're not under Ash's control anymore. You can do what you want."

Her expression is so distant, but a smile slowly crosses her lips. "I like that."

A few seconds pass and we sip our coffee in silence.

"Let me guess: you're going to read today."

"I *should* work out what to do next. There was no real time to think things out before I left, and I was told that someone would take care of me."

I grin. "I don't think they were talking about me, but I still think that you need to take a few days at least to get steady and decide your next move."

She laughs. "So far my next move has been cleaning the house."

I chuckle. "It looks good. I might just have to keep you on."

"I'd like that." Her eyes widen as if she's just realised what she's said. "I mean, thank you for giving me somewhere to stay."

"You're welcome. Treat my house like it's yours." I lean over. "Besides, it'll be good to have someone take care of the place while I'm working."

"You have to work. Of course you do." Her tone is almost disappointed.

I nod. "I have my own business doing pest control. Of the possum, deer, and stoat variety."

Constance frowns. "We had someone who used to do that for us occasionally. We went through a period of chicken eggs being stolen."

"That's what I take care of." I take a deep breath. "Unfortunately, it usually means I'm away at night."

Fear crosses her face, but she sits up straight. "I can handle that."

"I know you can. You're braver than most. And if you feel uncomfortable, I've got brothers in town and I'm sure you could stay with one of them."

She smiles, and I'm hit once again with just how pretty she is.

I'm going to enjoy having her around.

## 7

### CONSTANCE

I'VE BEEN INSIDE for the past week.

"Want to go for a walk?" Corey extends his hand.

Corey's offered to take me to his brother's place, to meet his sister-in-law and get me some clothes. But the threat of Ash has kept me from leaving the house.

Corey makes me feel safe, but fear has kept me on edge.

I don't know what I would have done without him. He's always with me, surrounding me with that calming manner that helps soothe my soul.

"Where?"

"Out the back door."

I stare at him. "But that's—"

"We'll stay away from the spot where I found you. I have something to show you."

I take his hand, using the leverage to pull myself to my feet.

For a moment, my feet won't move, but I nod and go to the back door to get my boots.

"Here you are." Corey dangles my socks in front of me.

"I didn't even notice they were missing."

He laughs. "I washed them the night I washed your dress. You left them on the bathroom floor."

"Thank you."

"You're welcome, Cinderella. Get your shoes on."

I grin as he pulls his own boots on and opens the back door.

The sunshine hits me before I step out into it. It's so warm on my skin, and I close my eyes and bathe in it for a moment. "This is nice."

"Told you." He laughs. "I bet it's good to get some fresh air."

"It is. Thank you."

Corey shakes his head. "No need. You just needed a little push. Now, come with me."

I follow him through his back yard—not that it's really a yard. There's a cleared spot behind his house before it goes straight into bush. Trees and ferns are everywhere, and it looks tamed in parts, unkempt in others.

Right before we hit the bush, I pause. There's a small pile of stones with a wooden cross on it, not dissimilar to the graveyard we have in the community.

"What's this?"

Corey frowns. "I used to have a dog."

"What happened?" I place my hand on his arm.

"He came hunting with me. And one day some, useless arsewipe in the wrong place mistook him for a pig."

My mouth falls open. "Oh, Corey."

"I brought him home to bury. I haven't had a dog since. I can't risk it."

I nod. "I can understand that."

He pauses for a moment and looks at the small cross in the ground. The pain is written all over his face. The death of his dog hurt him very deeply.

"What was his name?"

"Brutus." He gives me a wry smile. "I thought it was appropriate for a hunting dog."

I nod. "Very." Slipping my hand in his, I give it a squeeze.

"His grave needs cleaning up. The weeds go nuts when it rains."

"I'll help take care of it." I rest my head on his shoulder. "It's the least I can do. Do you have any other animals?"

He shakes his head. "There's never been any point. I'm here most of the time, but sometimes I go away for days. My family might pitch in and help, but I'd rather not rely on them. They have enough of their own crap to deal with."

"I could do it." I smile.

I close my eyes when Corey kisses me on the top of my head. "So, you're sticking around for a while."

"If you'll let me."

He squeezes my hand, mimicking my action. "I'll let you."

I look up at him. "Well, I do have all those books to read."

A contented smile spreads across his face. "I guess you do. And you know I can always find more."

I place my hand on my heart. "Why, Corey Campbell, anyone would think you wanted to keep me here."

He chuckles. "Maybe I do."

WE WALK for about ten minutes before he points into the distance. "This is what I want to show you."

I hear the water before I see it. There's a creek running through his property. Either side is lined by ferns, but there are gaps where you can reach the water.

"Just be careful down here. It's slippery after the rain." He holds out his hand, and I reach for him.

My feet slide out from underneath me. Pain shoots up my leg as I hit the ground.

"Constance," he cries out.

In an instant, he's beside me. "Are you okay?"

Taking a deep breath, I nod. "I think I twisted my ankle, but it's my pride that hurts the most." I widen my eyes as he bends, scooping me into his arms. "I'm covered in mud."

"I don't care. We need to get you back home and get that ankle seen to."

He cradles me in his arms, and I laugh into his neck as we move closer to the house.

"What's so funny?"

"I'm outside for, what? Ten minutes? And here you are carrying me back inside again."

His laughter sends shivers through me. Being in his arms is so intimate, and I hate the thought that in a few moments, he won't be carrying me.

Corey's boots leave muddy footprints across the polished wooden kitchen floor.

"I just mopped that floor this morning." I sigh.

"Tough. I'll sort it out later." He lowers me gently onto the couch.

"Corey, the couch."

"The couch can be wiped clean. Your foot needs to be elevated." He unlaces my boots and pulls them from my feet.

"Wait here, and I'll get something cold from the freezer to ice it."

"I'm not exactly going anywhere." I grump because it hurts, but when Corey returns, he's got a smile on his face.

"No, and you won't be for a while." He lays a tea towel over my ankle and places a bag of frozen peas on it.

"I'll get you a drink. Want me to turn the TV on?"

The back of the long, checked shirt I'm wearing and my legs are still wet from the mud, and he just doesn't care. I guess he's right. It'll all wash out. It's not comfortable, but the ache of my ankle overrides my discomfort. "Uhh, sure."

"I'll make some coffee. Want anything else?"

I run my gaze from his feet up to his face. His expression is so open and caring. It's confusing. Maybe because the only people who ever cared for me in this way were my parents.

Shaking my head, I look back down. "Thank you."

"I should have known better than to go down there after it'd been raining." He sighs. "And you're not familiar with the area."

"No. I should have been more careful. You did warn me."

For a moment, he just stands there. There's sorrow in his eyes, and I just want to laugh and tell him it'll be okay. But I also don't want to make him feel worse than he clearly already is. "Corey?"

He smiles. "I'll go and get that coffee."

I lie back and sigh. For just a little while, the sun and fresh air were so good to feel and breathe again. It just reinforces how much I love living on this mountain. Even if I'm not home anymore.

*I wonder how Mum and Dad are doing.*

That thought pains me. Ash will know I'm gone.

"Are you okay?" Corey asks, placing a cup on the coffee table.

I shrug. "Just thinking about home."

He sits on one of the chairs. "I hope you're not thinking about going back."

"No. Not at all. But there are people still in there who I love. It worries me."

He nods. "I'm sure it does. The police will get to the bottom of it. Sure, sometimes I think they couldn't find their arse with both hands, but I'm sure the detectives are better than that."

I laugh. "That's a terrible expression."

"In my opinion, Ash Harris should be a distant memory by now. But then, what would I know?"

"I think you know a lot about a lot of things."

His gaze catches mine when I look up, and I blush at the intensity of it. There are times when I catch him looking at me when he thinks I'm not aware of it. But then, I do the same to him.

Those awkward silences don't last long. But we seem to be circling each other, as if waiting for something to happen.

"You know a lot, considering your limited exposure to the world." He stretches out. "And you won't get more exposure if you're stuck inside with your ankle for a couple of days. Don't you dare think about vacuuming or tidying or any of that other stuff you've been doing either."

"Yes, boss."

He grins. "Maybe that's the way you should respond to everything."

I laugh, picking up a cushion and throwing it at his head.

"You cult girls. So violent."

"Oh, shut up." I laugh again.

He stands and makes his way to the couch. I shuffle over so he can sit next to me. "I just want you to know if I tease you, I'm not trying to be mean. I prefer you smiling and laughing to being grumpy at me."

"I know. I'm so glad I'm here."

"You are?"

"I can't imagine that I'd have so much fun anywhere else. Where else can I injure myself the first time I step out the door?" I grin at him. It's nice. I feel so relaxed and safe here. Even outside the house.

He looks down at my ankle. "I don't know if I'd call that fun."

"You know what I mean. I have a seemingly unlimited supply of books. That's pretty much all I need. Oh, and then there's the television."

Corey shakes his head. "You'll never leave the house again, then."

"Probably not."

He scans my expression, a fond smile on his face as he rests his hand on my cheek. Just like he did the second night I was here, he runs this thumb along my cheekbone. "That's fine with me."

I want to close my eyes and revel in his touch, but it's too much.

"I need a shower. This dried mud is driving me crazy."

He leans back as I push myself up into a seated position, then moves out of the way so I can stand.

"Want some help getting in the shower?" he asks. His

mouths cracks into a smile as I stare wide-eyed. "I didn't mean … well, okay, I didn't think that out before I said it." He laughs.

I roll my eyes. "I think I'll be fine."

"Yell out if you need anything."

I nod. "What I really need is to get all this mud off me. I'm sure I'll feel better once I'm clean."

"I'll sort out the couch. Make it habitable for when you come back out."

"Thank you."

His expression softens. "What for? It's my fault this happened."

"No, you're only looking out for me. You were right to talk me into going outside. I needed the sunshine more than I realised."

His lips twitch. "So, I'm not doing too bad a job after all?"

"What job?"

"Taking care of you. Thought I blew it this afternoon."

Laughing, I shake my head. "No, you're doing a pretty decent job."

"Room for improvement, then?"

I shrug, and I can't help the grin on my face. "I can't think of anything you could do better."

"Except not take you anywhere that you can fall and twist your ankle."

Raising my index finger to my lips, I look up at the ceiling as if pondering a response. "I'm pretty sure I could have done that anywhere."

Corey laughs. "Maybe you're right. Doesn't make me feel any less guilty."

Turning, I limp toward the hallway that leads to the bathroom. "Well, I feel guilty for all the hot water I'm about to use. Let's call it even."

I smile when I close the door behind me. While I was joking, it does concern me that I'm staying here for nothing. How will I ever pay Corey back?

I need clothing, and I need a job, or some way to make some money to pay him back.

My ankle screams as I strip off and take a step into the shower.

I'm not doing anything until this is better.

***

THE HEAT of the shower felt good on my ankle.

When I limp back to the living room, Corey's been as good as his word. The couch is clean, and scent of chocolate hits me. "That smells amazing."

"I forgot I had a tin of hot chocolate in the cupboard. After a crappy day, I figured it'd be good." Corey comes up behind me, grabbing my arm and pulling it around his waist as he helps me back to the couch. Two cups sit steaming on the coffee table.

"I think this and a good sleep and I'll be alright," I reply. He lowers me onto the couch and takes the bundle of clothing from my hands. "Oh, I was going to put that in the washing machine."

"I'll take care of it." He smiles. "Sit there and drink your hot chocolate. I'll help you to bed, or you can sleep on the couch if you like."

"Thank you."

"I'll make sure it's all dry for the morning. And if your ankle's no better, I'll take you down to see Doc Paton."

Tears prick my eyes, and his eyebrows dip as his expression changes to one of concern. "What's wrong?"

"Why are you being so good to me? I mean, it's wonderful, Corey, it really is, but this is way beyond ..."

He places my things on the table and takes a seat beside me on the couch. Letting out a sigh, he slips his arm around my shoulders. For a moment, I search his eyes and all I see is a sweet, caring man. He doesn't have an ulterior motive. He's doing this because it comes naturally to him. "You have nothing. Or, should I say, had nothing. When you came through that fence, you had no plans and nowhere to go. But now, you have me."

I lick my lips and keep my gaze on his. In such a short time, he's come to mean so much to me. He's become my friend.

"I like you, Constance. You keep me on my toes, and I like you being around. I know you've been through a lot, and I'll be damned if you have to go through any more."

Tears roll down my cheeks, and he catches them on his index finger.

"Thank—"

"Don't you dare say thank you again. You don't owe me anything. I'm here for you as long as you need. I promise."

His breath catches as I wrap my arms around his neck and lay my head on his chest. I've never felt so comfortable with anyone else before.

I think I love him.

**8**

---

OWEN

My little girl is five.

It's hard to believe she's only been in my life for the past year, but now I get to celebrate a milestone that I would have never known about if things hadn't happened the way they did.

I'm only sorry that her other parents don't get to see it.

"Ready." She grabs her backpack and puts it on. Her blonde hair is tied in pigtails, and her blue eyes shine with excitement. All of a sudden, she looks so grown up, I don't know if I can handle it.

"Well, Ginny's not quite ready yet, sweet pea." I laugh. I squat in front of her, holding my arms open. "Give me a big hug. I'll be thinking about you all day."

She throws herself at me, and I hold her, bag and all. How did I ever survive without Ava? My prior life is so distant now, it's almost as if it never happened.

I love my family.

"Are you ready … oh." Ginny's voice comes from the hallway. I look up to see her approaching, amusement written all over her face.

"She was ready before you were."

"I can see."

"Are we going to school now?" Ava asks.

Ginny nods. "It's exciting. You're going to love your teacher. Miss Anderton is lovely, and she knows all about you."

Ava's eyes widen. "I want you to be my teacher."

Ginny shakes her head. "It doesn't work that way, baby. I teach older kids. You have a very special teacher who will help you to learn. And soon, you'll be reading that bedtime story to me." She extends her hand to Ava. "Shall we get going? Say goodbye to Daddy, and we'll go to school."

Ava's grip tightens around my neck.

"You be a good girl, and I want to hear all about school when you come home. Okay?" I ask.

Ava nods, and I plant a kiss in her hair.

"Love you." I give her a squeeze and let her go.

I stand and lean over, giving Ginny a tender kiss. "You be a good girl, too."

"I'm always good at school. It's the night-time you have to worry about."

I grin. "I'll look forward to it."

A little piece of my heart walks out with them. Ava turns at the door and waves. I blow her a kiss and she's gone.

For a moment, I stare at the closed door before shaking my head and heading into the bakery kitchen.

Mel fixes a sympathetic gaze on me. "How'd it go?"

"Today is going to be the longest day ever."

"You know Ginny will make sure she's okay."

I nod. "Yeah, but it's a big step. Maybe I should have gone to—"

Mel shrugs. "You don't know how she's going to react. If you're there, she might make a scene. At least she knows Ginny's at school all day and she can go to her if she has any problems."

Sighing, I lean against the door. "You're right. I know you are."

She nods. "Get to work. That always takes my mind off things."

I tap my fingers against the doorframe. "You know what? I'm going, too."

Mel grins. "See you soon."

I run through the house and grab my car keys. I jump in my car, starting it up and backing down the driveway.

I swing into the car park and pull into a visitor spot. Ava and Ginny are already out of the car.

"Daddy." Ava laughs. She runs for me, and I pull her up and onto my hip.

Ginny's lips twitch. "I thought you were leaving me to take care of this?"

I shrug. "I changed my mind."

A smile crosses her face, and she grasps my chin, planting a tender kiss on my lips. "I love you."

"I have the best girls in the world. And I want to be there for the big things," I say. Ginny slides her arm around my waist. I tilt my head to kiss Ava. "Besides, I think I missed enough of those big things already."

I drop Ava to the ground, and she slots her hand in mine. Ginny positions herself on the other side of our daughter, and the three of us walk toward the classroom together.

My heart's settled.

After this, I think I'll be okay.

———

"Daddy."

I already know it's quarter past three from the clock I've been watching all day, and the sound of Ava's voice fills me with joy.

"Who's that?" I look around as if I don't see her.

She giggles. "It's me. Ava."

"Where's Ava? I can't see her?"

Ava grabs hold of my hand and tugs on it. "I'm here."

I look at her with wide eyes. "Oh. There's Ava."

She grins as I sweep her into my arms and bury my face in her neck.

"Did you have a good day?"

Her mouth falls open. "It was awesome. I can read."

I laugh. "Can you now? I thought you could already read. Ginny's been teaching you for months."

"I can read better now. I'm a year one."

Nodding, I suppress my laughter. "I'm sure that's right. You can read me a book tonight at bedtime."

She rolls her eyes. "I can't read a whole book *yet*."

"Oh, silly me. Maybe that happens in year two. Want a cookie?"

Her blonde pigtails swing as she nods with enthusiasm.

I let her down to the floor. "You know where they are."

"Do I have to use the tongs?"

"Even year-one girls have to use tongs."

She heads straight for the display cabinet, and I don't need to look to see she's picking a gingerbread man. It's always the same choice. I'm not exactly sure if it's because she loves them as much as she says she does, or if it's because they're the biggest cookies in the cabinet. Either way, she takes a huge bite and gives me a grin full of crumbs.

"Love you, sweet pea. Go and chill out with Ginny, and I'll be home soon."

"We *are* home."

"Do you sleep in the bakery?"

She shakes her head and sprays crumbs everywhere.

"Neither do I. So I'll be home in a little while." I let out a contented sigh as I watch her disappear back through the kitchen and into the flat. In the distance, the sound of the television starts up, and I shake my head with a smile.

"Do I get a cookie too?" Ginny's voice comes from behind me.

"Only good girls get cookies. Have you been a good girl?"

She grins. "Like I told you. Always, during the daytime."

I wrap my arms around her waist and close my eyes as I hold her tight.

"I've told you before. No canoodling in the shop." Mel walks past us, coming in from the kitchen with Tammy in tow.

"I'll leave the shop to you and canoodle in my home, then."

She laughs. "Later, boss. I'll close up today."

Ginny detaches from me, grabs a cookie and disappears back through the kitchen. I shake my head.

"Go on," Mel says.

"Don't have to tell me twice. See you in the morning."

I walk through the kitchen and into my flat. Ginny's sprawled on the couch, Ava on the floor in front of her, and they're both watching cartoons.

Shaking my head, I lift Ginny's head and slide my legs underneath, dropping her back onto my lap.

"Hello," she mumbles with a mouth full of food.

"Hi." I grin.

She snuggles against my legs, and I stroke her hair while we all watch television.

It's the simple things in life that are the best.

---

AVA'S HAD A BIG DAY, and she falls asleep curled up on my lap. I carry her to bed, and Ginny tucks her in as I return to the couch.

When Ginny appears, she looks tired, too. She nestles in against me.

"How was your day?" I ask.

"Long. I keep thinking about this appointment with Doctor Phillips. I'm so scared, Owen."

I take a deep breath as I stroke her hair. "Me too. I want so much to be the man to give you what you need."

"It's not your fault."

Grasping her chin, I pull her gaze to meet mine. "We're in this together. No matter what."

"I love you."

I smile. Every single time she says those words, it puts a

smile on my face. "I love you, too. More than anything. Don't you ever forget that."

Ginny shakes her head, and I lower my mouth to hers for a tender kiss that leaves her breathless.

"Let's get to bed. Miss Ava has her second day of school tomorrow, and it would be terrible if you were late for it." I grin.

She laughs. "Heaven forbid."

"You know, next thing she'll have boobs and the boys will be hanging around. I'll have to buy a shotgun."

Ginny rolls her eyes. "I'm pretty sure you're safe for a while. Besides, Uncle Corey already has a shotgun, and he'll be very protective of his favourite girl."

"I'm sure you're right." I lean my head against hers. "I wonder if Corey will ever find his perfect woman. He's in town more often since Adam came back, and it's been good to see him. But I always wonder if he's lonely."

"He must enjoy his own company living up the mountain by himself. Maybe he just needs to find another loner."

I smile. "Probably. And I'm not sure why I'm worrying about my brother's love life when I've got my girl in my arms and I could be indulging in some insanely amazing sex."

Ginny laughs. "So, what are you going to do about it?"

"Drag her off to bed and show her what amazing sex is like."

"Oh, really?" She sucks on her top lip to stop herself from smiling.

"I find it offensive that you think that's funny. And that thing you're doing with your lips is just making it worse."

"Come on then, big man. Show me what you're made of." She stands, holding her hand out for me to take. It wasn't that long ago that the love in her eyes would have terrified me. I'd have made an excuse and bailed if any other woman looked at me like that.

But I'm as smitten today as the night I met her.

"Big man, huh?" I take her hand and pull myself up.

"It's just an expression."

"Sure."

## 9

### COREY

"ARE YOU OKAY? You've been staring at that cup of coffee for at least ten minutes."

Lily's voice knocks me out of my stupor, and I look up and smile at her.

"I'm fine. Just got a lot on my mind."

"Do you want me to get Adam? I know he's in the middle of an engine rebuild, but I'm pretty sure his brother is more important than that."

I shake my head. "Nah. I came to have coffee with my favourite sister-in-law, and I'm sorry if I'm flaking out."

She leans over, grasping my hand. It's funny how things change so quickly. Three weeks ago, my body would have reacted to her touch.

It's actually a relief for her hand on mine to not affect me.

"What's going on?" Her blue eyes search mine as she releases my hand.

I swore to do everything I could to protect Constance,

but I know I can trust Lily. For years, we've confided in each other as friends. "I've met someone."

A smile spreads across Lily's face. "Is that good? Bad? You're so hard to read sometimes."

"I think it's good." I avert my gaze. "It *is* good." Reaching out, I take a sip of my coffee.

"Tell me about her."

I can't help but smile thinking about Constance. "She's feisty. She gives as good as she gets. And she's sweet. Really sweet."

"Sounds lovely," Lily says.

"She is. We haven't known each other that long, but I really like her." I take another sip of coffee. "She's younger than me, only twenty-two, which worries me a bit, but the heart wants what it wants, right?"

Lily grins. "How long have you known her? You haven't mentioned her before."

"About three weeks."

Her eyebrows creep up. "Three weeks?"

"How long was it that you and Adam knew? You were kids, but you were practically tied to each other as soon as you met."

She laughs. "I guess you're right."

"I just have to keep her safe."

"What do you mean?"

I sigh. "She's from next door."

Lily's eyes widen. "You mean …?"

"She came through the fence one night about three weeks ago with nothing but the clothes she was wearing."

Lily's mouth falls open. "What did the police say?"

"I haven't told them."

She sits back in her seat. "Corey. She could help them put Ash Harris away."

"Maybe, but I don't want her interrogated. There's not a lot she knows about whatever Ash is up to."

Lily nods. "I'm not surprised. But there might be something she does know that could help. You have to tell Graham about her. Why isn't she with you?"

"She hasn't left the house yet. Well, she has, but she had a fall and hurt her ankle."

"So she's been stuck in your house for three weeks?"

I nod. "She's happy. I think she's scared that if she goes out, Ash will see her, and he'll try something."

"She must be terrified."

I sigh. "I can see the fear in her face when she talks about it. I promised her I'd keep her safe."

"You can't let her live like this." She lets out a loud breath. "Tell you what. I'll get some of my clothes together so she's got something to wear, and I'll drive her to Carlstown to get new clothes myself."

"That might be a lot for Constance to deal with."

Lily cocks her head. "I know you want to protect her, but you can't smother her while you do it. She's never been free to dress the way she wants, to live her life the way she needs to."

"You're telling me I have to let go of her, aren't you?"

She shakes her head. "No. But I am telling you that she'll need more than to be trapped inside your house wearing your things. She needs to find herself to live a full life."

"How'd you get to be so wise?"

"It wasn't until I came here with Adam that I felt free.

Maybe before then I had all the freedom to do what I wanted, but for many years I struggled. I was trapped in a world I couldn't see my way out of." She licks her lips. "My circumstances might have been different to Constance's, but I think I can relate to her. And she's so much younger than I am."

I fist my hands under the table to squeeze out the stress. I can't pretend that the age gap between Constance and me hasn't played on my mind. But at the same time, we seem to be bridging it just fine.

"If she's okay with it, you can come over and take her shopping. I'll give you some money."

Lily nods.

"She's got nothing. Literally just the dress and boots she wore when she arrived. She had to leave in a hurry, and she had nothing planned on the other side. So, I'm it."

With a sigh, she nods. "I really feel for her. We'll shop for some bargains and get as much value for money as we can. Might as well grab her as many things as we can while you're paying."

I chuckle. "Whatever you ladies decide is best. I just want her to be happy."

"You really do like her." Her eyes shine with joy.

"It's a bit more than that. No. A lot more than that. But she's been through so much."

"Want my advice?"

"Please."

"Let her come to you. I know you're not patient at the best of times, but if she shares your feelings, she'll tell you when she's brave enough. Or she'll give you a sign. Just pay attention."

Nodding, I reach for her hand. "Thank you. I really don't know what I'd do without having you to talk to."

"You'd work it out. You are the second smartest Campbell boy, after all."

My eyebrows shoot up. "Who's the smartest?"

She grins. "Adam, of course. He picked me."

I laugh as she gives my hand a squeeze and lets go. "I'm sure you're right."

The whole way home, all I can think about is what Lily said. Maybe I need to let Constance come to me.

Maybe I need to let her go and hope to hell she comes back.

# 10

## CONSTANCE

"IT's time you got out of the house."

I look up from the book I'm reading. I've been engrossed in Middle Earth since yesterday, devouring the first book and moving on to the second. Corey's bookcases contain a wealth of fiction and I want to read it all. He seems to read a range of genres, and I'm enjoying the variety.

"Do I have to?"

He raises his eyebrows. "It's been three weeks, and you haven't gone anywhere. Like I said, it's time."

I pout. He can't really complain. I've slowly taken over looking after this place. I cook, and he does the dishes, and vice versa. The bathroom is spotless, and in what seems to be a change, his laundry is up to date.

"You can't stay inside forever. You're safe."

Standing, I try and plead with my eyes. "I need to feel safe. I'm still scared."

"It's not good for you to stay here."

My head spins. Does he want me to leave? I thought he'd said I could stay for as long as I needed. "What do you mean?"

His Adam's apple bobs as he swallows. "You need to get out and about to start living your life. It's not like you'll be living in my house forever."

"Why not?" Tears prick my eyes.

"You're smart, and you're hard working. Look at what you've done around here. There are a million opportunities out there for someone like you."

I shake my head. "I like being here."

"I know, but you're better than this. There's no future in being my cleaning lady."

Standing, I place the book back on the couch. He's a good foot taller than me, but he doesn't scare me. I know Corey has a big heart, and I'd hoped it was one that had space for me. "I don't want to be your cleaning lady, but I'll do what I can to pay my way."

"That's not what I want for you."

"Maybe it's what I want."

He runs his fingers through his hair. "God. Sometimes you are so annoying."

"That makes two of us." I can see something's bothering him. It's written all over his face. He's so bad at hiding things.

"Do you want me to leave, Corey?"

He sighs. "No."

"So, what's this all about?"

He swallows hard. "This. Us. You being here. It's a lot to handle."

"I don't understand."

His eyes drink me in, as if he's never going to see me

again. "You're under my skin, Con. I know that it'd be best for you if you moved on, but I'm struggling to let you go. I'm so fucking torn."

My mouth goes dry, and my eyes widen. "You want me?"

He closes his eyes for a moment. "Just forget I said that."

"I can't. How can I? Did you ever think that maybe I don't want to leave this house because I *like* being here with you?"

He sighs. "I'm not pushing you out. I told you that you could stay as long as you wanted, and I stand by that." Corey reaches out and grips my chin. "You're so young, and I won't be what holds you back."

"If you think you're doing that, you're an idiot."

His lips twitch in amusement. "Maybe I am. I just know that at twenty-two, I didn't know what I wanted, and I didn't take all the opportunities I probably should have."

"So, now you're acting like my dad."

He shakes his head. "No. If I was your father I would have got you out of that place years ago."

"It's not his fault." My voice drops to a whisper.

"It is. You should never have been in a position where you had to escape. What kind of life is that?"

Tears roll down my cheeks. "It was a good life when I was a kid. You don't understand."

He drops his hand. "No. I guess I never will."

I wipe my face with my palms.

"Come here."

I gasp as he wraps his arms around my waist and pulls me to the couch and onto his lap. Being this close to him is overwhelming, and a smile spreads on his lips as my breathing falls to pieces.

He lets go of my waist, but I stay still as he raises his

hands. Cupping my face, he runs his thumbs across my cheeks. "You're not going anywhere."

"Corey, I—"

"I'm not holding you prisoner, but you're safe here. I might not have much, but you're welcome to live here as long as you need."

My shoulders slump. I was so sure he'd tell me to leave, and I blink back more tears.

"Lily, my brother's partner, is coming to take you to buy some new clothes."

I shake my head. "I don't have any money."

"I'm paying. You need time to sort yourself out, and I'll take care of things until then."

"You can't—"

"I can, and I will. If you're starting a new life away from that place, you need to have more than the literal shirt off my back."

Biting back my lip, I stifle a laugh. "I like your shirts."

"I like you in my shirts. It drives me insane looking at you wearing them. So, for my sanity, I'm asking you to go and buy some more clothing." He drops his hands. His eyes search mine, and I melt into his in response. "Having you on my lap isn't helping either."

My eyes widen as I realise that it's not just his leg pressing against my thigh. Corey Campbell wants me, and I already know I want him.

I don't really know what to do, so I wriggle, and his lips part.

"I wouldn't do that if I was you."

"Why? What's going to happen to me?" I shoot him the most innocent look I can muster.

His lips curl into a sly smile. I want to dig my fingers into that beard and pull his face to mine. I've been attracted to men in the past, but never have I felt like this before.

"Well …" He leans closer.

A tap on the door leaves him chuckling. "That'll be Lily. I'm not sure if her timing is good or bad."

"We're going now? You didn't think it would be a good idea to give me a bit more warning?"

He runs his hand down my back. "I'm sorry. She offered, and then got a chance to get away without the kids."

"And am I supposed to wear this shirt to go out with her? What if Ash sees me? What if someone else sees me from—"

He places his hands on my shoulders. "She said she'd bring some of her clothes over so you'll have something to wear in public until you get your own stuff. Relax. We can trust her."

This time, there's a louder tap on the door, and Corey sighs. "As much as I like you sitting on my lap, I'd better go open the door."

He's so close, and he plants a kiss on my nose before gently lifting me off his lap and standing. Adjusting his trackpants, he heads to the door and pulls it open.

I follow and laugh at the look on Lily's face as he stands there, half-naked. Her mouth hangs open, and her eyes are wide. "You took so long to open the door, I thought you might have finished getting dressed."

He chuckles. "I was telling Con what you were here for."

She shakes her head and pushes past him, holding a bag out at me. "Here. I've brought a few things. There should be something in there that fits you, and once you're wearing a proper outfit we can go and get you some new things."

"Thank you."

She frowns, searching my expression. "Are you okay? You look like you've been crying."

I nod. "I'm fine. Just a little disagreement with Corey."

Lily arches an eyebrow. "I hope you won. He's a stubborn bastard, and sometimes he's wrong."

I laugh. "What do you mean, sometimes?"

Lily claps her hand across her mouth. "Oh, I like this one, Corey. She's a keeper."

He rolls his eyes, shaking his head with a smile on his face.

"Go and get changed, and let's get going. We can have lunch while we're out. There's this great little place where Adam and I go that has the best burgers."

"Sounds amazing."

I take the bag she offers and turn toward the bedroom. When I get to the door, I turn. Corey's in conversation with Lily, and although I was literally just in his lap, I hate the way they're so at ease with each other. *I'm jealous.*

This is something new, and I doubt I have any need to be. Corey's told me how happy she and Adam are together. Is this what a real extended family's like?

Shaking my head to focus, I place the bag of clothes on the bed and close the door behind me.

I smile as I pull everything out. Lily's brought a variety of outfits. I grab the jeans and a T-shirt that look like they'll fit.

The jeans fit beautifully. I've always worn dresses in the past, so wearing pants is a bit weird. I run my hands over my hips and thighs. These are something I definitely need for myself. The T-shirt is a little tight across the front, but it'll do the job. I feel like a completely different person.

Corey's eyebrows rise as I walk back in the room, and Lily smiles.

"You look great. Let's go get you some things of your own," she says.

I nod. "I'll just grab my boots."

"You're getting some of those jeans, right? Or keeping Lily's?" Corey says.

I roll my eyes, pulling on my socks and boots.

"I don't know how she puts up with you." Lily laughs.

"It's tough, I tell you." I stand.

Corey grips my shoulder. "Have fun, and make sure you get what you want."

"Oh, she will. I'll make sure she spends all the money you gave me." Lily laughs.

Corey grins. "Good." His gaze fixes on mine. "You deserve to be spoiled. I don't know if you've had too much of that."

"She will today. Adam's at home with the kids if you want to go and see him." She nods toward me. "If you're ready, Constance, let's go."

"See you later." Corey smiles at me. I hate saying goodbye, even for a little while. It's crazy. He's left me in the house alone while he's gone into town quite a few times now, but I hate the thought of him being here by himself.

"Bye."

With one last look at Corey, I follow Lily out the door and to her car.

It's the weirdest sensation leaving this place, even for a little while. This house has been my sanctuary, and maybe Corey's right in that I need to spread my wings a little.

But I'm content to roost here.

LILY'S NICE.

Really nice.

I can see why Corey's such good friends with her.

She knows enough to understand that I haven't really seen anything outside of the mountain, and she points out everything along the way to Carlstown.

"It's nice to have some company. I'm at home a lot of the time with my little girl, Rose, and while I love her to bits, it's so good to have some time out."

"Where is she?" I ask.

"With Adam. He worked last weekend and he hates missing out on his time with her. So, I could have brought her, but I thought it'd be a good chance for him to catch up." She shoots a glance at me. "I also didn't want you over-whelmed with family."

I smile. "The thought of being out and meeting other people has been a bit overwhelming. But it's nice to meet another woman. Corey's good company, but he can be a bit … well, he's such a man."

She laughs. "Can I say something? And you promise not to freak out?"

"Sure."

"I love watching Corey with you. People look at him, and they see that tall, bearded, muscular guy who kinda looks scary, when you don't know the real him. But you know he's a real sweetheart. And …" She takes a breath. "He has a lot of affection for you. It's written all over his face."

My cheeks burn. "He's taken good care of me. I'm not

sure what I'll do in the future, but he's been wonderfully accommodating."

"I've known Corey more than half my life, and I've seen him in relationships before. There's something really special about what you two have."

I sigh. "I don't even know what that is."

Lily pulls into a park, bringing the car to a halt. She fixes her blue eyes on me. "I doubt you have to worry much about the future. You'll have him behind you no matter what. And I wouldn't be surprised if you don't move out of his home." Her lips curl into a smile. "I was with you both for what, five minutes? You two will burn that house down with the way you look at each other before you move anywhere else."

I swallow. Does she think me being there is a bad thing? I can't tell from her words and the calm expression on her face.

She places her hand over mine. "Corey's been up there and alone for far too long. I don't know much about you, but I think you're good for him. And he's good for you. So, let's go and spend his money."

I laugh. It's good to have someone else on my side.

---

I HAVE no idea what to spend Corey's money on.

Every single piece of clothing I look at, I love. It's such a massive change from the garments I used to wear.

I'm overwhelmed by how everything I try on feels so freeing.

"Is there anything you want?" Lily asks.

"Just the whole shop."

She laughs. "Well, maybe I can tell you what I think looks best."

"I'd like that."

Lily smiles. "Corey told me a little about what you'd come from. I hope we can be friends. Sounds like you need a few."

"I'd really like that." I lick my lips. "He seems close to you."

"Corey's one of my best friends. I hope he wasn't being too much of a dick earlier."

For a moment, I'm confused. "Oh, when you arrived."

"You were clearly upset."

I sigh. "I think we're both a bit all over the place. He thought maybe I should leave, but then he doesn't want me to."

She scrunches her nose. "Leave?"

"Yeah. I think that he thinks that being there isn't enough. Like I should branch out and find something else. Live my life."

Lily shakes her head. "And you're happy right where you are, right?"

"Very." I pluck a shirt from a coat hanger.

"Maybe he's just a little confused. He's never lived with a girlfriend before."

I turn to see her shrug.

"I mean, he's had girlfriends, and they've stayed there for extended periods of time, but I always thought the one he ended up living with would probably be *the* one."

"I'm not his girlfriend." *Am I? Maybe I am.* "Do you think that's why he's confused? Maybe I'm not—"

She grips my arm. "Constance, I've never seen him talk about anyone the way he talks about you. There's so much pride and affection in his voice whenever he mentions your name. I think maybe he wants to give it a go."

"Then why can't he tell me that?"

A smile crosses her lips. "I think he's trying."

"Very trying," I mumble.

Laughing, she nods at the shirt. "That's nice, and a good price. You should try it on."

She points toward the changing room, and I take a couple of steps toward it before she calls me. "Oh, Constance."

"Yes?"

"Welcome to the family."

By the time we leave the store, our arms are full of bags, and Lily catches my gaze.

"Let's go and get some more things that you'll need. I don't know how you've survived three weeks in that man-cave."

I laugh. "It's not been that bad. I've got stuck into Corey's books."

She nods. "He's always been a big reader. But a girl has needs that he's just not going to understand. Let's go get you some toiletries. Oh, and shoes. You need shoes."

"My boots are nearly new."

"Yeah, but who wants to wear boots all the time? Live a little."

I can't help but smile.

And I can't help but think that I've made a friend.

## 11

COREY

I'm in the kitchen when I hear the crunch of gravel outside, and I smile at the thought of Con being home.

My thoughts are completely about her when in the past, Lily's arrival would have been the thing that made me smile.

I turn as the door opens, and the rustle of bags signals Constance's arrival.

What I see takes my breath away.

There's a shine in her eyes, and a grin on her face that sends thrills through me. I always want to see her this happy.

And she looks so different.

Those shirts of mine have engulfed her, and before that she wore that long dress. Now she's in a tank top and shorts. And with her change in outfit, there seems to be a new confidence radiating from her.

"Have fun?"

"We got so much stuff. I kept saying to Lily that we had

enough, but she told me that we weren't leaving until we'd spent all the money."

I laugh. Lily follows behind, her hands also full of bags.

"It's true. How often do you get to go shopping with someone else's cash?" She fixes her gaze on me. "We got some amazing bargains. Constance isn't going to need new clothes for a very long time."

I sigh. "I'm going to miss you hanging around in my shirts."

Lily rolls her eyes, and Con blushes. She's more beautiful than ever.

"Well now you can let her out of the house and not act so much like a caveman." Lily winks at Constance.

Constance giggles.

"She'd know if I was acting like a caveman. She wouldn't have even had my shirts to wear." Lily drops the bags on the floor beside the door, shaking her head as she laughs loudly.

"Well, with that thought I'll leave you two to it." She squeezes Constance's arm. "If you need anything, call me. Adam's never far away so I can leave the kids with him or bring them with me."

"I'm looking forward to meeting your family," Con says.

"We'll all get together really soon so you can meet everyone." Lily shoots a look at me. "Don't let him hide you away up here."

"I won't."

I step behind Constance, placing my hands on her shoulders. "We'll come and see you guys soon."

"You'd better." With a wave, she disappears out the front door, and for a moment we stand there.

I close my eyes. Constance doesn't smell like she did when she left the house. There's a sweet scent coming off her like perfume. I'm not sure how I feel about it.

"What else did you two buy?" I ask.

"Lily took me to get some shower gel and shampoo. So I don't smell so much like you anymore."

I lean over, my chin brushing her hair. "I liked the way you smelt."

"Then you probably hate the way I smell right now because I tried about fifty perfume samples."

I laugh. "But did you enjoy yourself?"

She turns, and she doesn't need to reply. Her eyes sparkle with happiness. "It was so much fun. Lily's so nice. I'm looking forward to meeting her family."

"They're the best. Max is ... well, Max is hard to explain sometimes. He's very full on, and you can't argue with him because he's always right. Rose is Lily, only smaller."

She laughs. "And Adam?"

"Adam is an idiot." I pause. "Was an idiot. They were apart a lot of years unnecessarily, and sometimes I think he's still trying to make up for it. He dotes on all of them."

"He's your younger brother, right?"

I nod. "One of them."

She smiles. We've talked about family, and I can almost see her piecing it all together in her head. "And you're the oldest."

"Yep. That's me. Old and living alone on the mountain."

She shakes her head. "No. Not alone anymore."

I reach and push a lock of hair back behind her ear.

"I guess not."

SHE INSISTS ON MAKING DINNER.

All the shopping bags still lie on the floor by the door, and I'm content just to see how happy she is. Today's been good for her. A break away from the house has done her the world of good. Constance is a woman who needs to bathe in the sun—not hide in the shadows like she has been these past few weeks.

It might just break me to let her go, but maybe I should.

My feelings are conflicted like they never have been before. I've always known my own mind, but she clouds my judgement.

I watch her from the doorway. The smell of onions and bacon fills the air, and she moves around the kitchen like she owns it.

It's hers. She owns me.

She moves to the fridge, turning and smiling as she sees me.

"Smells good. What are you making?"

"Well, we're kinda limited for choice. Someone needs to go grocery shopping."

I laugh. "I'm really bad at that."

"I'm making mac and cheese. I made sure the bacon and milk were out of the freezer this morning."

"What would I do without you?"

She crosses the room, and wraps her arms around my waist, leaning her head on my chest. "I don't know. What would you do without me?"

I close my eyes as I plant a kiss on the top of her head. "I like you being here. I'm sorry for what I said earlier. I'm so torn about everything right now."

"I'm sorry too. Thank you for organising today. I promise when I work out what I'm doing, I'll pay you back."

"You don't need to."

She breaks away, nodding. "I do. You've given me so much, and I don't ever want you to think I've taken any of it for granted."

I grasp her chin, pulling her face to look into my eyes. "I don't think you take anything for granted. Besides, I like taking care of you. You don't ever have to leave if you don't want to."

She licks her lips. I want to kiss her—take her in my arms and never let her go. But the last thing I want is to freak her out when I've sworn she'll be safe here.

"Thank you." Her words are soft, and her eyes are so full of warmth I get lost in them for a moment. "I don't know if I can ever express how grateful I am."

"You needed help. Still do. I'll be here for however long you need me."

She wraps her arms around my waist again. "You make me feel safe."

I hope she always feels that way.

---

"I don't know if I can get up." I laugh, placing my fork on the plate.

"Well, somehow there are still leftovers. I made a double helping, too." Constance grins.

"Are you saying I eat a lot?"

She nods, a huge grin on her face. "I'm not saying anything of the sort."

My jaw drops. "What is this? Make-fun-of-Corey time?"

With the sweetest smile, she reaches across the table and lays her hand on mine. "Would I do that?"

She stands, reaching for my plate, but I'm faster. I grab her around the waist and pull her onto my lap. "Yes, you would."

Laughing, she wriggles to get away, but my grasp is firm.

"And here we are again."

Her lips twitch. "Here we are again."

"I'll clear the dishes. You go and bury your nose in your book."

Constance wraps her arms around my neck. "You're so good to me."

I run my hands up her spine. "I could say the same about you."

She swallows and looks down. It's like her confidence wanes when we're so close. Again, I want to take things in hand, but I need to let her come to me.

That's if she wants what I want.

"Now, are you going to get off my lap, or do I have to do the dishes with you attached to me?" I laugh.

She smiles. "I'll go and read my book. Thanks, Corey."

My cheek burns with the kiss her lips brush me with, and in an instant, the warmth of her is gone.

She leaves me with more hope than I can bear.

CONSTANCE PUTS down her book when I walk into the room, a contented smile on her face.

I sit on the couch, facing her chair. "How's the book going?"

"I'm nearly finished book two."

I nod. "We can watch the movies if you want."

Her eyes widen. "There are movies?"

"We haven't even touched the surface, babe."

She grins. "I can't wait."

Licking her lips, she stands and takes a step toward the couch. There's hesitation in her face, and she clasps her hands tight together.

My cock stirs at her demure demeanour. "What's wrong, Con?"

"I don't want to sleep in that room anymore."

She's so nervous, and I give her what I hope is a reassuring smile. "If you're going to be here long-term, I can get a new mattress for the bed."

"You want me to be here long-term?"

I nod. "You need time to get on your feet, and there's plenty of space."

She licks her lips. "I still don't want to sleep in that room anymore."

"It's the only spare room. I …" I pause, swallowing hard as the penny drops. "Where do you want to sleep?"

Her cheeks pink up, and she squeezes her hands together. She opens her mouth only to close it again before taking a deep breath. "Your room."

*Shit.* The thought of her in my bed makes my erection even more painful. "Are you sure that's what you want?"

"Yes."

She shivers. If I'm reading her right, I think she wants this, but she's fighting her upbringing. If they had arranged marriages, I doubt there was much pre-marital sex.

"You know you don't have to do anything like this to stay here. I'll go and get a new mattress tomorrow if it's about the bed."

"It's not about the bed." Her eyes mist over.

*Shit. She thinks I'm rejecting her.* "I'm gonna ask you again. Are you really sure this is what you want, Constance?"

She nods. "But you don't. You only use my full name when you're trying to make a point."

"I never said I don't want you in my room."

Her eyes widen.

"But I want you to be one hundred per cent sure that I'm what you want."

"I am sure." She lets out a small sigh. "These past few weeks, I've learned a lot about myself. I wasn't a big fan of letting anyone pick who I should be with, but it's the way I was raised. Now I get to make my own decisions, and I choose you." She lowers her gaze, and then looks up at me through those long eyelashes. "That's if you want me."

I swallow, hard. "Come here."

She takes hesitant steps toward me, stopping well before she gets to the couch.

"You really want to know what I want?"

She nods. It's hard not to notice her breasts rising and falling in that tank top.

"I want to peel those shorts off you and lick your pussy until you're squirming beneath me."

The way she swallows tells me that while she's led a sheltered life, she knows exactly what I mean. Being so forward with her will either scare her off or show me what she's made of.

She takes a step forward. "What else?"

My lips curl into a smile. This shopping trip *has* left her full of confidence. I'm as hard as a rock, and I haven't even touched her yet. I'm bewitched by this woman who has lived so little and wants to explore everything. From the look in her eyes, that includes me.

"Do you want me to talk dirty to you, *Constance*?"

Her eyes widen, and she shrugs, breaking eye contact and looking away shyly. My cock twitches. She'll be the end of me. "Come here. I'll show you."

She walks toward me confidently, but fear is clear in her eyes.

"You never need to be afraid." I lick my lips as she reaches me. Leaning forward, I grip her arse. She spreads her legs and straddles my lap. "Is this really what you want?"

She nods, her lips parting as she catches her breath. I press against her shorts and settle back in the couch.

"You've shown me. Now tell me."

"I want this." She's breathless. "I want you."

"Are you sure?"

Constance slips her arms around my neck. "I'm sure."

"You know there's no going back after this."

She nods, grinding her hips against me. I catch my breath. If she keeps this up, I'll be finished before we start.

I press my hands to her waist, pushing her tank top up and over her head. Underneath, she's wearing a white, lacy bra that I'm sure came from her shopping expedition. But right now it's in the way, and I'm not stopping to admire it.

She beats me to the clip at the back, throwing the bra on the floor.

My reaction to her seems to have stirred her confidence.

*I want her.*

Her breasts are full, with pale pink nipples, and I close my mouth around one of them and suck gently. She sucks in a breath, and I grip her hips, pulling her down harder on me.

"I'm pretty full on, Constance. Are you sure you can handle me?" I tease.

"I have no idea."

I cup her face, pulling her toward me to kiss her. Her breathing's shallow, and I stop, my face close to hers. "I'll give you everything, sweetness. But I want everything in return."

She swallows, and I don't know if she had anything planned to say because my mouth's covering hers, my tongue sliding in between her lips.

"There's something you should know," she whispers when the kiss ends.

"What is it?"

"I've never done this before."

*Woah.* I was right. "Never?"

"There were rules. I couldn't ..." Her voice tapers off, and my heart aches for her. "I was supposed to wait until I was married."

"You're an adult."

"You don't know what it's like there. Ash controls everything."

Fire burns in my gut. It seems like it was Ash's need to control that led to what he tried with Hayley. When he couldn't get what he wanted, he drugged her in an attempt to claim her as his own.

The man's a pig.

"Well, I'm telling you now that your life belongs to you. You don't have to have sex with me to prove anything. You're so strong, Constance. You walked away from that life and left everything you ever knew behind, and—"

She presses her lips to mine. She moans a little as her tongue slips into my mouth. The woman's a fast learner. And it seems she knows exactly what she wants.

She pulls back, panting. "I'm not trying to prove anything. I want to be with you."

"Sweetness, you could have your pick of men. You haven't even been out in the world yet."

"I don't want anyone else. You're not the only man I've ever met, you know." Her lips curl into a smile. "But you are the most annoying."

I laugh, pulling her to me for another kiss. "You're so beautiful, and you don't even know it." I cup her breasts and look into her eyes. "What made you brave enough to do this?"

She licks her lips. "I feel like I've wasted enough of my life."

"You're young."

Constance raises her chin. "Maybe, but I know what I want."

"I believe you do."

She gasps as I suck one nipple into my mouth, then the other.

"I know what I want, too," I whisper. "I knew the night you arrived."

"Really? I thought you didn't like me at first."

I grin. "Do you think I'd let you stay here, and wear my clothes if I didn't like you? All I want to do is protect you."

"Are you sure that's *all* you want to do?"

I'll give her one thing. She's not afraid to speak her mind. In that regard, we're a lot alike.

"No. That's not all I want to do."

Constance presses her breasts against my chest, her face centimetres from mine.

"I want everything. You're moving in to my room. That's where you'll stay from now on."

She nods, shrieking as I stand up, her legs hooked around me. "Are you taking me to your bed?"

"No." I grab hold of a couple of the couch cushions and throw them on the floor. "In front of the fire."

She shivers. The room's so warm, I know it's not because she's cold.

"At any time, if you want to stop, just tell me. We don't have to rush this."

I close my eyes as she wraps her arms around my neck and says, "This is why I want it to be you. You care."

I shake my head. "You're everything to me." I take two steps toward the sheepskin rug, and lower her gently onto it.

"Corey." Tears well in her eyes, and I brush them away with my fingers.

"Are you sure this is what you want?"

"Yes, it's just …" She swallows. "You're everything to me, too."

I place a hand between her breasts, spreading my fingers. A gasp escapes her throat, but her eyes never leave mine. This woman belongs with me.

I reach for the button on her shorts, sliding them down her legs with her panties.

"You need to get undressed too." She looks so beautiful in the flickering light of the fire, and I smile at her words.

"Of course." I pull my shirt over my head, and she runs her gaze down my chest.

"Corey."

I stand, pushing my trackpants and briefs to the floor. Her eyes widen as she takes me in. Fisting my cock, I look down at her. "Is this what you wanted?"

She swallows, slowly nodding. I need to be inside her, to claim her, to do every wanton thing she wants me to.

I need her to touch me.

Kneeling, and then lying beside her, I place one hand on her torso. Even though she must be expecting it, she jumps, and I smile.

"Come here." I roll her onto her side facing me.

I kiss her, my tongue in her mouth as she strokes one bicep, her fingers dancing tentatively across my skin.

"Don't be afraid to touch me. I'll hardly be holding back," I say.

Her laughter is breathless as her touches become more than mere brushes, and her hand makes its way down my abs and toward my cock. I hold my breath in anticipation, closing my eyes as her hand closes around it.

Her touch sends shockwaves through my body. I run my tongue down her neck as she explores me, tasting her sweet flesh. Small gasps echo through the quiet room as I run my hands over her body, nipping at her skin as I go.

"Corey," she whispers.

My patience runs out. I need to taste her.

She whimpers as I pull away, spreading her legs and exposing her core.

I move down the rug, dipping my head between her legs, inhaling her scent.

Maybe this is wrong. She's more than ten years younger than me with zero experience of the real world. But I've wanted her since she arrived that first night, bluster covering her fear. She never needs to be afraid with me.

I grasp her thighs as she shivers.

I don't know what's a bigger turn-on: that she wants me as badly as I want her, or that this is virgin territory. Literally.

The thought that Ash Harris controlled her life grates on me. Who the hell was he to decide who she was to marry, who she was to fuck? Pride swells in my chest that my girl ran rather than did as she was told.

She picked the right time to get away. The gnawing pain in my chest reminds me that if she hadn't, if she'd gone along with Ash's wishes or been caught by him, her fate would have been a lot worse than this.

At that thought, I throw all doubts from my head and plunge my face into her pussy. She's all kinds of sweet, and wetter than I'd realised, but then it's not like she's had a man's hands all over her body before. And I've touched her nearly everywhere.

I moan at her taste, her clit swelling as I tease it with my tongue. Tonight, Constance Shaw gets everything I'm able to give her. She deserves that.

"Corey." She reaches down and grips my hair as she bucks her hips. My senses in overload, I push her harder, licking her like an ice cream, plunging my tongue as deep inside her as I can get. I want it all, and as much as I take, she's prepared to give me more.

Her body tenses, and I suck on her clit gently as she lets out a cry. *She's all mine.* She shudders under me, and I smile to myself in the hope that I'm the first one to make her come.

"Corey." There's so much emotion in her voice when she says my name this time. I slip a finger into her as I look into her eyes. She shivers when I stroke her clit with my thumb.

"Feel good?"

She's breathless. "That was amazing. Can we do it again?"

"We can do that as many times as you want, sweetness. Next time I want to see your face when you come."

Her eyes search mine.

"Right now, I need to get a condom. Should have thought about that before we ended up here." I chuckle against her thigh.

"I'm on the injection. Ash—"

"The last person whose medical advice I trust is Ash Harris. I'll go and grab one."

She nods, and I sprint to the bedroom and grab the condom box from the bedside cabinet. I grin as I return. "Hope I haven't broken the moment too much."

She shakes her head, sucking in a deep breath.

"It's okay, Con." I kneel between her legs, taking a condom from the box and tearing the wrapper. She watches as I roll it down my cock, her eyes wide. "We'll take it slow."

She trembles as I lower myself over her, and meets my gaze. There's fire in that look, and a little bit of fear. She's scared, but she wants this, wants me.

"It might hurt a little at first, but I promise it'll get better."

She gives me a small nod, and I line myself up with her

entrance. Her heat makes me gasp as I dip into her, the head of my cock finding warmth inside. She feels like heaven.

She feels like home.

I move slow, pushing my way inside. She reaches for my biceps and grips them as we meet.

"You're really tight, sweetness. Just relax."

"I'm trying."

Bending, I run my tongue over one of her nipples before finding her mouth with mine. She'll taste herself on my lips, smell herself on my beard, and she moans when I flick my tongue across hers.

Her body loses tension, and I give it one final thrust to take myself all the way in.

She's around me. Despite me being the one who needs to take the lead, I want to melt into her and let her do what she wants. Maybe next time.

I move slowly, savouring every movement. She's snug around me, her body coaxing mine to let go, but I won't give it that satisfaction yet.

She lets out a contented sigh, and I look into her eyes. They're so full of emotion, drawing me in as her body does.

"I hope I didn't hurt you."

She shakes her head. "I just feel really … full of you." A smile crosses her lips, and I laugh.

"As long as you're okay."

She reaches for my beard, looping her fingers into it and pulling my face back to hers.

"I'm more than okay," she whispers.

I kiss her again, moaning my release into her mouth. Relief floods through me as the pressure that began to build earlier in the evening is released, and I give myself to her, ecstasy rolling through me in waves.

Pausing, I scan her expression. Her breasts heave as she takes a deep breath.

"Thank you," she whispers.

"For what?"

"For taking me seriously. For giving me what I wanted."

I smile. "I wanted it, too."

"I know, but …" Tears roll down her cheeks, and I roll to her side, swiping them away with my fingers. "I'm so glad it's you, Corey. If I'd stayed, I'd have had sex with a stranger and given myself to a man I didn't want."

My insides burn at the thought. "You will never have to do anything you don't want. I promise you that. If you let me, I'll give you everything, but I'll never expect you to stay if you change your mind about this, about us."

She shakes her head. "I'll never change my mind."

"Never is a long time, sweetness." I pull myself out of her arms.

"Where are you going?"

"To get rid of the condom. I'll be back in a second."

When I return, I watch her for the moment. She's pulled the blanket down that lives on the back of the couch, and she's lying on her side just watching the fire.

I've already given my heart to her. There's no way I can deny it. I was never one to fall fast, but with her, there's been no thinking about it. It just happened.

Now, I just need to keep on keeping her safe.

"What are you thinking about?" I kneel on the floor beside her, pulling her into my arms as I lie down.

"Everything. How it was so dark that night I ran, and when the rain hit, I considered turning back. It all just seemed impossible." She smiles. "And then there was you. You were there when I needed you, and you've not hesitated since."

"I'll be there for as long as you need me."

Her eyebrows twitch. "Well, Corey Campbell, I think that might be a very long time."

———

THE EMBERS ARE DYING in the fire, and as much as I love lying here, stroking her body, it's time to move.

"What are you doing?" She laughs as I stand and lift her off the floor, scooping her into my arms, blanket and all.

"We're going to bed. It's going to get cold here."

"It'll be cold in the bed."

"Just as well I have you to keep me warm."

I walk her down the hall and into my room. Tugging back the bedclothes, I place her gently on the sheet.

"So, this is Corey Campbell's comfortable bed," she says, wriggling around as if she's testing it out.

"I told you it was better than the one in the other room." I slip in beside her, pulling her into my arms. Despite her concern, the bed is warm. I might have a fire to heat the house, but I still love my electric blanket.

"So much better." Her eyes search mine, and she reaches up, raking her fingers through my beard. "I don't know what to say to you because I'm unsure of how I feel. Thank you for being so wonderful."

"Thank you for stumbling into my life."

She smiles. "It's so weird. I thought I'd be scared until I was miles away from that place. But you make me feel safe."

"You are safe. I'll make sure of it."

She nods. "If I know anything, it's that."

I lean over, pressing my lips to hers. It's a gentle kiss, and when I pull away I realise just how exhausted she looks, her eyes hooding over with tiredness.

"You don't have to sleep on that uncomfortable bed anymore," I murmur.

With a faint smile, she snuggles into my chest and closes her eyes.

It only takes me a few minutes to join her in sleep.

# 12

## CONSTANCE

Corey's breathing evens out, but I can't sleep.

He has one arm under my neck, the other draped across my chest, and I lie on my back and stare at the ceiling.

I don't regret what we've done. Being with him was everything I ever dreamed of. But the very nature of my upbringing leaves me with a sense of guilt.

Ash and before him, his father, made all the decisions in the community about who married who. Chastity was drummed into us, although when Ash took over, his little harem was an obvious breach of that. Except that was okay, because it was the leader. He was different. The girls he picked usually thought it was some kind of honour.

The idea of Ash Harris's hands on me makes me nauseas.

*Corey's, on the other hand ...*

"Con." Corey's deep voice rumbles in my ear, and his lips brush my neck. "Having trouble sleeping?"

"I thought you were asleep."

"I'm a pretty light sleeper. Pays to be when I sleep rough while working nights."

I turn my head. The room's so dark, I can't see anything, but Corey's all around me.

"Are you okay?" he asks.

"I'm fine."

"But you can't sleep."

I sigh. "I've barely left this house, but this world is so different to the one I grew up in."

"You're feeling guilty because we had sex."

I wish I could see his expression. How the hell does he know that?

"A little. I'm glad we did it." I close my eyes. "Being with you is the best thing that's ever happened to me."

"Sweetness," he murmurs. His lips land on mine, and he gives me a gentle kiss. It's not filled with the urgency of his earlier kisses, but then again, it's for a different reason. This is why I have no regrets about being with Corey. While there's this raw attraction between us, it's not just sex. He cares.

"I don't regret walking away from the life I had, but I do miss Mum and Dad."

"Do you think they'll ever leave?"

I shrug. "They were there long before I was born. They've lived there for probably forty years. It's the life they know. I remember my dad saying ages ago that he didn't know how they'd cope out in the world. It's so isolated inside those walls."

"Maybe now you're here, they'll change their minds. We can help them if they want to go."

My heart thuds. "I can't go back to talk to them."

"No, but maybe I can."

"You'd do that for me?"

His breath is hot on my cheek. The ache in my core which has existed since that first night when he put his arms around me gets worse. I've gone from one extreme to the other.

I want him again.

*Now.*

"I'd probably do anything for you, sweetness."

I melt at his words. "There's only one thing I want," I whisper.

"What's that?"

I choke on the words. This is so unlike me, but if I don't show Corey, he's never going to know. Turning the rest of my body to face him, I hook my ankle around his calf.

"Oh." He shifts his hand to pinch a nipple, and I gasp. "You want me inside you again?"

"Yes." The word is strained, but it's clear, and before I can say anything else, his mouth is on mine. Every lash of his tongue, I meet with mine. I'm so determined to prove I'm his equal in this.

"Jesus, woman, you undo me."

"I hope that's a good thing."

"It's a spread-your-legs-for-me-and-I'll-take-care-of-you kind of thing."

I roll onto my back, and Corey moves quickly, quietly. I don't even hear him lift off the bed, but his breath moves from my cheek to between my legs.

I arch my back as he plays me with his tongue. I never imagined sex could be this good. Back home, it wasn't talked about much once a couple was matched. The descriptions I'd heard had sounded clinical.

There's nothing clinical about the way Corey's touching me.

He grips my thighs, his face pressing into my flesh. I tear up, loving that he's the only man to touch me this way. He's the only man I ever want to touch me.

"Hey." His voice is in my ear again, and I turn my head despite the darkness of the room. "Are you okay?"

"How did you know?"

"You sniffed. It wasn't loud, but I happen to have excellent hearing." His tone is kind and loving. I'm the luckiest woman alive right now.

"I'm just really happy," I whisper.

"I'm glad." He captures my mouth with his, and I surrender to my feelings. Nothing else in the world can compare to this.

In the dark, the drawer opens, and his weight's on me. I want this—I want *him* so much. He's so gentle despite his size, and I part my legs wider to let him all the way in.

"Fuck you feel good," he murmurs in my ear. I close my eyes as his lips graze my neck. He lingers, his breath floating above my skin as he moves inside me slowly. "Can't believe I could have fallen asleep and missed this."

I laugh. "I'm sure there'll be plenty of other opportunities."

His face is so close to mine as he speaks. "This is still our first night together. We only get one of these."

He speeds up, his weight lifting from me as he moves. I want to see this, want to see him, but the room's so dark, and even though my eyes have adjusted, I can't see enough.

I meet him with every thrust, and he groans. "Keep that up and I'll be finished before I've started."

But I can't stop. I'm way past my initial discomfort when he was first inside me, and the sensation of him moving in and out feels so good.

This is what sex should be like.

He finds my mouth with his, and his hand slips between us. I moan when his thumb strokes my clit.

"Come for me, Constance." His voice is right in my ear, and I spread my legs a little wider to give him more access.

Butterflies build in my stomach again, and when my climax hits it comes in waves, my body clenching around him.

"Holy shit." He slams into me and stops. His movements become slow and small, and I wish that I could see his face in the dark.

When he shifts off of me and to my side, I sigh. There's something comforting about having his body pressed against mine.

"Tomorrow, I'll go and get my annual check-up out of the way. It's a little early, but if you're on the injection, then we can ditch the condoms." He runs his hand up my neck. "I want to be buried deep inside you with nothing between us."

My breath catches. "I want that, too." I squeak, and he laughs.

"I think I've completely corrupted you." Corey plants a kiss on my forehead.

"You just woke me up."

"I like you being awake."

Corey was right.

His bed is a million times more comfortable than the spare bed is.

On the much softer mattress, I'm surrounded by him. He's so tall and well-built that I'm cocooned against his chest, wrapped in his body.

I feel safer than ever.

I didn't plan for this to happen. Maybe it was inevitable with the electricity between us. Though, until yesterday, I didn't know for sure it went both ways.

Now I do.

Corey stirs, burying his face in my neck, his lips grazing my skin. "Good morning," he murmurs.

"Good morning."

"I'm glad you're still here. I thought you might run in the night."

"Is that why I'm trapped underneath you?"

He gives me that throaty chuckle I love. "You're free to get out any time. I just like sleeping like this with you." His mouth latches onto my earlobe as his hand dips down between my legs. "Are you sore this morning?"

"A little. Not that I want to let it stop me."

"Good." He teases my clit with his index finger. "I don't know about you, but I could do with more of this."

"Me too," I whisper.

"But I also have things to do today and lying in bed isn't going to help." He leaps out of bed, and pulls back the curtains.

I roll until I'm looking at him, and pout. The morning sun catches his loving eyes, his broad shoulders—he's so beautiful.

"You can stay in bed. Get some rest before tonight." He waggles his eyebrows, and I laugh.

"Will I need it?"

"Yes. So, stay here and I'll bring you breakfast in bed."

"Really?" I tap my forehead. "I should have moved in here on my first night."

Corey chuckles. "I'm glad we got to know each other first. At least I know what you like for breakfast now."

I grin as he exits the room. The sight of him naked makes me sigh.

There's no way I could get rid of my grin, even if I tried. Last night was everything I ever imagined could be possible. My heart's a goner.

"Before I cook bacon, I should probably put on some clothes. That stuff spits."

I laugh as Corey flops back onto the bed. "That doesn't look like getting dressed."

He looks up. "Maybe I don't want to." Desire flashes in his eyes, and he crawls up the bed, pulling the duvet off me as he goes.

"What are you doing?"

"I want to love you in the daylight, sweetness. Then we can have breakfast."

I squeal as he keeps coming toward me, lowering himself next to me and draping his arm over my chest.

"Mine."

*What does he mean?*

I relax and close my eyes as he sucks gently on my neck. It hasn't taken him long to find the parts of my body that make me sigh when he pays attention to them.

"All mine," he murmurs in my ear.

No.

I don't want to be owned.

I can't help tensing up.

"Constance?"

I open my eyes to see his concerned expression, and a look of understanding crosses his face. "You might be mine, but I will never make you do anything against your will. Do you understand?"

Slowly, I nod. The memory of my last encounter with Ash is so fresh, and his insistence that he had complete control of me still rings in my ears.

"You're in charge of your own life now. And I promise that I'll always listen to you. If there's ever anything you don't want me to do, then tell me. I'll respect you."

As the tears well, I rest my head on his chest.

Maybe I should say something to him and acknowledge what he's said. But any words I have are lost in the overwhelming affection I have for him.

He considers me his equal.

---

DESPITE HIM TELLING me to stay in bed, I make my way into the kitchen. The smell of toast and bacon fills the air, and I breathe in deep as Corey turns to look over his shoulder.

"What are you doing in here?" he asks.

I wrap my arms around his waist, burying my face in his back. "I missed you."

"Missed me, or was your stomach grumbling?"

"My stomach doesn't grumble."

He laughs. "Are you sure? I thought I heard it from out here."

I slap his back. "No more teasing."

Corey turns and plants a kiss on my nose. "There'll always be teasing." His lips quirk. "But only the kind that gets you hot."

I roll my eyes, pressing my body against his. When I got out of bed, I stole one of his T-shirts from a drawer, and my nipples rub against the thin fabric, against him.

"That's cheating," he says.

"How?"

He captures my arms, holding them behind my back. My body's aching to be touched. All it's taken is one night, and I want more.

"Now you can't touch me," he says.

"I'm still touching you." I rub my breasts against him and he catches his breath.

"I need breakfast. And then I might need some more of you." He sucks my lower lip into his mouth before giving me a tender kiss. "But that's all you're getting for now, because I'm starving. You wore me out."

"I wore *you* out?" I laugh as he lets go of me and steps back.

"Yeah. You're insatiable. Can't get enough of me." He winks before turning back to the stove, and I grin as I take a seat at the table.

This house looks different today. Before, it was somewhere to stay, but this thing between Corey and me makes it home.

*My home.*

"I made you coffee." Corey places a steaming mug in front

of me, and drops a plate stacked with toast and grilled bacon on the table. "Are you okay?"

"Just thinking."

"About what?"

"How happy I am here. How everything in my life seems to have fallen into place when I was so lost."

He smiles. "I hope that includes me."

"It *is* you. The night I ran away, I panicked when I realised what I'd done. It all happened so quickly. But you've never wavered in taking care of me."

Corey nods. "Whether we'd ended up in bed or not, I'd never have let anything hurt you."

"I know." A thought I don't like crosses my mind. "This isn't just sex for you, is it? Because I can't—"

"If you think last night was just about sex, you're crazy," he says. I close my eyes, and he cups my cheek. "I'm not one to take advantage. Not like that."

"Corey," I whisper.

"I would never have slept with you if I didn't want more out of this. You showed up here scared and vulnerable, and all I've wanted since the day we met is to protect you."

I open my eyes and look into his. I've been here long enough to know how open he is—about everything. He's not the type to hold back and given that he's already extended an open-ended invitation for me to live here, I think I can trust what he's telling me.

"The only reason why last night happened is because we wanted each other. If you'd come here and thrown yourself at me at the start, I would have said no."

I can't breathe. "No?"

"You weren't ready. But we've spent the last few weeks

like an old married couple. You fight me on everything, and you know better even though you've only been outside those gates a short time. You're what I need." He lowers his voice. "You're who I need."

Tears blur my vision, and Corey runs a thumb under my left eye. "If you're not a match for me, Con, then I don't know who is."

I sniff, laughing, as he smiles. "Let's have something to eat."

Nodding, I pick up a fork. "I'm starving."

"I knew I wasn't the only one left tired by your neverending need for me."

As I stab a piece of bacon, I roll my eyes.

This is the life I always wanted—not full of fear or worry about what's coming next.

This is freedom.

**13**

---

COREY

I GO to the doctor in the morning.

"Corey." Doc Paton smiles as I walk into his office.

"How are you, doc?" I ask.

He nods. "Good. You're here early."

"I want a full work-up. Everything."

"Everything?"

I take a seat. "I'm in a relationship now, and she's on the injection."

He nods. "Fair enough. It's good to make sure you're safe."

I shrug. "I'm her first sexual partner, and she had the injection maybe a month ago?"

Smiling, he stands. "Well, the injection lasts three months. So, if she wants to make an appointment for two months' time, I'd be happy to see her."

"Sounds good."

"Let's get this done. The courier picks up for the lab this

afternoon, so we'll have your results in few days, with any luck."

"Thanks. Appreciate it."

I let him do everything he needs to. It amuses me that he checks my height every time I'm here. It's been the same since I was eighteen.

"Let me guess. Two point zero three metres."

The doctor gives me a weary look. I do this to him every single time. "Good guess."

I stay silent the rest of the appointment, pee in the cup when he wants me to, and let him poke and prod me.

"You know you're in perfect health, Corey. You always are."

I smile. "I know, but it pays to check. Look at Mum."

"Very true." He sighs. "It's tough. Just when you think you've gotten rid of it …"

"I'm going there after this."

He nods. "She's lucky she has all of you."

"Well, her illness seems to have brought us closer together." I lick my lips. "How long do you think she's got?"

"That's something your parents need to talk to you about." He looks over his glasses at me, as if telling me off.

"Fine."

"Want my nurse to call you with your results?"

I nod. "That would be good."

"Sure thing. Give your parents my regards."

"No problem."

---

It pains me to see my mother declining.

She's stubborn and won't be anywhere else but home. Dad's at home full-time now to care for her, living on their investment income. At least they're not short of money.

There can't be long to go now.

She's pale and struggling to keep her eyes open as I approach.

I'm going to miss her. We clashed all the time in my teenage years, but our relationship has mellowed over time.

"Hey, you old bitch. How are you?"

Despite her obvious tiredness, she smiles. Mum and I have always had an open and honest relationship. Or at least, I thought so until I discovered the line of crap she'd fed Adam for years. It's the one thing I know of that she kept from me.

"A box of fluffies. Isn't that what the Kiwis say?"

I sit on the side of the bed and lean over to kiss her temple. "You're as much of a Kiwi as I am, Mum."

"Maybe." She raises a hand and palms my cheek. "It's so good to see you."

"Now I know you're like this, I'll visit every day."

"We both know you won't. You'll get caught up somewhere in the bush and disappear for days at a time."

I shake my head. "Not anymore. Not unless I've got a job."

"What's changed?"

I can't fight the grin on my face. "I met someone."

"It's about time. Who is she?"

"She's one of my next-door neighbours."

Mum's mouth falls open. "No. From that weird place?"

"The very same. She left it behind, and she's been living at my place ever since. It was a natural progression to us being together."

"Are you going to bring her to meet me?"

I nod. "Another day. I wanted to check in to see how you were doing."

She grimaces, and rolls onto her back. "The days are so long now, Corey."

"I bet."

"I don't know how much longer I can fight this."

It hurts my heart to hear her say that, but Mum's never been a quitter. I swallow. "Then, don't."

Her lips twitch.

"I hate seeing you in pain. You should be in a hospital."

She nods. "Maybe. But I don't want to die in a hospital."

"You're so stubborn."

"I know."

Sighing, I reach out, flicking her hair off her face. "Love you, you stubborn cow."

She chuckles. "I love you, too. You boys are my world. I hope you know that."

"We all know it a little too well, Mum."

"Tell me all about your lady."

***

My youngest brother, James is home.

Since he went to university, we've barely seen him, but with Mum getting worse and him having finished his current year, he's been here for an extended time.

We haven't spent much time together.

Growing up, we weren't that close. I was thirteen when he was born, and much more interested in girls and my friends than my pesky baby brother.

It was when he was older that we became closer.

When Mum first fell ill, James fretted. He used to come up to my place and we'd go hunting, or just hang out.

I've missed him.

Tapping on his bedroom door, I don't give him a chance to respond before I push it open. "Hey, dude."

He's sitting on the edge of his bed, facing away from the door, his mobile to his ear. I shake my head in amusement, as he very clearly didn't hear me.

"Do you really want to hear what I want to do to you?"

Oh, Jesus. I need to make myself known before this turns into full-blown phone sex and he has his cock out.

I lean over. "What do you want to do to me, James?"

He leaps off the bed as I roar with laugher.

"My brother's here. I'll have to call you back." He ends the call and glares at me.

"I'm sorry. It was just too good an opportunity to pass up."

He frowns. "I didn't hear you."

"No, you were too busy sexing up whoever was on the other end of that phone. Got something to tell me, little brother?"

He shrugs. "What are you doing here?"

"I came to visit Mum, and to check in on my baby bro. You know, seeing as he hasn't come to see me in forever. Thought you might want to go for a beer."

He glances at his phone. "Sure. That sounds good."

"You're old enough to drink now, right?"

James rolls his eyes. "I'll just send a quick text and I'll be ready."

I nod. "Say hello to her for me."

His cheeks redden as he types his text, and I try to suppress a smirk. "Come on, let's go. We'll take my truck, and I'll drop you off before I head home."

"Sounds like a plan."

We head outside, and he cracks a smile as he climbs into the ute. "I thought you might have traded this thing in by now."

"And get what? She's never skipped a beat."

He nods. "I guess. Suppose it helps that Adam's around now to fix her when she does break down."

"Is this a diversion tactic to make me forget about that phone call?" I start up the car and back down the driveway, onto the road.

James laughs. "I guess it's not working."

"Memory like an elephant. You should know that."

"Fair enough. How have you been, anyway? Adam said you've got a new girlfriend."

I chuckle, moving into gear and pulling into the road. "Adam's right."

"He also told me where she's from."

I nod. "Uh-huh."

"You're not going to talk about her, are you?"

"Depends on if you ask the right questions." I laugh. "But seriously, I'm trying to look forward and not back for her. She's so much better off out of that place."

"I bet she is. What happened? Adam said something about her coming through the wall?"

"The cops loosened it not far from their little hideout, to give their guys the ability to come and go if they had to. She was sent through to escape an arranged marriage."

His eyes widen. "Woah. I knew that place was weird, but …"

"Yeah. To be honest, I think most of it's pretty harmless. They work the land and largely live off the food they grow. But something else is going on in that place. I'm just glad she's with me now and not still there."

He grins. "I can't wait to meet her."

"Maybe you can when I meet your lady."

James laughs, and looks out the window as we draw closer to the pub.

I guess that's a no.

———

WE GRAB a booth in the corner.

There aren't a lot of people in the pub at this time of day. It's mostly the old fellas from the cove who come here to bet on the horses and watch the racing.

"Thank you," James says.

"What for?"

"For inviting me out. I'm glad to be home, but it gets a bit hard sometimes. I hate seeing Mum like this."

I nod. "I get that. Any time you want to come up to my place, you know you're welcome."

"Even with your new girlfriend?"

I take a sip of beer. "She'd love to meet you. I think you'd really like her. She's a reader, like you." *And closer in age to you.*

"And you."

"We do have that in common." I pause. "So, who was that on the phone?" His eyes shoot to the ceiling, and I grin.

"Dude, it's okay. I'm your big brother. You can tell me anything."

"I met someone."

"I guessed that. You moped around after Ashley left for long enough. If it makes you happy, I'm happy."

He smiles, running his finger around the rim of his beer glass. "Thanks."

"Are you going to bring her home to meet us?"

I swear, there's terror in his eyes for a fleeting moment. He shrugs. "Not yet. It's … complicated."

Nodding, I take a sip of my beer. "Well, if you ever need to talk about anything, you know where I am."

"Thanks, Corey. I want to, but …"

"It's okay. Just remember that if the shit hits the fan, we're all here for you. You've been gone so long, man. It's so good to see you."

He forces a smile. "I wanted to see Mum before, well—you know."

"I sure do."

"Do you think she's got long left?"

I shrug. "You know her. She'll hang on as long as possible. But who knows? I'm glad her and Dad have got to spend time with Max and Rose. I only wish it had happened sooner."

He nods. "If Adam hadn't come back, I might not have started studying."

"Is that where you met your new lady?"

James might be older now, but his cheeks still go red when he's got something to hide. "Umm, well …"

"It's okay. You don't have to answer that."

He looks so relieved, I laugh.

"Look. Whatever's going on, you don't have to tell me. But know that I'm here for you if you need it. Okay?"

James nods. "Thanks."

"It's pointless asking Dad for advice. He won't be thinking about anything other than Mum. Plus, I think he's a bit out of date. So, if you need an ear …"

"I know. I'm glad I have you guys if I need you." He sighs. "I love being back home. It feels like I've been away forever, but at the same time, this isn't home anymore."

I chuckle. "I'm sure. Just don't forget us when you leave uni and go on to some amazing career."

"Like Drew?"

Grinning, I slap him on the back. "Just like that."

"I do get to see him and Hayley from time to time. She makes a fuss over me, and it drives him insane."

"Good. Maybe it'll keep him on his toes. He'll hate her attention being on anyone but him."

James takes a sip of his beer. "You know, even a few years ago, I'd never have picked that we'd all be doing what we are. Adam's back, and with Lily. Owen, of all people, is settled down. Drew, I'm not surprised about." He focuses his gaze on me. "And then there's you. I'm glad you've found some-one, Corey. It always seemed like there was something missing from your life."

I nod. "I didn't know what it was until I found it. I've never been so happy."

"Good for you."

When I drop him off, I don't muck around anymore in town.

There's only one place I want to be right now.

*Constance.*

## 14

### COREY

HER NOSE TWITCHES in her sleep, and it's the most adorable thing I think I've ever seen.

There's no point fighting it. I'm smitten.

I love sex, but I also love my solitude. It's led to a life that doesn't usually involve women. The ones I meet don't tend to understand my need to live away from everything and everyone. I'm not that far from town, but far enough that I have my privacy up here.

Mum and Dad helped me out buying my block of land years ago, and with land being the price it is out in the middle of nowhere, I paid them back pretty quickly. It's ten hectares of mainly bush, and it's great for getting lost in when I need some time out. I know it all like the back of my hand.

I trace circles around Con's nipple. The last few nights have been the most incredible nights of my life, and my only concern is whether or not she'll want to stay on the mountain with me once she discovers just how much she's missing out on.

When she came home from her shopping expedition with Lily she was so animated. I'm sure she'll want to get away again soon.

I'm loathe to tell Graham about her because I know that he'll have a million questions, and even though she's strong, it's a lot to put someone through.

I know I have to tell him.

She could be the difference between cracking the mystery of what's happening next door and their investigation dragging on for God knows how long. I'm torn between knowing that and just wanting to hide her from the world and protect her.

At least when they arrest Ash for whatever shitty things he's been doing, the police will pack up and leave my property, and Con and I can get on with our lives—together and alone.

If that's what she wants.

"Morning." Her soft voice breaks me out of my thoughts, and I fix my gaze on her smile.

"Good morning."

"What are you doing?"

I bend, sucking her nipple into my mouth and letting it go with a pop. "Playing with you."

"Didn't you get enough last night?"

Raising my hand to her cheek, I smile. "I don't know if I can ever get enough."

"Feeling's mutual."

I kiss her, long and deep and never wanting to stop. When I'm working, I sleep rough, at the most in a tent, and usually I don't mind that. Comfortable in bed with her, I don't know if I ever want to do that again. In a few weeks, I've got a week-long hunting trip planned to cull possums. It's good money, and it's never bothered me to be away from home before. This time, I'm reluctant.

But it'll put food on the table, and as it's my contract I'll make some extra money from the pelts. It's a tough job, but I love working outdoors, and it beats using poison the way some landowners do. At least other animals aren't at risk.

My stomach grumbles.

"Want some breakfast?" I ask.

"I'll make it." She sits up.

"Don't you dare get out of bed." I run a finger up her leg until I reach her pussy. "I'll make breakfast, and then I'll take care of our other needs."

She laughs. "Sounds good to me."

Inserting a finger inside her, I grin. "Or I could take care of this need and then make breakfast."

Her breathing quickens, and I close my eyes as her hand closes around my cock. I wrap one hand around her hand and guide her, moving it up and down, gentle and slow. With my other hand I insert another finger, tilting the tips, my thumb rubbing her clit.

She moans, her movements becoming more urgent. Pressure builds in my body, and I fight my release. I pump my fingers in and out of her, and her hips slam into my hand.

"Let it go," I murmur, determined not to come before she does. The dirty thought of coming all over her hand creeps into my mind, and I strain to hold on.

"No, you let it go."

I laugh as she echoes my words back at me. "It's not a race."

"Are you sure about that?"

God, she's going to drive me insane, but if it means getting a hand-job to prove who's better at masturbating the other, I'm all for it.

"Corey," she cries as her body shakes.

"I … win." Relief floods me as I let go of my own release, and I chuckle at the thought of having to change the sheets. It's worth it to see Constance let go. She's a different person to the one who landed on my doorstep a few weeks ago, but no less determined.

She's a lot like me.

I love it.

She licks her lips. "Try again?"

I can't help but grin. "How about we have some breakfast? I want to take you for a drive today."

"Where?"

"To the cove."

She grins. "I haven't been there since I was little."

"That's what I figured, if you'd been there at all. It's a nice day, and we can go get our feet wet." I smirk. "As opposed to the bed."

It takes her a moment, but she blushes and laughs. "I hope I'm not too demanding," she says softly.

"I'm pretty sure I can keep up."

Her expression turns serious. "You must think I'm crazy at times."

I shake my head. "I think you're a twenty-two-year-old woman who's lived a very sheltered life. I'm pretty sure it's normal to enjoy exploring your sexuality."

"I'm glad it's you." She digs her fingers into my beard, and I love it.

"I'm glad it's me too. The alternative really disturbs me."

She licks her lips. "Do you think the police should know I'm here?"

I let out a sigh. "Yeah, they should. I've been weighing that up since you got here. I want that bastard taken down for what he tried on my sister-in-law, but at the same time I want to protect you."

"If you think talking to them will help, I will."

My heart swells with pride when I think back to her first days and how scared she was, comparing them to now. Now, she's so much braver.

I don't think she knows just how strong she is.

AFTER LUNCH, I take her for the promised drive.

Since she got all her new clothes, she's not been as scared of going outside. That dress had so much of her identity tied up in it, and wearing my shirts didn't ease her mind as much as having her own things. I guess adopting her own style has helped her confidence, or maybe it's just the feeling that she's less recognisable as 'one of them' now.

Whatever the reason, it's so good to see her shine.

We pull up at the cove and hop out of the car, walking across the parking lot to the beach.

"I remember coming here when I was little." She slips out of her jandals and digs her toes into the golden sand. "It's so peaceful."

"Sometimes. Other times it gets a bit crazy around here."

We walk along the beach. I like coming down here during the week while everyone else is working. There's barely anyone around, and it's so peaceful. She's so quiet, and I nudge her arm.

"I was just thinking that I could do with a little crazy. It'll be good to be around other people, and noise. I like the noise," she says.

"Noise?"

"My life feels like it's been so quiet. I didn't realise how isolating it was even though there were plenty of people around. Just being out like this is … liberating."

I grin. "I'm glad. If you ever get overwhelmed when we're out, tell me, and I'll take you home."

She shrugs. "I survived the shopping trip. I can survive anything."

Laughing, I wrap my arms around her waist and pull her into me. "I'm so proud of you."

"Are you teasing—"

She doesn't finish her sentence as I silence her with a kiss. Everything's perfect.

When I pull away, she looks at me with those big grey eyes full of affection. "That's cheating."

"Want me to do it again?"

Constance smiles. "As if I'd say no."

She laughs as I press my lips to hers.

We walk for a little longer, until she yawns.

"Tired already?" I ask.

"It's all this fresh air. I'm not used to it."

I shake my head. "What am I going to do with you? I can't take you anywhere. Come on. Let's get home."

She smiles. "Home."

On the way back, she falls behind, and I slow.

"Your steps are too big."

"Maybe yours are too small."

She pokes her tongue out at me, and I laugh.

"This is sounding a bit like *Goldilocks and the Three Bears.*" I grin. "I could always throw you over my shoulder like I did the night we met."

Constance laughs, squealing when I tackle her. I pick her up by the legs and throw her over my shoulder.

"Corey, put me down. Is it too late to tell you I'm afraid of heights?"

I spin her around and drop her to her feet. Her eyes show me just how happy she is, and that smile bores straight into my heart.

"There's not far to go. I'll make my steps just right," I say.

She links her fingers behind my neck. "Maybe we can have a nap when we get home. In your bed that's just right."

I grin. "Sounds good to me."

Holding hands, we walk the rest of the way back to the car park.

I reach for her hand when we climb in the truck and place it on top of the gearstick. She grins as I place my hand over hers and put the truck in gear to leave.

"I should learn to drive."

"That would be a really good idea. Then you wouldn't be so dependent on me." I shoot a glance at her. "Not that it's a bad thing right now. I kinda like it."

She smacks her lips together. "When we get home, can you call the police and tell them about me?"

I grip her hand tight. "Are you sure you're ready?"

She nods. "It's time for me to move on with my life."

GRAHAM'S on my doorstep after dinner, and not too happy.

He glares as I open the door.

"Graham."

"Corey. I'm still pissed you didn't tell me about your visitor."

"She walked in straight under your noses."

"You're so smug sometimes."

"I have every right to be. My only concern has been protecting Constance. She's safe with me."

He nods. "I have no doubt about that. You still lied to me."

I shrug. "What would you guys have done? She needed to feel safe, not be harassed about what she knew. Not at first. And I'm still going to be all over you if you give her too much shit."

A smile spreads across his face. "That's not the only reason you've kept her hidden, is it?"

"I don't know what you mean."

"I'm a married man. I know what that look means."

"What about it?" I snap.

He shakes his head. "Corey, as long as you're both happy and it's legal, I have no issues with it. I always thought it must be lonely living up here by yourself."

"It wasn't until she arrived." I lick my lips. "Graham, she'll tell you everything she knows. You don't have to be hard on her."

"From what I've heard of that place, she's probably been through enough. I just want a chat. There might be something that she thinks is insignificant, but is important to us."

I nod. "Better come in, then."

Constance is standing in the middle of the living room when we walk in the door, her hands clasped together. She would have heard a fair bit of Graham and my conversation.

I give her a wink, and her shoulders relax. "Graham, this is Constance."

He nods. "Nice to meet you."

Constance links her arm in mine, and Graham nods, as if acknowledging our relationship.

"You can ask me anything you want," she says.

"How about we sit at the table? I'll make coffee. You'll be pleased to know I've become quite domesticated since this one moved in," I say.

Graham chuckles. "You mean, you have milk *and* sugar?"

I nod. "Constance takes both. I'm not taking the risk of getting in trouble with her."

She laughs as she sits down. "I'm not as bad as he's making me out to be."

"Well, I already know Corey has trouble with the truth," Graham says. Thankfully his tone is amused and not angry. I should have told him earlier. I know that, but the thought of him talking to her now sets me on edge.

By the time I make the coffee, the pair of them are chatting like old friends. I place the cups down and sit between them.

"I was just telling Constance that this is an informal chat. Obviously she's not in any trouble, but I just wanted to reassure both of you that's the case. I'll take notes, but I just want to get some background."

I nod. "That's fine."

He directs his gaze to Constance. "So, I guess you already know my first question. Why did you leave?"

Constance flicks a glance at me. "Ash told me who I was to marry."

"You never thought it was unusual he was the one to pick out your husband?"

Con shrugs. "It's the way I was brought up. There are a few families that have been there since Ash's father, Robert, started the place, and they decided that was how things were to be."

"But you didn't want that?" Graham's eyes are full of empathy. I know he's interviewed a few former members of the group, and I'm sure he's heard stories.

She shakes her head. "I liked a couple of the boys when I was young, and then they were married to other people." She meets my gaze before looking back at Graham. "The more I thought about it, the less I liked the idea of having Ash pick my husband. I wanted to choose someone for myself."

"And you left when he picked a man for you?"

Her eyes glisten with tears and she nods. "The man he picked is around the same age as my father. I thought if I could keep my head down and under Ash's radar he might forget I exist. But he told me he was saving me for something special."

Graham's eyebrows rise. "Did he ever touch you?"

She shakes her head. "No, but he told me that John would be a safe choice, after …" Her cheeks flame with colour.

"After what?"

"There's someone Ash was doing business with. The guy spent the night with a couple of Ash's girls, and then wanted someone a little more … inexperienced."

"He was pimping you out?" I ask.

For a moment, she looks confused, and then she nods. "I

guess that's as good a word as any. It would be for one night, and then I'd be safely married to a man who didn't care if I was a virgin or not."

I have the biggest knot in my throat. "You didn't tell me that part."

She shakes her head, and looks down at her hands. "I was ashamed."

"Of what? You did nothing wrong."

Graham grips my arm. "I think Constance knows that. But can you imagine telling that story to someone you just met?"

"She just told you."

"Maybe because I'm the one involved in investigating that dodgy bastard. The more info she gives me, the better."

I nod, reaching for Constance's hand. "I'm sorry. It just drives me a little crazy that he thought he could run your life in this way. That he's run other people's lives."

Those grey eyes I adore are fixed on me, and she gives me a small smile. "I know."

"So where to next?" I ask.

"I've got a blueprint of the complex with me. We've gathered quite a picture of it, but I want to know if there's something we don't know about. Maybe Constance can fill in some of the gaps."

I squeeze Con's hand. "Are you good with that?"

She nods. "I'll do whatever I can. My parents are still in there."

"Do they want to leave?" Graham asks.

Shrugging, she sighs. "It would be difficult for them to do. They've been there for most of their adult lives. It's what they know. They don't trust Ash the way they trusted his father, but surviving in the real world would be a challenge." Her eyebrows twitch. "My mother was diagnosed with multiple sclerosis a few years ago. She has good and bad patches. I always thought we'd be better off closer to real medical care, but that's been their life for so long."

Graham lets out a loud breath. "It's a tough situation, alright. I'll talk it all through with my superiors and see what we can do."

"Thank you. If you can get an update on how my parents are doing, I'd be grateful."

"I'll ask." He turns over his papers. "I've managed to leave the blueprint in the car. I'll go and grab it."

Constance nods as Graham stands, and as he walks from the room, I take her hand in mine. "You okay?"

She gives me a small smile. "It actually feels good to get it all out. And I feel like I might finally be some help."

I lean closer, stroking her hair and planting a kiss on her forehead. "Remember, if it gets too much, I'll tell him to piss off."

"You're so good to me."

"You're good to me." Her smile grows, and I give her another kiss, this time on the lips. "I'm so proud of what you're doing."

I turn at the sound of paper hitting the table. Graham gives me a sheepish look. "Sorry."

"Let's get this over with," I say.

"Constance, can you please take a close look at this and tell me if there's anything we've missed?"

Taking a deep breath, she stands and leans over the table, running her index finger over the map and naming the buildings as she goes. "I can't think of anything else. I mean, I know this place like the back of my hand."

Graham frowns. "It's okay. I can't help but feel we've missed something, you know?"

"Let me take another look." She points at one part of the map. "There's the big house. It used to house quite a few families, but Ash took over the whole thing for himself and his girls."

Graham nods.

"Those buildings are for communal living. They're the original ones, where everyone used to live. And then the houses around, like my mum and dad's, they built over time when the families wanted a bit more privacy."

"Ahhh," Graham says. "I did wonder about that."

"It's usually the older couples who have their own homes. They take priority."

I place my hand on hers, resting on the table. She shoots me a small smile.

"There's the food hall, where everyone eats. And those buildings are laundry, just like you've marked." Her eyebrows knit.

"What is it?" he asks.

"That spot there by the greenhouse. It says storage."

He nods. "That's where the gardening implements for the greenhouse are. Right?"

"Yes, but there's more to it than that."

"Like what?"

"Under the greenhouses, there are bunkers. Ash's father was convinced one day the world would end horribly, and so he made concrete bunkers underneath. We used to play in them when we were kids, but it's a maze down there."

"How big are we talking?"

She traces her finger around the large greenhouses. "The whole way under the greenhouses. It looks like there's a concrete foundation, but it goes down into the ground. They were shut off when one of the smaller kids wandered off and got lost."

"You know your way around them?"

"It's been a while, but I used to know them like the back of my hand."

"Do you think there's anything down there now?"

She shrugs. "They were meant to house us, so there are bedrooms as well as storage rooms. I remember there being rooms of canned food."

"That's a great help, Constance. I'll leave a copy of this with you, and if you think of anything else, let me know."

Constance nods. "I'm more than happy to help. Sorry we didn't tell you earlier that I was here."

He gives her a reassuring smile. "I understand. This whole thing must have been terrifying. I'm glad you have Corey here for you. He might be a pain in my arse, but he's a good man."

She laughs.

Graham drains his coffee. "I'll get this info fed through, and hopefully we can get a damn breakthrough."

"It'd be good. Then you guys could get the fuck off my land." I chuckle.

"Yes. Yes, we could."

AFTER DINNER, I watch Constance as she lies in bed and pulls the duvet over her. It's been a long day.

"You okay?" I ask as I climb in beside her, my clothes discarded in a pile on the floor.

She's naked under the covers, and I suck in a deep breath at the feeling of her bare skin against mine. There's nothing better.

"Tired. I hope what I've given Graham helps."

"I'm sure it will." I stroke her face, and palm her cheek as she closes her eyes.

"I love being here with you," she whispers.

"I love you being here."

She opens her eyes and meets my gaze. "Do you really think they'll be able to find out what Ash is doing?"

"I hope so. Everyone deserves better. That wall needs to be taken down."

Her eyes well with tears.

"Hey." I kiss her cheek. "What's going on?"

"I feel so guilty, Corey. I got away weeks ago, and only now am I helping do something about Ash."

I raise my hand to her hair and sweep a stray lock behind her ear. "You shouldn't feel guilty. You were scared, and you didn't know for sure who you could trust."

"I trust you."

I pull her into my arms, and she rests her head on my chest. "You'll always be able to trust me, Con. I'll always believe you."

She's so tired she falls asleep within minutes, and I kiss the top of her head.

"Always," I whisper.

# 15

CONSTANCE



When I first got here, we'd watch television after dinner, or Corey would put on a DVD and we'd watch a movie.

Now, every night we lie in front of the fire. It's so cosy while the world around us gets colder the closer winter comes. He covers me with kisses all over my body, and I explore him in return. Corey knows me better than anyone ever has, and has learned how to thrill me in such a short space of time.

I fall a little more in love every single day.

Graham's spoken to me a couple more times since the first interview to get further details, but he's kept his distance other than that.

It's been two weeks since I first spoke to him, and we're snuggled on the couch watching a movie. My world's become so much bigger since I came here, and Corey has as many DVDs as he does books.

They could make a movie of what Ash is doing to our community.

I wonder if it's my fault he's like that. I turned him down.

*What if he's hurt my parents?*

"What's wrong?" Corey snaps me out of my thoughts.

"It's my fault."

He frowns. "What's your fault?"

"Ash. The way he is. I'm partly to blame."

Corey kisses my shoulder. "Con, he's nuts. There's no way you can be responsible for that. It's all on Ash."

"I rejected him," I whisper.

"Good." He searches my eyes, shaking his head.

"I was thirteen."

His eyebrows rise. "Pardon?"

"Ash was the guy that all the girls my age liked. He was a lot different back then, or at least, he seemed different." I sigh. "Everyone knows everyone there, so of course he knew who I was. When I turned thirteen, it seemed like my body flipped a switch. I had boobs, and I grew a half a foot in a few months."

"So you looked older than you were."

I nod.

"But he knew how old you were."

"Yes." I pause. "He was sweet. And I liked him. Really liked him."

"What happened?"

"He was my first kiss," I say. Corey tenses beside me. "And he wanted me to tell my father that when I was old enough, I wanted to marry him."

"Did you?"

I shake my head. "Even at thirteen, I think I was far too

sensible for that. My dad would never have listened. Besides, it was Ash's father who made those decisions, and he didn't take kindly to pressure from anyone."

Snuggling into Corey's chest, I link my fingers in his. "Ash spoke to his father, and he dismissed him. There was already someone closer to Ash's age who he had in mind. I'd have to wait until I was older to find out who he'd match me with."

Corey raises my hand to his lips, planting kisses on my fingers. "Ash didn't suggest you to be together after his father died?"

"No. That was four years later, and in that time Ash grew to realise what kind of power he'd have over people. He was so angry at me for not going to my father. He blamed me for his father saying no."

"This man he wanted you to marry?"

"John Parsons beat his first wife to the point where either he killed her, or she killed herself. The second one ran away —she was so scared. Ash took his time getting his revenge, but he still harbours a grudge. He'll always remember I rejected him, and that's why he chose me to be next."

Corey runs his finger under my jaw, tilting my head so my gaze meets his. "You were a child."

"That didn't matter to Ash." I swallow. "When he told me about his plans for me, I basically threw myself at him. As much as I grew to hate him, living in Ash's little harem would have been preferable to the fate he'd prepared for me."

His eyes are so full of sorrow. "He turned you down."

"I'm so thankful that he did. If he hadn't, I never would have found you. And I wouldn't have been happy. So, when I tell you how happy you make me, Corey, it's because I came so close to never coming through that wall."

His lips are on mine in an instant, and then he brushes them over my cheeks, removing the tears that fall. "Don't you ever blame yourself for Ash."

"I'm scared, Corey. I haven't heard anything, and I don't know how my parents are doing."

He wraps his arms around me and makes me feel safe. As he always does. "I'm sure if anything had happened to them, Graham would know."

I nod. "I guess."

"I'll ask him in the morning if he can get an update from his guys."

"Thank you."

He's right. That wall does need to come down.

**16**

___

OWEN

Visiting Drew is a rare trip.

He makes it home on a fairly frequent basis. The twins love the car, and he likes getting Hayley away from it all. Plus, he's trying to squeeze in as many visits with Mum before it's too late.

This time, it's Ginny and me visiting him, but first, we have our appointment with his friend.

I can tell by the bright, shiny, new-looking building we pull up out the front of that this isn't going to be cheap.

But I'll do whatever it takes to give my girl what she needs.

We dropped Ava with Hayley on the way. She doesn't need to sit through a clinical visit. Earlier in the week, Ginny filled in some paperwork so that Doctor Phillips could pull her medical records.

When her previous relationship fell apart, she continued down the treatment path her doctor at the time had set.

She'd been offered surgery then, but broken, she'd moved to Copper Creek to start a new life instead. It was my gain, but at what cost to her?

The receptionist gives us a warm smile.

"Ginny Robinson to see Doctor Phillips," she says.

The receptionist nods. "Take a seat. I'll let him know you're here."

I take Ginny's hand in mine. Her chest rises dramatically as she takes a deep breath.

"It'll all be over soon." I kiss the back of her hand.

"I know. It's just … I was on the waiting list for a while just to see a gynaecologist. This is so quick."

I grin. "Pays to know someone in the business."

She laughs.

"That's better." I kiss her on the temple.

"Ginny, Owen," a tall, blond man greets us.

"Doctor Phillips?" I ask.

"Please, call me Dion. Drew's told me all about you two." He holds out his hand, and I shake it, followed by Ginny.

"Don't believe anything he says." I let out a nervous laugh.

Dion laughs. "Come through, and we'll talk."

He leads us into a luxurious office, and I shoot Ginny a *What the hell are we doing here?* look. It's all a bit overwhelming. This might be Drew's life, but it's a long way from mine.

We sit on the large black leather couch Dion points to, and he picks up a file from his desk and sits in a matching chair opposite.

"So, I'll just tell you a little bit about me, and then we can talk about why you're here." He smiles.

I nod. Ginny reaches for my hand, and I squeeze it tight.

"I worked with Drew at the hospital, but since leaving

there, I've specialised in dealing with couples with fertility issues, and specifically endometriosis. That's where my focus is, and that's why Drew's sent you to me."

"Okay," Ginny says.

"So, Ginny, I requested your medical files from your previous doctor. You didn't have surgery when diagnosed?"

She shakes her head. "I had the ultrasound. My life got a bit complicated shortly afterward. The doctor suggested surgery, but I didn't follow through with it."

"Well, surgery is the only way to really confirm an endometriosis diagnosis. Although, looking at your symptoms, if I had to guess, they got it right."

She licks her lips. "Is there anything else you can do?"

He leans forward. "You already know what you're dealing with, so I'm just going to cut to the chase. In a nutshell, we can perform laparoscopic surgery to confirm the diagnosis and remove the endometriosis. And we recommend after the surgery for you to try to become pregnant in the first six to twelve months of the operation. That's when you have the best chance."

"Then we can have a baby?" Ginny's tone is hopeful.

"There's a much better chance of it happening if we do this procedure, yes. I know Drew would have told you that I can't promise anything, but I have a good success rate with this method. At the very least, it'll give you some relief from the symptoms."

She shoots me a smile. "I can live with that. It's worth a go, right?"

He nods. "Definitely. Now, we could do it on the public system, but there's a wait, and I can't tell you how long that will be. The alternative is to do it privately."

I swallow. "How much would that cost? We don't have medical insurance."

"I'll get my assistant to put it all together if you'd like to know. It's not cheap, but I think it's your best shot."

I nod.

Ginny snuggles into my side, and I slip an arm around her waist.

"Thanks for seeing us."

"It's no problem. Your brother and I go way back, and whatever I can do, I'll help." He smiles. "It's not going to be easy, whatever you do. But I can promise you that I'll do the best job I can."

I lean my head on Ginny's. I'm already calculating the figures.

It's not pretty, whatever the cost.

---

THE CAR RIDE back to Drew's is quiet until we get close to his place.

"Do you think we can do this?" Ginny's so quiet, and I know she's thinking what I am.

"Gin, we can't afford to go private. At least, not for a while. We'll have to save."

"Maybe we could get a loan?"

I nod. "Maybe. It's a lot of money when everything's tied up in the new house."

She sighs.

I reach for her hand and bring it to my lips. "Let's see how much it comes to. We'll know in a couple of days what it'll cost, and we can make a decision then."

Ginny rests her head on my shoulder. "It's okay. I mean, it doesn't have to happen now if we can't afford it."

"I'm sorry, babe."

"There's nothing to be sorry about. We're in this together." She sits back up, and I turn into Drew's driveway.

"Let's go and enjoy our evening with Drew and Hayley," I say.

She nods.

"Love you." I turn my head as I switch off the engine.

Her face lights up. "Love you, too."

---

DREW OPENS the door and ushers us into the living room.

Ava sits in the middle of the floor. She's got her big colouring book open, and pencils everywhere. "Hi, Daddy."

"What are you doing?" Ginny asks.

"I did so much colouring." Ava's eyes grow wide. "Logan tried to eat one of my pencils."

"Yes, he did." Drew laughs.

I nod at Drew. "Look at you, at home in the middle of the afternoon."

He shrugs. "Gotta be some perks to working for myself."

We sit on the couch, and he sits in a nearby chair. Hayley appears in the doorway leading to the hall, a big smile on her face.

"Ava's been good as gold. She let the twins climb all over her, and Logan did indeed try and eat a pencil."

"He's got no teeth." Ava laughs.

Hayley shakes her head. "No, thankfully he has no teeth. Yet. Do you two want a coffee?"

"I'd love one," Ginny says.

"I'll go and sort that out."

Drew leans forward. "What did he say?"

"He told us about the surgery option." I sigh. "There's the waiting list, but at least it gives us a bit of hope." Turning to Ginny, I squeeze her hand. She smiles at me, all the love in her eyes clear to see.

"I thought he might. So, Hayley and I have been talking about it …"

I cock my head. "Talking about what?"

"We'll pay for you to go private. It means you could have the surgery in the next few weeks, and—"

"Oh, Drew, it's so generous, but we can't accept that," Ginny says.

"Yeah, you can. Family looks after family, and I can't tell you how long that wait will be otherwise." Drew grins. "Maybe Owen can pay us back in bread or something."

"That's a lot of bread." I catch Ginny's gaze again, and this time it's so full of hope, I can't bear it.

"We love you guys," Hayley says, placing steaming mugs in front of us. "There's no obligation to pay us back. We just want to help give you the best advantage you can get to end up with what you want."

I swallow. My pride would usually stop me from accepting something like this, but it's Ginny, and I want to give her everything. Maybe even after the surgery we'll still fail, but at least we tried.

"How much do you think it'll be?" I ask.

"Don't worry about it." Drew fixes his gaze on me.

"Well, I am going to worry about it and the clinic will call me and tell me in a few days anyway."

"I'll pay it. You just get Ginny to where you're told to take her on time. That's all you need to do."

Beside me, Ginny lets out a pained breath.

I nod. "Thank you. Okay. Let's do it."

Ginny's grip on my hand is vice-like, and she leans her head on my shoulder. "Thank you," she whispers.

"Thank Drew. He's the one bankrolling this. Wait—does this make my brother your sugar daddy?"

"What's a sugar daddy? I have a cookie daddy." Ava giggles.

Ginny laughs, slapping me on the arm. "Look what you did."

"We are in *so* much trouble when the twins are old enough to pick up on the random things Drew says." Hayley grins. "But seriously, you guys, we're more than happy to help out. You've already got so much on your plate."

I exchange a look with Drew to try and convey my gratitude.

The truth is saying thanks will never be enough.

# 17

## COREY

I SPEND SO much time at home wrapped up in Constance, things are piling up for me to take care of. We're out of basic groceries again.

She's into her next book, so I leave her at home to go into town.

When I drive past the medical centre, I slow.

*Shit.*

I stockpiled on condoms last time I was in town, and time has passed so fast, I've forgotten all about my test results—the ones I don't have yet.

I pull into the car park and walk into the building. It's feast or famine in this place. It's either packed with people or empty.

Thankfully, it's empty this time.

Doc Paton stands in front of his reception desk.

"I don't think you've ever visited me twice in one year before." He laughs.

"I'm in town for a few things, and I realised I haven't had my test results back."

His mouth falls open. "Let me take a look. Sorry, Corey, we just got a new nurse and she's still learning the ropes."

I shrug. "It's okay. I should have followed up a week ago."

He walks behind the reception desk and taps on the keyboard. "It's all clear. The results came back fine."

"Thanks."

"Sorry again for the delay."

"It's no problem, really."

"Are you going to see your mum today?"

I sigh. "I popped in, but she's asleep."

He nods. "I think that'll happen a lot more from here on in."

"She's not got long, does she?"

He pauses for a moment, and shakes his head. "I'm sorry about that, too. She's always been a force of nature."

"Thanks for letting me know. I thought that might be the case, but Dad hates talking about it."

"I'm sure he does."

***

THE LAST TIME I had no beard, I was about twenty-two, and my girlfriend at the time hated facial hair. When we got to the point where there were more things she hated about me than liked, I grew the beard back and ditched the girlfriend.

Now, I stroll into the town barber like it's no big deal.

"Trim as usual?" Chris asks.

"Nope. Shave the beard off, and tidy up the hair."

The expression on his face makes me laugh. He doesn't need to ask me what the fuck I'm doing out loud.

"I want to tidy up for Adam and Lily's wedding. I know it's still a while away, but no time like the present, right?"

Chris laughs. He's been trimming my beard for the last seven years or so. "If you're sure."

"It'll grow back."

It takes a while as he cuts it back and then shaves me before giving me a haircut that makes me look more respectable than I have done in a long time.

I thought I might regret this, but I don't. My life is changing, and I want to change with it.

"Corey?" I look up from paying Chris and grin.

"Rob. Long time, no see."

"Dude. I can't even remember the last time I saw your chin."

"Me either. But it's all for a good cause. You know Adam's getting married in a couple of months?"

He nods. "I had heard. Bit early to get ready for that."

"I also have a lady at home."

A grin spreads across his face. "Anyone I know?"

"No, actually. I'm sure you'll meet her at some point."

He sits in the barber chair. "I'll look forward to it. Amy's planning a party soon. You guys should come to it."

"When?"

"I'm not exactly sure, but I can text you the date."

I nod. It'd be the perfect opportunity for Constance to meet my friends in a relaxed atmosphere. If she's not comfortable, we can always make it a quick visit. "Sounds good."

"You still up for Bruce's job? Now that you have a new

lady at home …" He turns his head. "Does she mind you being away for a whole week?"

Laughing, I shake my head. "I'm sure she thinks I do nothing at the moment. I haven't been on a job in weeks thanks to our haul at Bruce's place last time. Done a few day jobs, but nothing at night."

"Well, he bought more land and expanded his property. This trip might be even more successful than the last."

I nod. "Sounds good. Anyway, I should get going. I've got a few places to stop before I get home. Text me the details of your party."

"Will do."

I head out the door and down the road to the bakery. Owen makes these cheese and bacon croissants that are heaven on earth, and I have a sudden craving for one.

He does a double take when I walk in the door.

"Who are you, and what have you done with my brother?" He laughs.

I roll my eyes. "All I did was shave."

"And the rest," Mel says. "You scrub up pretty well. Who's the girl?"

"No one you know." I grin.

I don't have to see her to know she's watching. Those big blue eyes bore through me from the doorway to the kitchen.

"I thought you'd be at day care, Ava." I peek over the counter at my niece. Her gaze is fixed on me. She's such a sweetheart, and she usually throws herself at me to pick her up.

Instead, she inches toward Owen until she's tucked behind his leg. Her eyes never move from my face, and it registers with me why she's staring as Owen laughs. "It's not day care anymore. Ava's at school."

My mouth falls open. "School? How did I miss my girl starting school?"

"You're scaring her. Ginny's home today as she's not feeling well, and Ava's helping me now school's finished for the day.."

"It's Corey, honey." I smile. Owen shuffles around the side of the counter, bringing Ava with him. I squat in front of her.

She still stares in silence until I wink.

"Corey?"

I nod. "I cleaned up for Uncle Adam and Auntie Lily's wedding. Owen tells me you're going to be a flower girl."

She nods, still wide-eyed, but steps out from behind Owen. I open up my arms, and she falls into them.

"That's my girl. How's Ginny?"

"She's asleep," she whispers.

"Is she?" I scoop her up and onto my hip, and she squeals in delight. Riding on my shoulders is her favourite pastime. I think she likes lording over Max that she's taller than him when she's up there.

She pats my cheek. "The beard's all gone. It looks funny." She giggles.

"I'm sure it does." I pick up her hand and plant a kiss on her palm. I look over at Owen. "I just wanted to pop in and say hi while I was in town."

"You after any food?"

"Yeah, I could kill one of those cheese and bacon croissants. Or three."

He chuckles. "There are some in the kitchen that were

baked this morning. I'll throw some in a bag for you, and the lady I hear you have stashed away in your house."

"Stashed away?" Mel asks.

"She just prefers my company to anyone else's"

"Wow. That's as amazing as this one settling down." She nods at Owen.

"Miracles do happen, Mel. You just have to believe."

Ava cups my face and steers my gaze back to her. "I'm helping in the bakery today."

"Are you, sweetheart? I bet lots of people buy things from you."

She nods. "And I ate three cookies."

"I swear to God you'll turn into a cookie one day."

She rests her head in my neck, and I sigh. "It doesn't tickle anymore."

"That's the plan. Do you like it?"

Ava looks up. "No."

---

AFTER GRABBING SOME GROCERIES, I head to Adam's place. I want his help looking out for a small car for Constance.

I'm not teaching her to drive in my truck. It's a lot to handle for a learner. Especially on some of the roads around Copper Creek. The road up the mountain is windy, and I handle it because I know it so well. A new driver might not be so lucky.

When I walk in the door, one of Lily's eyebrows arches so far, it's like it's going to disappear from her face. "I can't even remember the last time I saw you clean-shaven. I don't know if I like it."

Shrugging, I grin. "Con will like it. My beard scratches her when I—"

Her second eyebrow joins the first. "I don't want to know."

"You'll get used to it. Or she'll decide she likes the beard after all."

Lily's eyes shine, and she smiles widely. She reaches for my face, running her palm down my cheek. "I love that you love her so much you'd make this change. Even if I'm not sure about it."

"Lily, have you seen my …" Adam walks into the room, his eyes narrowing in confusion. It takes a second for him to register who I am. "Corey?"

"The one and only. Bet you'd forgotten what I looked like."

He laughs.

Lily withdraws her hand, turning her attention to him. "What are you looking for?"

"Uhh." He shakes his head as if to remember. "My tape measure. I remember using it on the deck last, but I can't find it."

She smiles. "It's on the bench by the microwave."

His gaze shoots across the room. "Oh, it is too. Thanks."

"I came to see you, actually," I say.

He grins. "Walk with me. I'm measuring up for some new shelves in the workshop."

Once he's got his tape measure, we walk back out to the garage. It's so busy here, and a pleasure to see.

The workshop's full of cars, and there are a couple more waiting outside. Adam started off by himself and now has two assistants.

"Can you hold the tape measure there?" He points to the wall, and I take one end and do as instructed. "What's up?"

"I wondered if you could keep an eye out for a car for Constance. Something small and easy to drive."

"Does she drive?" He takes his phone out of his pocket to make a note of his measurement, and nods to indicate to me to drop the tape measure.

"Not yet, but can you imagine me teaching her in my ute?"

He shakes his head. "Good point. I'll keep an eye out. Things pretty serious with you two?"

I nod. "Very."

"Good for you, dude. I'm glad you're happy. I was worried you'd end up being some crazy old hermit up that mountain."

"Well, that's still a possibility. Less likely now, though. I even shaved for your wedding."

He gives me a sideways glance. "That's not for a while."

"I know, but I'm prepared. It'll be easier to maintain like this until the big day."

"I'm glad you're ready for it. I don't know if I am."

I stare at him, but all he does is laugh.

"Not that. I'd marry Lily tomorrow if I could. It's all the stuff that goes with it. Max and I are going to Carlstown next week for suit fittings."

"I've got to get that done, too."

"You feel my pain." He grins. "But I know it'll all be worth it. Lily will get a better wedding today than if we had got married all those years ago. I can't say it was worth the wait because I'd rather we'd got married back then, but I'm glad I can give her more this time."

I grip his shoulder. "Let me know if there's anything we can do."

"Will do."

# 18

## CONSTANCE

I'M NOT USED to late nights, and having so many of them are catching up to me.

Some evenings, Corey and I just sit up and talk. He tells me stories of his childhood, and I tell him what life was like for me.

His life sounds like so much more fun.

Right now, all I want to do is sleep.

I'm just drifting off when I feel the bed sink. Warm breath floats over my neck, and I smile at the lips that are right behind it.

But something's wrong.

The tickle doesn't come. I'm used to Corey's beard against my skin. Sometimes it's soft; other times, it's scratchy. But it's not there.

*Ash.*

I spring off the bed. My eyes struggle to focus at first.

"Con?"

*Corey*. I let out a loud breath of relief. What on earth has he done? My unkempt, bearded mountain man is clean-shaven and his hair's tidy.

"Corey?"

He chuckles. "I thought it was about time I tidied up. Lily and Adam's wedding is coming up, and ..." He reaches for my hand.. "I know the beard was a bit scratchy sometimes." His gaze shoots down between my legs, and the heat rises in my cheeks at the thought of what he means.

"You look so weird."

"It's still me. Come here and I'll prove it."

Before I know it, I'm on the bed and his lips are on mine. His tongue probes my mouth with gentle, tentative moves. It's like he's being shy with me when he knows me better than anyone.

"I love kissing you," he murmurs, dropping his head to my neck. I sigh as he nips at my skin. "I'll grow the beard back after Adam and Lily's wedding if you want me to."

"Yes, please."

His throaty chuckle sets my heart alight. I know now more than ever that this is where I'm meant to be: in Corey's arms, in Corey's bed.

"I even like it when it's scratchy," I whisper.

Corey rolls onto his back, pulling me with him so I end up lying on top of him. "Do you now?" He waggles his eyebrows. "Wanna try it when it's not?"

Despite my tiredness, I laugh. "Sure. Why not?"

---

WE NAP MOST of the afternoon..

When I wake again, the air is full of food smells, and I open my eyes to find a large paper package next to me.

"Hey," I say. "I didn't hear you leave."

"Hey," Corey says. He sits on the bed and opens the package. "I got a few things. There are fish, chips, scallops, and there's a bag with some donuts."

My mouth waters at the smell. "So, what did you get for you?"

He laughs. "There's plenty there. Are you hungry or something?"

"I think I could eat a horse and the rider."

Corey leans over, pressing his lips to mine. "Only if I'm the rider."

I lick my lips. "You cheated. How many chips did you eat?"

"I don't know what you're talking about." He picks up a chip and gives me a wink.

"You taste of salt."

He chuckles. "Fine. You caught me. I might have had a few. But there are heaps. I promise."

"Better be." I poke my tongue at him.

My stomach grumbles.

"Wow, you really are hungry."

"Told you." I pick up a chip and moan as I slide it between my lips. Nothing has ever tasted this good. It's a delicious mix of potato, fat and salt.

"You're so dirty, Constance."

"I'm only eating a chip."

"Want some sauce? I should go and get the sauce."

"Hmmm, sounds good."

"This is gonna be a really long night if you eat them all the way you ate that last one," he says as he leaves the room.

I laugh as I pick up another chip.

This is heaven.

---

I GO from being hungry to being bloated in the space of about fifteen minutes.

Lying back on the bed, I rub my stomach.

"Better?" Corey teases.

"Much. I'm ready for a nap now."

He chuckles. "I'll go and get rid of the rubbish and be right back."

Moments later, he returns, pulling his shirt over his head. I smile, placing my palm on his chest as he climbs into bed.

"Still sleepy?" he asks.

"After all that food? I could sleep for a week."

"Was that the first time you've had fish and chips? From the shop, I mean."

I shrug. "Possibly. I have memories of us going to town and to the cove when I was little, but they're not quite that detailed."

"I'm trying to think of everything we can do that you've never done before."

I pull him over for a kiss, then stroke his face. "Why?"

"I want you to be happy, and I want to make the most of the time we have together."

My heart stops. Does he expect this to end? "What do you mean?"

"I mean that you haven't seen the world yet. You've

moved less than a kilometre from where you've lived your whole life. You left the community behind, and there's so much out there for you to see."

I blink back tears. "Do you want me to go?"

A look of horror crosses his face. "No. Shit no. But I'm not so naive that I expect you'll be here twenty-four hours a day, seven days a week."

"I don't want to go anywhere."

"That's what you say now." Corey lets out a sigh. "I've seen enough of the world that I am happy. I was born in the States, came here as a kid, and I've travelled the length of New Zealand. It's enough for me."

"Why can't this town be enough for me?"

He smiles. "Maybe it is. You're so much younger than me, though. There's a whole world out there waiting for you to experience it. I won't be the one to hold you back."

I sniff. "You'd let me go."

Corey runs his index finger down the side of my face. "I'm just saying if you want to explore, I'll be right here."

I swallow. "I was born on this mountain, and I'll die on this mountain. The only question is where."

His eyes search mine. "Constance …"

"I'm right where I need to be, Corey. If I wanted to be out exploring the world, I would be." I reach up and palm his cheek. "I don't want to be anywhere else but here."

His face is so smooth, and I smile at the change he's made for me. For *me*. I didn't ask him to shave, but that he did it says a lot.

I trace my hand down over his smooth chin and up the other side of his face.

"I'm not sure if I like this."

He chuckles. "Lily said the same thing."

"You showed Lily?"

"I was in town getting it done. Figured I'd drop in and see how the wedding preparation was going."

*She saw him first.*

I have no doubt Lily's in love with Adam and not Corey, but my thoughts are tinged with jealousy.

"You could never play poker." He says it so gently. "There's nothing to be jealous about. I didn't go there to show her what I'd done. I dropped in to see my brother." He turns his head, planting a kiss on my palm. "And then I came straight home to you."

I catch his gaze as he looks at me, and for the longest moment, we just stare at one another.

Corey licks his lips. "Look, I don't know what to call this thing between us yet, but I do know that you are who I want to be with. This is the clearest my path has ever been. And if you stay, I'll give you everything I can."

"I just want you."

"You have me. You have all of me." He's so sincere, and my heart swells at the earnest expression on his face. If I know anything, it's that Corey's honest with me.

And that's why I love this man so much.

**19**

---

CONSTANCE

IT WASN'T JUST the dresses that were drab back home.

When we went shopping, Lily helped me find two beautiful lacy nightgowns. I'd never owned anything like them in my entire life—and I haven't worn either of them since trying them on in the store.

Later that night, I stare into the flames, sighing a contented sigh as Corey covers my body in kisses. It's hard to stay focused when his tongue skirts my bellybutton.

"We should just give up and bring the mattress from the bedroom in here." He laughs against my skin.

I reach for him, running my fingers through his hair. "It's not a silly idea."

"Do you remember the night we met?" He plants gentle kisses on my stomach.

"How can I forget? You threw me over your shoulder."

He chuckles. "Remember how we argued over the odds of being struck by lightning?"

"Of course."

"I don't know about you, but that night, I was."

For a moment, I'm confused. "You were what?"

"You're my lightning bolt."

My heart melts at his words. I don't even notice my tears until Corey kisses them from my cheeks.

"Don't cry, sweetness."

Sighing, I stroke his face. "I'm just so happy."

"I am, too. You make me happy. I can't even imagine what my life was like without you." He sucks in his bottom lip. "I've also got other news."

"What's that?"

He runs his hand up my stomach, cupping my breast. "My check-up was fine. If, and only if you decide to, we can ditch the condoms."

"Is that right?"

"Doc Paton says the contraceptive injection lasts three months, so if you had it the day you came here, you can go and get it again when the time comes. If you want to."

I smile. "It doesn't seem to disagree with me so far."

"All I want is to bury myself deep inside you. Become a part of you. With nothing between us." His lips brush my neck. "I want to come in you."

"Yes." The word comes out as a breathy whisper.

"What was that?"

"I want you inside me."

He doesn't wait. Holding my leg up, he guides himself into me. This is the two of us with nothing between us. He fills me as he always does, driving in deep. Nothing's ever felt so good.

"Fuck, you feel amazing," he says.

I moan as he thrusts slowly.

"Sweetness," he moans. I arch my back, needing every little bit of him.

Corey's mouth covers mine, and I fall apart underneath him. This is what I've spent my life waiting for—*him*. We're in our own little bubble where the outside world can't touch us. I want it forever.

"Constance," Corey moans in my ear.

I'm undone. I push up to meet him as he slams into me one last time.

We both breathe deep as he slowly pulls out and rolls to my side.

He pulls me toward him. His tongue runs across the seam of my lips before he kisses me again.

"Every time it gets better," he whispers.

"For me, too."

"All I know is that I don't know if I've ever felt like this before. We're so in tune. It's been a long time since I felt anything, really. Not since …" His voice trails off, but I know what, or rather who has crossed his thoughts.

"Lily," I finish his sentence, and he raises his head. He has such a wounded expression, but I'm not sure if it's because of his pain, or my own at knowing.

"How did you …?"

"The way you were with her that first day I met her. I know now that you had feelings for me, but the way you felt about her was written all over your face."

He swallows, and it only confirms what I thought. "Constance, I swear it's only you. It's been you since the night we met."

I nod, running my fingers through his hair.

"I already knew I was over my feelings for her when she took you shopping."

My eyebrows shoot up of their own volition.

"I'll always love Lily. But as a sister, not as anything else. The day before she came over, we had coffee and I knew then. Because all I could think about was you."

Tears fill my eyes.

"You're my girl, Constance. And the only one I want."

"I know," I whisper. "I know."

**20**

───────

COREY

I HATE BEING AWAY for the night. It's the first job I've been on since Constance arrived. I'm mindful of the fact that I'll have to work more often now I'm supporting both of us.

While I don't mind working, I'm not enjoying being away from her.

I'm just grateful that I told Graham about Constance. At least he knows she's there and maybe he can protect her, should anything go wrong.

*I should have got another dog.*

The thought twists my stomach.

For the first time in a long time, my head is back home and not where it's meant to be. I almost miss the sound I've been waiting for.

The branch above me creaks as the possum lands on it. I don't have to see it to know it's there.

I aim my rifle, using the night vision to locate him. In the silent night, the gunshot sounds like an explosion.

A thud comes from the forest floor, and I grab the torch, quickly finding him.

"Last one for the night I think." I mutter to myself.

I carry the possum to the back of the truck and drop him. Tomorrow, I'll take them to show the landowner. Then, I'll be off to Carlstown to see my contact who takes it from there. I'm paid for the pest eradication, and then I get paid for the fur, and sometimes for meat from the pet food factory.

It's not a nice business, but this land should be full of native birds. The possums kill everything they come across. The guy who farms this land has cattle, and the possums can carry bovine tuberculosis.

Our arrangement works out well for me—I'm just glad it's one night this time.

As I crawl inside the tent, my thoughts return to home. *What's Constance doing? Is she buried in a book? Or has she gone to bed, too?*

I check my watch. It's a little after two. I laugh, still not knowing the answer. She loves having so many books to read, and I love having that in common with her.

I've never really missed anyone like this before.

---

SHE'S on the couch when I walk in the door. My heart sings at the sight of her.

This is what I always wanted: someone to come home to. Someone who belongs here.

Nothing has ever felt as right as this.

"Corey?" Constance smiles, dropping her book to the

floor. She runs toward me, and I let my bags fall to the ground.

I need a shower, and sleep, but for now I wrap my arms around my girl and hold her, closing my eyes. She smells like my shower gel, and I bury my nose in her hair.

"Are you okay?" she asks.

"Never better. This is what I need." I let her go enough that she can look at me. Her eyes are full of affection, and I don't have to ask to know she's feeling the same way I am. "I've got a present for you."

"You do?" Her smile widens.

"I do, but I want a kiss first. And after I've given you your present, we can take a shower before bed."

Con snuggles into my chest. "I like that idea."

"I just need to go and get your present from the car. I couldn't carry it in with everything else."

Suspicion is written all over her face.

I grin as I grab the box from the car. She's gonna love this.

I get just inside the door, and she's by my side. "What's in the box?"

"Take a look and see." I hand it to her.

She opens the holey lid of the box, and the look on her face is priceless. Her mouth falls open, and I swear I can see the *awww* before she says it. "Chicks?"

"Trevor was frantic to get rid of the possums pestering his chickens, among other things. Spring chicks."

"This is my present?" She's completely focused on them, running her fingers over their fuzzy little yellow bodies. They don't have a lot of room, and they're jostling for space, making those high pitched chicken cheeps.

"We can find a bigger box for them for tonight, but we'll get something permanent in the ground in the morning. I figure they'll need plenty of space to run around, and we'll need somewhere for them to roost." I nudge her arm. "One day, we'll have fresh eggs every day."

"We will. Oh, Corey, they're gorgeous."

"You asked me once before about keeping animals here, and I told you I can't leave them alone for days. But you're here now, and I figure you're sticking around for a while."

She pecks me on the cheek. "Thank you."

I shrug. "Maybe I should have done it a long time ago. I'm sure Lily or one of the others would have been happy to check on any animals I had." I sigh. "I'm sure it gets boring being up here with just the two of us."

She shakes her head. "Believe it or not, I prefer it. I love being with you, and I miss you when you're not here, but for the first time ever I can hear myself think."

"That's why I like it, too."

"Let's go find a bigger box for them, and get in the shower. I could do with getting clean, and touching you." Con shivers, the smile on her face widening. "I've missed you."

"Missed you, too."

---

SHE'S STILL FUSSING with the chicks when I go to the bathroom and turn on the shower.

I sigh as the hot water hits me. My body aches from walking through the bush, and I know sleeping won't be an issue tonight.

Constance slips into the shower beside me.

"Let me show you just how much I missed you." I wrap my arms around her waist, and she giggles as I run my hands down to her thighs, pulling her legs up so she hooks them around me. I press her into the corner of the shower, cupping her arse, and kiss her, my tongue lashing over hers. This is turning into the perfect homecoming.

Dropping my head, I nuzzle her neck. I'm rock hard, and my cock is pressed against her pussy. I want in.

"I'm glad you're home," she whispers in my ear.

"Me too. I'm not sure how I'm going to survive a week away."

Her nails dig into my shoulders, and I raise my head. Her eyes search mine. "A week?"

"I've got a client that has trouble not just with possums, but stoats. And the area's so big, there are a couple of us who spend the week out there clearing it. I do it twice a year, and it pays well. It'll keep us going for the next six months, Con."

"Us?"

I press my forehead to hers. "Yes, us."

"Corey." There's so much affection in her voice as she cups my face.

I'm falling in love with this woman, and now is the time to show her that. "I want you to stay for good."

She nods. "That's what I want, too."

"Good." I shift my hand to her clit, and her lips part as I use my thumb to get her off. "Now that's settled, I'm going to give you the good fucking I think we both need."

She blushes when I talk like that, and now's no exception. Letting go of me, she slams her palms against the shower walls. Fuck, I love the way she looks when she comes. I might have given her multiple orgasms over the last few weeks, but it's like each one catches her by surprise.

"Come for me, Constance, and I'll fuck you."

She lets out a loud gasp. I've got her completely under my control. She can't move anywhere; she can't wiggle out of my grasp. I need to taste her. But that'll have to wait.

"Corey," she cries. Her body shudders, and she falls apart right in front of me. She hooks her arms over my shoulders, leaning her head against mine.

I pull my hips back, line up my cock, and drive into her, not giving her a moment to recover. I thrust, pushing her against the corner of the shower. She moans over and over again. She's so hot and tight around me, and I need my release as much as she needed hers.

"That feels so good," she says.

"You feel so good." I find her mouth with mine.

She breaks away to cry out as I bury myself deep inside her. She hooks her ankles together, pulling me in tight. I grin at her need for me being as great as mine for her.

I can't imagine ever being without her now.

When she giggles, I snap back to reality.

"What's so funny?"

"Nothing, really. Just that you're strong enough to hold me up like this."

"You weigh nothing, that's why."

She drapes her arms over my shoulders. When I look into her eyes, it calms me, brings me back to centre myself.

I slow. Her breath catches, and I close my eyes as I come.

Pulling out, I hold her while she drops down to stand in front of me.

"I think I'm a bit wobbly after that." She laughs.

"Me too. I'll sleep well tonight."

She picks up the sponge from the shelf, and squirts shower gel onto it. "Turn around?"

"What are you up to?"

"I thought I might scrub your back."

Her hand slides around my hip and I shudder. "Uhh, that's not my back."

Constance presses her lips to my shoulder. "I'll get to that. Promise."

I lean against her, closing my eyes as she runs her hands over me. It's like she's marking her territory, and I don't mind that at all. I already belong to her.

Afterward, she falls asleep first.

By all rights it should probably be me. I've had no sleep for nearly forty-eight hours, but I'm running on adrenalin.

I love watching her sleep.

She looks so peaceful, and I hope to hell she always feels that way.

This is it. *She's* it.

I slip my arm under her neck and curl my body around hers.

I've never slept better.

**21**

---

CONSTANCE

A PARTY.

I wasn't sure when Corey first suggested we go, but it's a chance to meet his friends. The thought of socialising terrifies me, but with Corey by my side, I'm pretty sure I can do anything.

"If you feel uncomfortable at any time, we can leave," he says for about the millionth time as we drive to his friend Rob's place.

"I know." I pat him on the hand.

"We've had this conversation, haven't we?"

I laugh. "Just a few times. It's okay, Corey. I'll let you know if I want to go home."

He grasps my hand in his, bringing it to his lips and grazing my knuckles with his kiss. "They can be a bit wild."

I take a deep breath. "I hope they like me."

"They'll love you." He pauses. "We're here."

We pull up to a large, old cream house. It's like a lot of the houses in Copper Creek—built a very long time ago, and taken care of. It looks like something out of the Victorian era, and it very likely is.

The sound of rock music lingers in the air.

Corey grabs my hand as I step out of the ute, and my stomach is a mess of butterflies as we walk to the front door.

He doesn't knock, turning the door handle and stepping inside, pulling me with him. "Hey guys."

I'm not surprised by the number of people here, judging from the cars outside, but for a moment, it's overwhelming. Men cluster around the chairs, some drinking beer, others with glasses of dark-coloured liquid. A few women drape off some of the guys; none of them seem to look up as I walk in.

"Come on. I'll introduce you to Rob."

There's a woman in the living room, sitting on the floor by the fireplace and talking to a guy. Her gaze flickers to Corey, and a sly smile appears on her face before she takes in the sight of him holding my hand. Her eyes narrow as she shoots daggers at me. I can't pretend it's not intimidating, but I know Corey will take care of me.

We reach the kitchen, and he finds who he's looking for. "Rob," he says.

Rob is around my height, with shaggy brown hair and a kind smile for me. The butterflies settle.

"Corey. This is your lady, I assume?"

Corey pulls me up next to him, hooking his arm around my shoulders. "Rob, this is Constance. Con, this is Rob."

"It's really nice to meet you."

"Good to meet you, too," he says. "When I ran into Corey the other day, I knew there was something different about him. I guess that's down to you."

I shrug. "I'm not sure about that."

"Well, you dragged him out of his house. It's been forever since he's been to one of my parties. I have them most weekends."

Corey turns his head, pressing a kiss into my hair. "I'm probably less likely to make it to them now. I've got an even better reason to stay home." He laughs.

"If I was you, I'd stay home, too." Rob grins. "Now, do you two want a drink? There's plenty of beer, and some vodka pre-mixes if you want one, Constance."

I look at Corey. There was very little alcohol in the community. I had a taste of beer once, but wasn't keen on it. Dad had laughed and said there would be more for him.

Corey smiles. "That sounds great."

"Who's driving?" Rob asks.

"Me," Corey says.

"Then Constance can drink whatever she likes. Come this way." He leads us to some big bins on the floor filled with ice and bottles. Corey leans over, grabbing two bottles and twisting the caps off.

"Here you go, babe," he says, handing me a clear drink with a silver label.

"Thank you."

He leans in. "Just take it slow. Okay?"

I nod.

"I'm not a big drinker," I say to Rob.

"No worries. Neither is Amy."

"That's Rob's wife," Corey says. "Where is she?"

"Around here somewhere." He twists his lips as if he's not sure if he should say what he's about to. "Did you see Tanya on the way in?"

"No. Shit." Corey's grip on me tightens.

Rob turns to me. "Tanya is Corey's stalker."

"You have a stalker?"

Corey laughs. "*Had* is probably a more appropriate word."

"She drove up the mountain while drunk and turned up on Corey's doorstep."

I widen my eyes at Corey. "Really?"

He nods. "Thankfully she didn't have an accident, but I made the mistake of letting her sleep in the spare room." Taking a sip of his beer, he chuckles. "I woke up at three in the morning with her wrapped around me. Fast asleep. Snoring."

"What did you do?"

"Moved to the spare room."

I slap his arm. "Seriously?"

"Wait until you hear what he did the next time." Rob laughs.

"I've got this two-person tent I take when I'm working. I made her stand on the front porch while I put it up, then threw a couple of pillows and a blanket in there and left her to it."

I slap my hand over my mouth, howling with laughter.

"But it didn't stop her. The next week she was there again. So, I called Graham Taylor and told him to come and pick her up for drink driving. He couldn't prove it, but he still took her home and sorted out someone to pick up her car." He chuckles. "She's barely spoken to me since."

"That'll be the woman who—" I start.

"Corey."

I turn my head. The woman from the living room's

heading toward us. I don't need to finish my sentence because it's pretty obvious who she is.

"What was that, babe?" Corey asks.

"Nothing." I give him a tight smile, and he winks at me.

"Tanya." He holds on to me, not giving her an inch.

She pouts. "It's been ages. Give me a hug."

"Nah, I'm alright. Constance, this is Tanya. Tanya, this is Constance. My girlfriend."

With zero shame, she gives him that sly look she did when we arrived. "Girlfriend? Another one?"

"*The* one," Corey says, and he says it without hesitation. My heart leaps as I exchange a loving smile with him. Her eyebrows shoot up.

Corey leans his head on mine, and I wrap my arms around his waist. When I look up, he plants a kiss on my lips.

"I just came to get a drink. Talk to you later, Corey." With a look over her shoulder, she goes back to the living room.

"You're such a stirrer." Rob chuckles.

"Everything I said was true." He gazes at me. "This one's pretty special."

"Good for you. I'm sure it beats being alone up on that mountain." He tilts his beer toward Corey. "At least she's human."

I stare at him with wide eyes, but Corey just laughs. "Did you also notice Tanya didn't take a drink with her?"

Rob grins, winking at me.

I think I'm going to enjoy myself here.

By the time I've finished my first drink, I'm warm and content. Corey's not left my side, and his arms have been around me more often than not. I'm so happy.

He does this for me.

It's not about the party, and socialising. It's about being with the man I'm falling in love with, and knowing he feels the same way about me.

Everyone is so nice. Tanya keeps her distance, but I catch her eye from time to time, and she's not looking any happier.

But it doesn't matter.

The second drink goes down as easily as the first one, and the buzz I'm on is incredible. Corey steers me into a corner, his arms around me, his hands resting on my arse. He's showing the world that I'm his and he's mine.

"Having a good time?" he asks.

I nod. "Your friends are so nice."

"You're nice." He brushes his lips against my neck, and I giggle. "I think you're also a little drunk."

"I've only had two drinks."

"And sometimes that's enough. Especially when you're not used to it." He raises one hand, palming my cheek. "God, you're so beautiful. I'm the luckiest man alive."

My cheeks burn. "You know you don't have to compliment me to get me into bed."

He chuckles. "You make me feel things I never knew I could. We should get out of here."

"What would we do at home?" I bite down on my bottom lip.

"I'll let you use your imagination."

"That might be dangerous."

Laughter rumbles in his chest. "I think we need to head

home. But I've got to go to the bathroom first. I'll be back in a minute."

He gives me a tender kiss before letting me go, and I watch him leave the living room, heading up the hall.

It takes about thirty seconds for her to show up.

"Constance, wasn't it?" Tanya asks, and I suck in a breath. "That's right."

"Corey seems really into you. Are you in town for long?"

I can't stop my eyebrows rising, although, I think that's because my face is feeling fuzzy and I've lost control of it. "I live here."

"Oh. I thought you must have been a tourist. He's hooked up with them before." She smiles her slimy smile.

"Nope. Born and bred in Copper Creek."

"Really?" She puts her finger to her chin. "I don't recognise you at all."

"I guess we don't hang out in the same places."

She nods. "Where do you live? I'm on Donovan's Road."

"At Corey's place. On McKenzie's Mountain."

It's her turn for her eyebrows to shoot up. "You're living together? It's that serious?"

I nod. "I'm meeting the rest of his family next week. The ones I haven't met yet."

Her eyes grow sad. "It must be so hard. I'd imagine it's very isolating up there, and you must miss having company."

*She'll dig her way to China if she keeps this up.* "No. We're good."

She leans in closer. I think Tanya's drunk a brewery's worth of beer. She reeks of it. "I still can't place you. Where do your parents live?"

"On the mountain."

She narrows her gaze. "Corey's the only one I know of who lives up there except for that bunch of weirdos …" Her eyes widen. "Oh my God. That's where you're from, isn't it? That explains your weird name."

"Excuse me?"

"There are so many stories about that place."

I frown. "What are you talking about?"

"Corey's not gone and hooked up with some inbred, has he?"

It's instinct. I know she's just doing her best to insult me, and I bite. But when I swing my hand, it never connects.

"How about we get you a seat, Constance?" Rob guides me to the couch.

"I'm sorry," I whisper.

"Not your fault. I'll get rid of her." He gives me a warm smile. "Corey's not far away."

I nod. "Thank you."

Tanya squawks as she's marched out of the room by Rob. I let out a breath.

"Constance, right?" A tall, dark-haired, bearded man sits beside me.

I nod.

"Corey's girlfriend."

"That's right." I hold my breath. This had better not be a repeat of what just happened.

"I'm Mark. Mark Malone. Corey and I go way back." He offers me his hand to shake, and when I take it, he lingers before letting it go.

"Where'd Corey go?" he asks.

"Bathroom. He'll be back in a minute."

"I think there's a bit of a queue."

He leans back on the couch, and takes something out of his pocket. "Want some?"

What he offers me looks like a fat cigarette. "What is it?"

"Weed." His eyes are glazed over, but his mouth moves quickly into a smile at my ignorance.

"I don't know if I should."

"It'll relax you. Corey does it sometimes."

"Really?" I look at his hand.

"Yeah. You seem to be having a good time. This'll make it even better."

I bite down on my bottom lip. My head's fuzzy with the alcohol, and although I know this is probably the wrong thing to do, it makes sense. Taking a deep breath, I reach for the drug.

"No way. There'll be none of that." Corey swoops in, placing his hand between myself and Mark.

"Dude. Your woman wants it."

"She's had too much to drink. She doesn't know what she wants." He takes my hand, and pulls me to my feet. "We're going home."

"You're no fun," Mark teases.

"I don't really care." Corey's tone is short, his words clipped. Tears well in my eyes at the sound.

Corey removes his jacket, placing it over my shoulders. I look up and into his eyes, thinking I'll see disappointment, but all I see is love.

"Let's go home." He bends, claiming my mouth in this room full of his drunk friends. It warms my heart to know he doesn't care if they see how he feels about me, and in that moment I don't feel self-conscious at all. The only thing that matters is the man whose arms I'm in, the man I'm going home with.

He leads me out of the house and toward the ute. After opening my door, he waits until I'm in my seat before rounding the car and getting in the driver's side.

"I'm sorry." I meet his gaze.

"You don't have anything to be sorry about."

"When he said you do it sometimes ..."

Corey grips my chin, pulling my face closer to his. "If you ever smoke that stuff, we do it at home, just the two of us. There's no way of telling how you'll react to it. I haven't smoked it in years."

"Really?"

He nods, pecking me on the lips.

"Mark's known me a long time. Truth is with the work I do, I can't afford to be stoned. There are guns in my house, and I had to go through all the police checks to get a license. I'm not about to screw that up." My eyes widen. How many guns does he have? He smiles, caressing my cheek. "From the look in your eyes, I think you're drunk, Ms Shaw."

I laugh. "Maybe. I feel warm."

"I'm going to get you home, get a big glass of water in you, and then you can sleep."

"I don't want water. I want you in me."

Corey chuckles. "You *are* drunk. You don't usually say things like that."

"Let's go home, and you can show me how much you want me."

"Oh, I do. Make no mistake about that. But I'm not having sex with you while you're drunk."

"Why not?"

Corey's gaze grows even more intense. "Because when we're together, I want you to feel everything. And I want you with me, not so out of your head you don't know where you are. Let's go."

I rest my temple on the car window all the way back to his place. My eyes grow heavy as we approach, and I don't even realise I'm falling asleep until we come to a halt.

Corey opens my door, holding me up as he gently pulls me out of the car. I lean on him, and he helps me up the steps and in the front door.

When we're inside, he scoops me into his arms, and I sigh when he places me on the bed.

"I want you," I say.

"You're slurring your words, sweetness. You'd be asleep before I was inside you."

I laugh, and my eyes are so heavy.

He has to hold me up to get me to take a sip of water. "That's not enough. You need to drink the whole glass."

"You can't make me."

He chuckles. "You'll regret it in the morning if you don't drink it."

I shake my head, flopping back on the pillow.

I don't know if he tries arguing anymore as I give in to sleep.

My head hurts.

I hold my hand over my eyes as I open them to shield them from the invasion of incoming light. Not that I really need to worry. Corey has this room so dark, very little light makes its way in.

I reach for him. Right now, all I want is to snuggle into his chest, feel his arms around me, and go back to sleep.

My hand hits the cold sheet.

"Corey?" I force myself into a seated position and look around. The sheet's crumpled. I can't remember much about going to sleep last night, but I'm sure he was with me. Although, that could be my mind playing tricks.

I shiver. Even on warm days, the mornings are cold here. Picking up a blanket and wrapping it around me, I make my way out into the living room.

There's no sign of him.

He's not in the kitchen or the spare room. I still don't like going outside on the off-chance Ash or one of his underlings might see me, but my heart sinks when I can't find Corey.

He was annoyed last night. I drank too much, and I nearly smoked drugs. He must think I'm some kind of child.

Planting myself in a chair, I pull my legs up underneath me and lean on the arm. He says he loves waking up with me, so I must have done something bad for him to leave before I woke. What on earth did I do last night?

I can't fight the tiredness anymore, and I close my eyes, feeling myself drifting off again.

The crunch of gravel outside brings me to my feet. I never checked if Corey's ute was there or not, but I can't assume it's him. *Please let it be Corey.*

My reaction time is slowed by this groggy feeling, and I hold my breath as the door opens.

Corey beams. "Hey, sweetness. How are you feeling?"

My breathing accelerates as I hold back the tears that threaten to leak from my tired eyes.

"Con?"

"Where were you?"

His brows knit as he frowns, and he steps toward me, holding up a plastic bag. "I thought I'd make you breakfast, but we were missing a few things. I'll get some toast and juice to help settle your stomach. I bet that's feeling a bit rough. And I got some ibuprofen. If I'm not mistaken, that's a killer headache you're sporting."

I let out a loud breath in relief, but I can't stop the hot tears that fall down my cheeks.

He drops the bag on a nearby chair. "What's wrong?"

"I thought … well, I didn't know what to think. You weren't happy with me last night, and I made a mess of things, and—"

"Who said I wasn't happy?" He places a hand either side of my face, wiping the tears with his thumbs.

"I must have embarrassed you."

"What makes you say that?"

I drop my gaze. "Everything's so new to me. I drank too much, and I would have taken drugs if you hadn't stopped me."

He sighs. "Con, you made mistakes. Everyone does that. I didn't think about the fact that you hadn't drunk alcohol, or that someone would have drugs there. But I never would have let anything bad happen to you, and you can chalk this one up to experience."

I look back at him. "I nearly punched Tanya."

Chuckling, he plants a kiss on my nose. "If you did, she

would have deserved it. I've had texts all morning checking on you to make sure you're okay."

"You have?"

"We're a close-knit bunch. Even if we're not all spending time together, everyone cares about one another."

"I feel awkward."

"I'm sure you do, but I'll be right here, taking care of my girl."

*His girl.*

He gives me a tender kiss, and I smile. "Now, let me get this bread in the toaster and pour some juice, and you can take some painkillers and go back to bed."

He turns, grabbing the bag and heading toward the kitchen.

"Corey?"

At the door, he stops, looking back at me. "Yes, babe?"

"Thank you for taking care of me. For everything."

A wide smile spreads across his face. "It's what I'm here for. Sit down, and I'll be back in a minute."

I can't help but give a little contented sigh as he disappears. Staying was the best decision I've ever made. I feel like I've wasted so much time stuck behind those walls when what I needed was right here.

Lying on the couch, I pull the blanket down from the back. My head thumps. "I am never drinking again."

"That's what everyone says." Corey chuckles as he places a glass of juice on the coffee table, and takes one of my hands in his. In it, he places two white tablets. "And maybe you won't, but it might be that you just need to find your limit."

He reaches down and strokes my hair. "I'll bring you out

some toast with marmite on it in a minute, and then you can get some more sleep."

I nod, pushing myself up to pick up the glass of juice. "Thanks."

"I'll always take care of you, Constance. If anything, I failed you last night by not paying attention to how even a small amount of alcohol was affecting you. I won't do that again."

I grab his hand. "You do take good care of me."

"I try."

He leans over, placing a kiss on the top of my head. "Just make sure you eat all the food. And when you get up, we'll have a bath. It'll make you feel better."

"You make me feel better. It must be like looking after a baby sometimes."

Corey smiles. "Not at all."

He turns and walks toward the kitchen before looking back over his shoulder. "Babies don't drink alcohol."

Despite my pounding headache, I laugh.

Payback will have to come later.

## 22

## CONSTANCE

I DON'T JUST LOVE BEING with Corey.

He comes with an entire family. It's clear they're all close, and they all love him.

And they all accept me without any hesitation.

At first, it was enough to make me want to weep.

I'm sitting in the living room at Lily's place with Lily and Ginny. The two women chat up a storm, and it takes a while for me to catch up sometimes, but they always stop to include me and explain what they're talking about.

"You know, for a while it was just me," Lily says. "The boys would get together, and I'd be the only woman. I liked talking with them, but it's nice to have you, Ginny. And Hayley when she's here." She smiles, and turns to me. "It's nice to have you here too now."

"I like spending time with you two. I'm looking forward to meeting Hayley. Corey tells me they have twins?"

Lily laughs. "Yep. Double trouble. Drew always wanted a big family. What about you? Do you have other family?"

I shrug. "Mum and Dad. If they have any family outside the community, they never told me about them."

"You might have grandparents, or cousins. Maybe we can help you find them."

I nod. "This new life is a little overwhelming. I'll look for them one day, but I just want to settle in." I miss Mum and Dad. Graham's last report was that they were doing okay, but I still worry. I'll ask Corey if he can get another update.

Lily pats me on the arm. "I'm sure. If any of us can do anything, just tell us. We all love how happy you make Corey."

"He makes me happy too."

She smiles. "I'm glad to hear it. I always knew it'd take someone special to settle down with him. He lives such a quiet life up there. I mean, I lived a little out of town, but I always had Max with me. Corey never even had a pet. Not after Brutus died."

"Well, we now have some chickens. And he's thinking about getting another dog."

Lily's mouth falls open. "No way. He said he'd never get another dog after …" I know she's thinking about what Corey must have gone through.

"He just wants to make sure I'm safe, with the threat right next door, and Corey working at night." I smile. "He hasn't decided yet, but I think he'll do it."

"If you ever need somewhere to stay when he's away, give me a call. You're always welcome here." She grins. "I'm sure Owen and Ginny don't mind giving up their couch either."

Ginny laughs. "Gladly." She takes a deep breath. "But we

recently bought the section behind ours, so our little place may not be so little for long."

"That's amazing." Lily clasps her hands together. "Owen's been in that flat for so long."

"Well, even if we don't have a baby, it'll be good for Ava to have more space. She'll have a bigger room, and a much larger yard to play in." Ginny's smile grows. "We're going to build a new house."

"Sounds perfect. I just love that you're not moving that far, so you're still near us." Lily laughs. She turns to look at me. "It's just a pain that you're up on that mountain, but if you want I can come and get you any time. We should have a girls' day out."

"I'd like that," I say.

"Me too." Ginny beams.

"Then, let's do it. And soon. Now, how about we open another bottle of wine?"

---

DINNER, dessert, and more chatting. I feel like I really fit in.

After a trip to the bathroom, I stand in the living room doorway for a moment. Owen and Ginny are sitting on the couch. Ava's fast asleep on Ginny's lap. It's such a sweet sight.

"Enjoying yourself?"

I close my eyes as Corey's lips brush my neck. "Very much. Lily and Ginny are lovely."

"You're lovely," he murmurs in my ear. His grip tightens around my waist. "I think we need to say our goodbyes and get out of here."

"Me too."

"I need to get you home and naked."

Laughing, I turn, and he loosens his grip. "Sometimes, I think that's all you want from me."

Corey shakes his head. I love him, and I think he might just love me.

He raises his hand to palm my cheek. "You mean everything to me."

"And you mean everything to me."

"I don't think I've ever been so happy. You appeared out of nowhere, and being with you is exactly what I've always wanted from a relationship. I love waking up with you, and I love that you're there when I come home from work." He bends, pecking me on the lips. "But I still want you home and naked."

I laugh, nestling into his chest.

"We need to make the most of the time we have together before I have to go away."

"Do you really have to?" I already know the answer, and I don't want to put pressure on him, but I can't help but ask.

"I wouldn't go if I didn't have to. We need the money."

Patting his arm, I look up into his eyes. "I know. I'm sorry."

"I get it, Con. I want to stay home with you, and if it were any other job, you might be able to convince me."

"Man make money to live." I grunt.

He laughs. "Are you trying to compare me to a caveman again?"

"Never. You have much more class than that."

"Well, this classy guy needs to get home."

After saying our goodbyes, we head out to the ute. Corey opens the door for me, as usual. I love his sweetness with me.

But that only makes the thought of being without him for a week even more painful. I want to be greedy and have all his time to myself.

When we pull into the driveway, Corey turns off the ute, and for a moment we sit in the dark. "Maybe I'll get a dog before I go."

I fix my gaze on him. It's a huge step for him to be thinking this way after what he told me about Brutus. His dog's death has haunted him for a long time.

"Are you ready for that?"

He shrugs. "Your safety's more important than anything else."

I wrap my arms around his neck. "Give it some time to be sure. There's a reason why you waited this long."

He nods. "I guess. Everything gets muddled in my head sometimes. I worry so much, but at least Graham and his guys know you're here."

"I'll be fine. We'll talk about it when you get back." I peck him on the cheek. "How about we get inside, and you show me how much you're going to miss me?"

He laughs. "Deal."

**23**

———————

CONSTANCE

"I WISH you didn't have to go."

Corey's leaving for work, and he'll be gone for five days. I've gotten used to spending every day with him.

I curl my arms around his neck and snuggle into his chest.

"I know. But this trip will keep us going for a few months. Longer, if we're frugal."

Raising my face to look into his eyes, I smile. "I'm good at that."

"I know you are. We make a great team."

He drops his head to meet mine, and gives me a kiss that curls my toes.

"I love you," I say.

His eyes search mine, and he nods, wrapping his arms around me tighter. "I'm going to miss you a lot. There are no warm bodies beside me out in the bush."

"I should hope not." I laugh.

His lips meet mine again, and he brushes his hands down my back until they rest just above my arse. Corey sighs. "I need to stop kissing you before we end up back in bed again."

"Would that be so bad?" I whisper.

"When I get home, I promise we won't leave the bed for a week."

I laugh. "I'll hold you to that."

With one last kiss, he's out the door, and I sigh as he pulls out of the driveway.

*He didn't say I love you back.*

This is going to be the longest week of my life.

---

I hate Corey being away.

While I don't mind being alone during the day, the nights are the worst. I lie in his bed and dream of him, his arms around me, his hands all over my body. I just miss him.

On day three, Graham Taylor knocks on the door. Since Corey told him I was here, I've answered questions for him whenever he's needed it. I want Ash taken down, too.

"Come to check on me?" I grin when I open the door. "I'll make you a coffee."

He shakes his head. "I've got to get back to town, but I wanted to give you some news." His tone's so grim.

"What's wrong?"

"One of our guys is missing."

I clap my hand to my mouth. I had no clue Jared and Kane were cops while I lived on the other side of that fence. Sure, it was unusual for young men to join us, but not unheard of. Most of the newer residents were female thanks to Ash, and Graham was the one to tell me his methods for finding them were dodgy.

All this stuff happening right under everyone's noses and we had no idea.

Most people in our community went about their daily lives, blissfully unaware anything untoward was going on. There was work to do, people to feed, the ongoing grind of life that kept us all busy. How were we all so blind?

"I'm so sorry," I say.

He licks his lips. "Thing is, I was wondering if you could tell us anything that might help."

"I've told you everything I know."

"He went missing after you gave us that information about the bunker." Graham sighs. "We have reason to believe that your parents are in danger, too. Ash's grown more agitated since you've left. Kane's told us that he's been threatening your mother."

"You have to get them out of there. Please, my mum, she's sick. They've done nothing."

"We know that. Ash doesn't." He places his hand on my arm. "Kane will do what he can to protect them. When's Corey back?"

"Umm, he's gone for three more days."

"Is there any way you can get in touch with him?"

I shake my head. "He said there was no phone coverage. I tried calling him just in case, but I got his voicemail."

He nods. "Okay. Well, it's a good idea if we can get you out of town."

"Corey's expecting me to be here."

"I'll tell him where you are."

I shake my head. "I'm not letting Ash Harris scare me away from my home."

His lips twitch as he seems to fight a smile. "I can't say I'm surprised. You seem as stubborn as Corey."

"I think that's why we get along so well."

Graham breaks into an all-out grin. "I'm sure." He sighs. "Anyway, I've got to get back. I've got an audio conference to discuss our missing officer and next moves. Do you have my number?"

I nod. "Corey wrote it down and stuck it on the fridge."

"You call me if you need anything. And if you change your mind about leaving here …"

"I'll let you know."

He gives me a nod and leaves me with my thoughts.

*What's happened to Jared?*

*Are my parents okay?*

I wish I could see them, but more than anything, I wish Corey was here.

**24**

---

COREY

I SHOULD HAVE TOLD her I love her.

The fire sparks as my fish cooks in the pan. There's a freshwater stream nearby, and I don't usually catch anything when we're out here, but by some miracle it happened today.

"Nearly done?" Rob walks out from his tent, and I nod.

"The potatoes boiled a while ago on the cooker. This thing only needs another thirty seconds, if that."

"I'm starving. Let's eat."

As I pull the pan away from the flames, my mind wanders back to Constance. There's no phone reception out here, and I can't just call her and tell her what I should have done. It wasn't until late afternoon, when we were getting ready to go hunting that I realised I didn't really reply.

I hate that I can't tell her until I get home.

"Corey?"

"Sorry, mate." I slide the fish fillets from the pan to the plates while he spoons up the boiled potatoes.

"You okay?"

"Just thinking about home. Well, Constance."

He nods. "I get that. I spent months wanting to get away from the noise of the kids, but it only takes a night away and I miss them."

I pick up the plate and a fork. The food might be basic, but it'll fill us up ready for hunting.

What I need to do is to focus. I've been coming up here for years, and this is the first time I've just wanted to get it over with and get home.

---

FIVE DAYS WITHOUT CONSTANCE.

We've had a huge haul of possum, and a fair few stoats. Those little bastards exceeded our expectations when it came to the damage they were doing.

Our find on the third day of a kiwi egg spurred me on. I haven't seen one out in the bush for years, but they're very obviously around, and this place needs to be as clear as we can get it. To protect them.

I think we've done the best job we ever have.

But my mind still turns to Constance on the way home.

When I pull into the driveway, I drive right up to the garage. In the back of the ute are two big chilly bins of meat, part of my payment for the job I've done. There's enough lamb and beef to keep us going for a few weeks.

Securing the meat in the freezer, I close the garage and head toward the house. Surely Constance has heard me by now. I'm surprised she's not out here already.

I'm tired, I smell, and I'm in desperate need of one of

those showers where you use all the hot water with no regrets, and I'm aching for Constance. Just the thought of her soft lips to kiss, and her hot, tight body makes me hard before I get to the front door. I turn the handle.

"Con?" I look around, but there's no sign of her. She's not in the living room, the kitchen or the bathroom.

The bed's a mess, which isn't like her. I never make the bed, but Con makes it religiously. My heart speeds up at this seemingly small thing. Something's not right.

My house seems too quiet. If I know Constance, I know her excitement levels will be off the charts to have me home. My hair stands on end. *Is she okay?* I've got a freezer full of meat and a healthy bank account, and right now I wish I had none of it. Leaving her even for a few days was a big mistake.

I search the bathroom, and step out the back door onto the deck.

"Con," I call before turning back inside. Plucking my phone from my pocket, I dial Lily.

"Hey, Corey," she says.

"Is Constance with you?"

"No. I visited her the day after you left for work, but haven't spoken to her since. Everything okay?"

"She's not here, and it's not like she can go far by herself. Maybe it shouldn't, but it worries me. She hasn't made the bed, which is so unlike her."

"That's weird. But there could be a good reason for it. Don't panic."

Unease prickles across my skin. Something's wrong. Really wrong.

*She's gone.*

I don't know how I know, but I do. When she's around, she fills my senses, and right now I can't sense her.

It's like hunting. I know how animals think, especially possums, and that's why I'm so good at what I do.

For the first time in a long time, I have no idea what to do.

A tap on the door knocks me out of my stupor. I turn to see Graham.

"Hey, I saw your car go past. I know you've been away, and there's something I need to tell you."

"Is it about Constance?"

"She's gone back."

My whole world falls apart. *What the hell? Why would she do that? Is she okay?*

"She's been spotted in the main house with Ash."

I shake my head. "No, she can't have gone back there."

"She's getting married in a month."

The ball in the pit of my stomach grows. For the first time in years, I've fallen in love with someone who I thought loved me back. "But I …"

Graham nods. "I know, and I'm so sorry, Corey. But there's one thing that's been nagging at me."

"What's that?"

"What if they planted her here? Jared disappeared following up the information she gave us."

I shake my head. "No, I can't believe it."

"Right now, it's the only thing that makes sense."

"You didn't see her when she thought they might have come after her."

He frowns.

"Graham, she was terrified. That first morning when you

came to the door? The day I lied to you? She had a full-on panic attack thinking you were Ash."

"Could she have been faking it?"

I shake my head. "It was a full-body reaction. Her palms were clammy when I held her hands afterward."

"Maybe that's how he's controlling her—fear."

"I can't believe that. With every little bit of freedom she's had, she opened up more."

He swallows, and grips my arm. "Corey, you're hardly going to see this objectively. You were sleeping with her."

"I believe her. I have to."

Letting go of my arm, he nods. "I understand. The intel we got said her parents were being threatened. Maybe that's her motivation. Whatever it is, I'm sorry."

I nod, but I'm hollow. There's nothing left of me without Constance. She's at the very core of my being. The one person who's all mine.

*Was.*

There's no way I can rest until I get to the bottom of this.

**25**

---

COREY

Adam.

I need to talk to Adam.

He's always been the brother who understood me best. Our falling out all those years ago pained me more than I ever let on, and then I was so angry that he walked away and didn't come back when Lily was found that I never bothered to go looking for him.

Now, I need him.

I pull up to the gate. Lucky runs up and watches as I unlatch. He wags his tail as if he's hugely excited to see me. This dog is the canine equivalent of Max.

Lily's standing in the kitchen when I get there.

"Is Adam here?"

Lily shakes her head. "He's over at Owen's. Ginny had some more problems with her car."

"Again? She needs a new one."

"I think that's what Adam's telling Owen." She smiles.

"Can I help?"

"I don't know. I wanted to talk to Adam."

It's as if she senses my agitation. Her eyebrows knit, and her eyes fill with concern. "How about I make a coffee? Go and sit in the living room. I'll be there in a minute."

I nod. "Sure."

Fidgeting as I look around the room, I realise what, or rather who, is missing. "Where's Rose?"

Lily grabs two mugs out of the cupboard. "She's fast asleep. We had a big morning at the park, and she's got molars coming through so she's not sleeping too well at night. I wore her out just so she could have a nap." She gives me a smile, but I can still see how worried she is about me.

I leave her in the kitchen and sit on the couch. My mind is going at a million miles a minute thinking about what Graham said. All I want is the truth.

*Why did she leave?*

I'm lost in my thoughts when Lily waves a cup of coffee under my nose. I smile, and she places it on the coffee table.

Sitting beside me, she takes a sip of her coffee. "Now, what's wrong?"

"She left me, Lily. She's gone back to her old life. Including the getting married part."

Lily's mouth falls open. She shifts her coffee to the table, and wraps her arms around my neck.

My whole life I've been the tough one. I've given people shit, without caring, especially when it comes to protecting my family.

But right now, my heart is broken, and the tears in my eyes are something new. I embrace them because this is the only way I can express myself. Even when Adam returned and Lily went back to him it didn't hurt this much.

"I'm so sorry, Corey. I don't get it. She's so in love with you."

I lick my dry lips. "Yeah, well, maybe she's not. I feel like shit, Lil. She told me she loved me before I left for work, and I never said it back."

"None of this makes sense."

"For days I was in the bush, thinking that was the most important thing to do when I got back. Tell her how I really felt. And now …"

I choke back the tears, and she grips me tighter. "I don't have any of the answers, but you know we're here for you. I wish I could talk to her and find out what's going on."

"You're not going anywhere near that place."

She shivers. "I wouldn't want to."

"Damn it. I just want to know why." Tears roll down my cheeks. Constance leaving has cut me to the core, and I have no idea how to recover from this. The thought of her marrying and sharing a bed with a man she barely knows makes my stomach roll. It makes no sense. She was scared because he was abusive. I want to kill him if he so much touches a hair on her head.

Lily lets go, raising her head to look at me. Tears are in her eyes, too. I know her well enough to know how much she feels. Seeing me like this is probably confusing.

"Do you want to stay for the night? Adam will be home soon, and you two can talk. We can have a family dinner."

I shake my head. "Maybe I should be at home. Just in case she comes back."

Lily sighs. "I can't even tell you how sad this makes me. She seemed really lovely."

"She is. I've never met anyone who pissed me off and made me want them all at the same time."

She laughs. "You two were really happy together. I just don't understand."

"That makes two of us."

"If you're going to go home, I'll talk to Adam. I'm sure he'll want to come and see you."

"I'd really appreciate it. I'm not sure how we all coped without him here."

Her face lights up. "It seems so long ago. But he's where he belongs now. I was sure Constance was, too."

"What am I going to do?"

"Oh, Corey, I don't know. It takes a long time to mend a broken heart. If it ever mends at all."

"Yours never did, did it?"

She shakes her head. "Not until Adam came back. And then, I was so scared. I thought if I took my eyes off him for even a second, he'd disappear."

"I hope you know now that there's no chance of that."

She gets this faraway look in her eyes. "We're really getting married this time. It feels like an eternity since we tried all those years ago." Her eyes turn sad. "I'm so heartbroken for you over Constance. You were in deep."

"It hurts so much."

She nods. "I know it does. I'll miss her. I didn't get to spend a lot of time with her, but I really liked her." She lets out a sigh. "I thought we were friends. Maybe she just needed to be back there, surrounded by people she knows well."

I nod. That's the hard part about living somewhere remote. It never even occurred to me that Constance would need more than just me.

I just don't know what to do.

---

It's dark when I find my way to the gap in the fence.

I've got no idea where I'm going, or where she is, but I'll turn this whole place upside down if I have to.

I need to know why.

Constance talked about walking through the maize field, and that's what I hit. I'm hidden here, and no one can see me. In the distance I can see lights, and at least I know which direction to go in.

The ground is soft beneath my feet, and I can't imagine what it was like for her that night, struggling in the weather all the way to the fence. I already know she's brave, but this sheds a whole new light on her fight to get out.

So why has she gone back?

All I can think is that she's returned to make sure her parents are safe. It's the only thing that makes sense.

Except for Graham's theory.

I don't even want to think about that.

"Graham thought you might be stupid enough to try this."

I hear the voice when I reach the edge of the maize. Someone's approaching in the dark. Someone who knows about me, and about Graham.

"Kane," I say.

As he reaches me, he pulls me back into the field, and flicks on his torch.

I recognise him from the day he turned up on my doorstep with Hayley. He's shorter than me, but the look he gives me is enough to make me raise my eyebrows. The guy's got balls.

"You need to turn around and go home," he says.

"No." I glower at him. He's not going to stand in my way.

"I'm trying to get close enough to talk to Constance. She's in the main house, and Ash has locked down access there since we got Hayley out."

I swallow. "She's with him?"

"I've seen them together. She's very hard to read, but she doesn't seem to be there under duress."

My heart aches. I teased her once about not being able to play poker. Every expression shows on her face. So if he can't see she's unhappy, maybe that means …

"Promise me that you'll make sure she's okay," I say.

He nods. "I will. The information she gave us was invaluable, and I'm sure Jared's disappearance has something to do with it. I'm so close. I'll protect Constance and her parents as much as I can."

I hesitate. I raise my right hand, and stab his chest with my index finger. "Do not screw this up. If anything happens to her, I'll hold you personally responsible."

He nods. "All I want is to solve this thing and get out of here."

Fisting my hands, I bite down the urge to ask why he hasn't already done it. I knew their investigation would take a long time, but the longer this drags out, the longer I may have to wait for answers.

"Go home, Corey. You're no good to her here. Ash has the

house tightly guarded. I'll get a message back through Graham when I know more. Okay?"

I look toward the lights in the distance. That house is there, and Constance is in it.

I need to know what happened.

I need her.

But I nod, and turn back.

As I reach the fence again, I pause. She's in there somewhere with answers for me.

But do I want to hear them?

# 26

## OWEN

"Owen, stop pacing. Come over here." Ginny pats the side of the bed, and reluctantly, I do as she tells me. Pacing helped with my tension.

"I just wish they'd hurry up."

She looks at me with all that love, and I realise I don't need to pace. "They'll be here soon, and I'll be fine. You heard the doctor. It's straightforward."

I nod. "I know. I'll just be glad when it's all over." Reaching for her face, I cup her chin. "Then I get to take my girl home and pamper her."

"Right now, your girl needs to go to the toilet, so get out of the way."

I take her hand and help her off the hospital bed. Why they always seem so damn high, I'll never know.

She shuffles from the bed toward the bathroom.

"Hey, Gin."

"Yes?" She turns as she reaches the door.

"Do you think you could bring home the hospital gown?"

She frowns. "What for?"

"Because I could watch your naked arse for hours."

Her mouth drops open, and she turns her head to check. When I meet her gaze, amusement is written all over her face.

"My bum is not on display." She laughs.

"Made you look."

As the door closes, I sigh. Making her laugh is important to me. I love seeing her eyes sparkle, and her cheeks flush pink.

I love her so much.

Today is important in so many ways. It'll give us both hope, and whether that turns into something beautiful or not, we'll always have that.

All I want is for Ginny to get pregnant and carry our child to term. It's not too much to ask. Surely.

And I want it for her sake. While I want to hold our baby in my arms, it'll be so good for her to have this happen. We grow closer all the time, but every now and then she stops and stares into the distance, this wistful expression on her face. I can't wipe it away, no matter how much I joke or tease.

I want in.

The door opens, and she does a little wiggle, holding her hands behind her back like she's covering her bum.

All I can do is laugh. "You are the most beautiful woman I think I've ever seen."

"Would I be even with my arse hanging out?"

I waggle my eyebrows. "Especially then." Grasping her

hands in mine, I squeeze them. "I hope they get this over with soon."

"So do I. I'm starving," she says.

"If you're a good girl, I'll bring you a cheeseburger for dinner."

The door opens, and a smiling Dion Philips enters the room with Drew.

"Hey, Gin." Drew grins.

Ginny drops my hand and turns toward Drew. He kisses her on the cheek. "I'm so glad you're here," she says.

"Me too. I can't be in the surgery, but I can take care of this one for you. Hayley's looking forward to seeing you both."

Dion nudges Drew's arm. "I've told Drew that if it goes well, I'll release you into his care for the night."

Ginny smiles. "We were just talking about that."

"You'll get the very best of care," Drew says.

"I'll just be glad when it's all over," she says. She's putting up a brave front, but I can see a little fear in her eyes.

He nods. "I bet. You'll be fine, Ginny. It's my pleasure to have you guys with us tonight."

"Thank you." She beams me a smile.

She's so damn happy to be having this surgery.

I hope this works.

***

DREW GETS PAGED ALMOST AS SOON as Ginny goes into theatre, and he doesn't come back for almost an hour.

"Hey." Drew grips my shoulder as he sits beside me.

"Hi."

"Sorry I had to go. Babies never stick to a damn timetable."

I laugh, despite my anxiety. "I'm just glad you're here now."

"Are you doing okay?"

I swallow hard, and close my eyes for a moment. "I had a bit of a realisation."

"What's that?"

"So, this whole thing. I want to make Ginny happy, and Ginny wants a baby."

"Okay."

"I hadn't actually thought about how much I want that, too." I turn my head to see my brother with a reassuring smile on his face.

"It's about time you realised that," he says.

"What do you mean?"

"You need this as much as she does. It's not like you had the chance to be there for Ava when she was a newborn. If you and Ginny work through this and it happens for you, you two get to do it together." He leans back. "And I can tell you now, there's nothing better on this planet."

"That good, huh?"

"Hayley and I grew closer when we had the twins. We bonded with them, and as a family. You guys already have a head start on that with Ava. Sharing this with her and Ginny will just bring you all closer."

I sigh. "I miss having Ava here."

"She would have hated sitting around the hospital, dude."

"I know."

Drew grabs my arm. "Want a coffee? I'll go get us one while we wait."

"That'd be great."

I look up to see Ginny's doctor walking toward us.

"Owen. Drew." He nods.

"How did it go?" I ask.

"It went well. She's just in recovery now, but she'll be brought in shortly."

"What happened?" Drew asks. I nod toward him as if asking the question too.

"Confirmed as endometriosis, and the removal of it was clean. It certainly isn't the worst case I've seen, but I can see why she'd have had pain and discomfort."

Drew nods.

"You know I can't make any promises, Owen, but if you and Ginny have any chance of having a baby, now's the time to try. After she recovers of course." The doctor grips my shoulder. The way he speaks to me makes me grateful he's a friend of Drew. At least I know he'll talk to us in plain English.

"Thank you for giving us hope," I say.

Drew throws his arm around my shoulders. "Our girl will be here in a minute, and once this guy clears her, we can take her back to my place. Just pamper her for the next couple of weeks."

"I pamper her all the time."

He leans his head against mine. "I know you do, bud. Just watch Ava doesn't jump all over her."

I nod. "She'll be so excited to see us when we get home."

"She sure will."

I extend a hand to Doctor Phillips. "Thanks, doc."

"You're welcome. I'll come back and see Ginny in a little while. In the meantime, hold tight."

"I'll grab that coffee," Drew says.

I nod, and sit down, letting out a loud breath. *It sounds good. Please let this work.*

Burying my face in my hands, I don't notice Drew's returned until he nudges my arm. I look up, and he hands me a takeaway cup.

"Here you go. You okay?"

I take the cup. "Nervous, but holding it together."

"When Hayley had that emergency caesarean, I was terrified. I mean, I was right there while she was having the surgery, and I could see how well it was going, but ..." He takes a sip of his coffee. "It's still scary."

"She's my whole life, you know?"

Drew nods. "I know. Believe me, I know." He grips my shoulder, and I meet his gaze. I'm so glad I have him with me.

Drew knocks my knee with his. "Now, drink up before it gets cold. I'm sure it won't be much longer."

I get down half of my coffee when they wheel Ginny back into her room.

Her eyes are closed, but I place the cup on the bedside cabinet and sit on the bed beside her anyway. I smile as those green eyes open, and I'm lost in all the love I have for Ginny.

I lean over and plant a lingering kiss on her forehead.

"Hey," she whispers.

"Hey. How are you feeling?"

"Pretty rough." Her eyes are still so hazy. "But not as sore as I thought I would be."

"We'll make sure you have plenty of pain relief," Drew says.

She shifts her gaze to him. "Thank you so much for everything. We owe you and Hayley big time."

He sits on the other side of the bed. "I hope it's successful. That's all the reward I want."

Ginny tears up, and he leans over to give her a hug.

"I'll do whatever I can to help you two get what you want. We won't give up, Ginny."

GINNY'S CLEARED to leave by early evening, and Drew goes ahead of us to his place.

As I'm driving, she closes her eyes. "I'm so glad that's over."

"So am I. I know that they're the experts, but I still sat and worried while you were in surgery."

She touches my arm. "I'd be the same if it was you. It's a scary thing."

"And now I get to take you home and treat you like you're made of china for a while."

Ginny laughs. "I might get used to that."

"I don't mind. But you'll have to be careful with Ava for the next few days at least."

"She's a good girl. Maybe we just need to tell her that I've been in the hospital and we all have to be gentle."

I nod. "You're right. She loves you so much that she'll hate the thought of hurting you." Flicking a glance at Ginny, I grin. "Our little girl."

We follow Drew into his driveway, and when I turn off the car, Ginny reaches for my hand. "Just give me a second."

"Sure." I reach for the door handle.

"No, I just want a second with you. In the quiet."

I nod, and lean over to kiss her. "Love you, beautiful."

"I love you, too. Do you think this is going to work?"

Shrugging, I reach up to palm her face. "There's only one way to find out. Once you're recovered, you're going to have a *lot* of sex with me."

She laughs. "Define a lot."

"At least three times a day. You might even have to sneak home in your lunch break for it."

"I only have half an hour."

I waggle my eyebrows. "Half an hour is all I need."

She grins, and inhales deeply. "Let's go and see Hayley."

"I thought you wanted a moment with me."

"I do, but …" She licks her lips. "I just need to pull myself together if we're going to see the twins. Today's been pretty emotional."

Suddenly, I feel like the biggest arsehole in the world. "Shit, babe. I didn't even think."

"I'll be okay. They're my beautiful niece and nephew. At least I'll be able to get cuddles."

I nod. "If you're ready, let's go. I'll just grab our bag from the boot."

She's already at the front door by the time I've rounded the car. Hayley's there, hugging Ginny and greeting her warmly. She ushers us both in.

Hayley smiles at me. "Want anything to eat?"

Ginny shakes her head. "I'd love a coffee."

"Coffee, coming right up." Hayley loops her arms around Drew's neck, giving him a kiss. "Good to have you home, too."

"I hope the twins have been behaving."

"We sat on the floor playing until they went to sleep."

He frowns. "I missed them?"

She laughs. "We both know they'll be up around two to have their night-time snack."

Grinning, he pecks her on the cheek. "Owen's used to getting up in the night. Defrost some expressed milk and he can feed them."

Hayley rolls her eyes, letting him go. "Do you want a coffee too, Owen?"

"That'd be great."

"Dinner's in the slow-cooker. If you're hungry, help yourself." She walks into the kitchen. I sit down.

"How are you doing?" Drew asks Ginny.

Ginny nods. "Sore and tired. You wouldn't think I'd be sleepy after being knocked out for so long."

"Anaesthetic will do that to you," Drew says. "If you need me to check anything, or if the pain gets worse, tell me."

She nods. "I will. I don't know if I can ever thank you enough for what you've done."

He smiles. "Told you, when you're being driven mad by a baby old enough to crawl, I'll be happy."

I laugh. "As awful as that sounds, it'll be great."

I catch Ginny's gaze. She does look tired, but so happy. If Drew thinks it's okay in the morning, we'll go back to Copper Creek.

I'm looking forward to being reunited with my daughter.

It'll be good to be home.

**27**

---

COREY

I miss her.

I've never had anyone under my skin as much as Constance Shaw is. I want to hate her for what she's done, but I can't.

All I do is miss her.

I bury myself in a bottle of bourbon or two. My phone rings, and it could be someone looking for me to work, but I don't care. I'm no use to anyone right now.

The hammering on the door starts when I'm lying on the couch. Some reality show's playing on the TV, but I'm not really paying attention.

"Go away."

"It's Adam."

Reluctantly, I drag myself off the couch and to the door.

He sighs when he lays eyes on me. "Dude."

"Come in."

I sit on the couch, and he sits beside me.

"I thought you didn't really drink," he says.

"There's not been any reason to until now."

"Still upset about Constance, then?" It's been two weeks, and the pain's not any better.

"Wouldn't you be upset if Lily left?" I close my eyes. "Shit. I forgot. Fuck. I'm sorry."

He gives me a small smile.

I run my fingers through my hair. "I miss her. I miss her arguing with me, and how she'd get so angry, and her face would get all red."

He nods.

"And then there's the sex. We couldn't get enough of each other. I miss her being torn between need and guilt." I pause. "And I miss that sweet, tight—"

"Dude. I get the point. You miss her. But right now, we have to get you together, because Mum needs us."

"Mum?" I press through the fog that surrounds me. *Mum.*

"This is it, Corey. We've all been trying to call you." Adam lays a hand on my shoulder. "It's time."

"Now?"

He nods. "Now."

"Adam, are you …?" Lily stands in the doorway. "Oh, Corey."

"Hey, Lil. Sorry, I'm a bit of a mess."

She sighs. "You've been drinking."

I nod. "Just a little bit."

Her annoyed expression falls as she looks at me with sympathy I don't want. "I'm sorry." She pushes Adam out of the way and sits beside me on the couch. He rolls his eyes as she pulls me into a hug. "It'll get better, Corey. I promise."

Adam sits in a chair—Constance's favourite chair.

"I don't know how. Everything makes me think of her," I reply.

She presses a kiss to my temple. "It will for a while. I've never seen you so down."

"I've never felt so bad. Not even when Adam came back to you." I shouldn't say it, but I can't help myself. It's how I feel.

Adam leans forward.

"I loved you," I say. "But you never loved me back. It was always Adam."

Lily wraps her arms around me tighter.

"I've got this," she says to Adam. His expression is tight, but he nods.

"I love you, Corey. You're like a brother to me. And you're one of the best friends I've ever had," she says gently.

Adam stands, sighing as he approaches. He squats in front of me, and Lily releases me from her grasp. "It may not seem like it, Corey, but I know what you're going through."

"Bullshit," I mutter.

"This is what it was like for me when I thought Lily had left me. I was so empty." He swallows. "I know you thought I was selfish for not coming back for so long, but I was just like you are now—completely and utterly lost."

I nod. "I guess you're right."

"I did some dumb stuff when all I should have done was come home. So, no more dumb stuff. Let's get you back on track." He smiles. "Who knows? Maybe Constance will realise what a mistake she's made and come home too."

Pushing myself up off Lily, I nod again. "I'll go and have a quick shower."

"See you in a minute. Everyone's at Mum and Dad's. We'll take you," Adam says.

"Thanks, Adam. Sorry about everything."

He shakes his head. "Don't worry about it. It's done with. We know you love Constance."

"I never told her that. I had so many opportunities, and I never said I love you. I'm an idiot."

"Yeah, you are. But right now, you need to get into that shower and change your clothing. We need to get to Mum and Dad's."

"Okay."

---

I STAGGER as we walk from the car to the house, and Adam stands by my side to hold me up. Of all the times to drink, I had to pick this one. But I didn't know better. Mum's been going downhill for so long, and I still didn't see this coming.

When I reach the living room, I see most of the family's here. By the time Adam came and got me, even Drew and Hayley had arrived.

"Where's James?"

"He's on his way."

"Is there time?"

Adam lets out a loud breath. "I don't know, mate. I hope so."

"He's a good kid. Maybe he has some secret girlfriend, but he's a good kid."

Adam chuckles. "Yeah, he is. He did stay here for a few weeks, so he's had a lot of time with Mum lately. I still hope he gets here."

"Where's Dad?"

"In with Mum. Let's get you seated, and try and sober you up a bit so you can see her."

Ginny and Hayley occupy the couch. Ginny's talking to Owen, and Hayley's talking to Drew, and there's a Corey-spaced gap between them. Of course, that's where I have to go.

"Hey." Hayley smiles.

I lean over and press a lingering kiss to her cheek. Enough to make Drew cock an eyebrow.

"Hey, princess," I say.

She clamps her lips together in obvious amusement.

"How are you doing? Adam and Lily told us about Constance. I'm so sorry, Corey."

I nod. "I miss her."

"Drew, is there anything more I can give him to sober him up? Before he starts talking about how much he misses sex again?" Adam says.

Drew shakes his head. "Not really. Just lots of water and hope for the best."

Ginny hands me her cup of coffee. "Here you go, Corey. Drink this."

I take the cup. "Thanks, Gin. You are so good for Owen. Did I ever tell you that? I've never seen him so crazy about someone." I pause. "Except maybe that girl he went out with when he finished high school. What was her name?"

"Pretty sure her name was Shut-The-Fuck-Up," says Owen.

"No. That can't have been it." I chuckle.

"Just drink the coffee." Hayley slips her arm around my shoulders.

"You're the best, Hayley. I don't know why you went back to that guy when you could have had me."

She laughs. "Sometimes, I don't know either."

"Oi." Drew narrows his eyes at her.

"But now you have those two beautiful babies. I want babies."

"Jesus. Can someone shut him the hell up?" Owen shakes his head.

I take a sip of the coffee, and sigh. "This is so good. Constance made good coffee."

"Glad to see you made it, Corey." Dad approaches the couch.

"He's a little worse for wear," Adam says.

"I can see. Sober up a bit before you see your mum, okay?"

I nod. "Of course."

Ava appears in the doorway. I gulp down my coffee, and hold my arms open for her. "Come here, little light of my life."

She runs toward me, grinding to a halt before she gets to the couch and screwing up her nose.

"It's okay, baby. I just need to drink some more water, or coffee, or something," I say. I must smell like a brewery.

"I'll get a glass of water," Ginny says.

"No. You stay there. I'll get it." Owen stands, shaking his head at me.

Ava climbs up and onto the couch. I settle her onto my lap, and kiss the top of her head.

"What are you up to?" I ask.

"Playing with Max and Rose," she says. "Why do you smell?"

"I'm terrible, aren't I? First I shave my beard and freak you out, then I come here all smelly. I'm just sad, sweetheart."

She pouts.

"I feel better now you're here." Tears prick my eyes as she climbs up and wraps her small arms around my neck.

"Here you go." Owen hands me a tall glass of water, and I guzzle it down.

"Thanks, guys. I really appreciate all of this. My timing sucks."

Hayley shakes her head. "That's what we're here for. I think we all understand."

Drew places his hand on her shoulder, and the look she exchanges with him is so full of love, it stabs me in the heart.

"I just thought I had what you guys have. So if I'm a little jealous today, I'm sure you'll understand," I say. Drew nods. "In the meantime, I have my girl with me and everything's better. Right Ava?"

Ava nods.

"She even loves me when I stink of alcohol." I laugh.

"She could probably get drunk on your fumes." Owen shakes his head.

"Nah," I reply. Ava snuggles in against me, her head against my chest, and I lean my chin on her head. "Where are the other kids?"

"Max has hooked up his Switch to the TV in Adam's old room, and Rose is with him. The twins are having their nap."

"They didn't sleep in the car?"

Drew shakes his head. "No way. They usually do, but today they were wide awake and making noise."

"They were snoring a minute ago," Ava says.

"Were they? Do you snore?"

She shakes her head. "No. Daddy does sometimes though. When he falls asleep on the couch."

I laugh. "Oh, does he now?"

"Don't tell him all my secrets." Owen narrows his eyes at Ava, but the smile on his face shows how amused he is.

"Tell me all of the secrets."

---

WHEN I'VE GOT ENOUGH of my shit together, Dad takes me in to see Mum.

I've watched all these months as the weight dropped off her, and she lost control. Her eyes are closed, and she's got no colour in her cheeks. Even if I hadn't been told, I'd probably think this was it.

"Mum," I say gently, sitting on the side of the bed.

"She knows you're here. Doc Paton was in earlier, and gave her some pain relief. She's been sleeping ever since." Dad rests his hand on my shoulder.

Tears prick my eyes. I always knew it would come down to this, but now it's here on top of the pain I'm already in. I hate it.

Mum was the one who pushed Dad to take the job and move us here. She was the one who wanted more for me, for all of us. Maybe she pushed and interfered in our lives a bit too much for our liking, but she always loved us.

"I wish this wasn't happening," I say.

He sighs. Exhaustion haunts his face. My heart aches for him. "Me too. But she won't be in any pain soon, Corey. God, she loves you boys so much."

"I'm sorry, Dad. I'm sorry I'm such a mess."

"Broken hearts will do that to you, Corey. I understand better than you know. I'm sorry for what you're going through."

I stand, and wrap my arms around my father's shoulders.

"You want to stay here for a bit with your mum?"

"Don't you want to be in here, too?"

"You all need some time with her. The others have been in, and James isn't too far away. Then I'll sit with her."

I nod. "Thanks, Dad."

He smiles. "You know, I remember the day you were born. Your mother was so happy. She took one look at you and fell in love. Oh, she loves the others fiercely, but you— you are so special to her."

His words stab me right in the heart. I gave them both trouble when I was younger, and although that's way behind me, it leaves me full of guilt.

With a sigh, he pats my chest. "I hope you sort things out with your girlfriend. I'm sure she's as upset as you are about things."

"She left me, Dad."

"You know, I wasn't always good to your mother. But we worked things out. You never know."

I sit back down as he leaves the room, and it's quiet, just the slow and steady sound of Mum's breathing filling the room.

Knowing that breathing will come to a stop soon is breaking my heart.

Right when I thought I had nothing left to break.

Drew and Dad are with Mum when she passes away in the evening.

It seems apt that she has a doctor with her—her beloved son, whom she was so proud of, alongside the man she loved more than anything.

I look around the room.

Drew has Hayley.

Owen has Ginny.

Adam has Lily.

They comfort each other while we respect Dad's privacy as he sits with Mum and waits for Doc Paton to come back.

I'm lost in my thoughts when there's a tap on my knee. Ava's got her arms open again, and I smile as I pick her up and hug her.

"You know just what I need." I chuckle.

"You look sad."

"I am sad, sweetheart."

"Why?"

I catch Owen's gaze. She's loud enough that's he's heard. I don't think she knew Mum that well, but this kid already lost her parents a year ago. She knows what grief is.

"Ava, come over here for a second." Owen takes her from my arms, and he, Ginny, and Ava disappear outside. I sigh at the thought of her understanding what he's about to tell her. It's hard when you can't protect the little ones.

"Here you go." Lily hands over a smiling Rose, who buries her face in my neck.

"Hey, pumpkin." I give Lily a smile. "Thanks."

"Everyone needs someone." She gives me a pat on the back, and I'm left with my other favourite girl—the one who no longer has a beard to tug on.

"Dad, Dad." Her eyes grow big.

"Yes, your dad's right over there." I point at Adam.

She points, too. "Dad, Dad."

"Are you going to abandon me for your father?" I grin.

She wriggles in my arms, and I drop her down so she can run to him. Oh, to have the energy of a two-year-old.

I'm filled with an overwhelming urge to go back to the bottle and drink myself into oblivion again tonight. But surrounded by my family, my brothers who have so much love—I can't waste my opportunities. I can't fall to pieces when even without Constance, I have these great people to live for.

But I can't let my mood win.

**28**

———————

COREY

I FEEL NUMB.

Even when you expect death to come, when it does, it still hits hard.

"Corey." I look up to see the minister nodding, indicating that it's my turn to speak.

Hayley reaches for my hand and squeezes it before I stand. The walk to the lectern is the longest of my life. I'm going to say goodbye to my mother.

I've spent the last couple of days at Dad's place. I'm not stupid. Constance isn't coming back. And Dad needs me right now.

I clear my throat and look around. Copper Creek might be a small town, but there's always a decent turnout for a funeral. There are those who knew Mum, and those who are just here being nosey.

"In case anyone doesn't know who I am, I'm Corey, Joanna's eldest son." I take a deep breath. "Mum was tough. She called a spade a spade, and she fought right till the end. But she loved us. Endlessly. She was merciless when it came to fighting for her children, often to the detriment of our own relationships."

I meet Lily's gaze, and she gives me a small nod. "But all that did was bring us closer together. And it meant we were all together at the end for her. She died surrounded by her children and grandchildren, and that would have meant the world to her."

I swallow. "And then there's Dad. Dad was by her side for nearly forty years, and I can only hope that we're all so lucky —to have someone stick with us for all that time. Living with Mum can't have been easy, especially in her final years, but my dad held his head up high even when it must have felt like he was punched in the face repeatedly. We love you, Dad."

Dad's gaze is fixed on me, and the pride in his expression is obvious.

"So, on behalf of myself, Adam and Lily, Drew and Hayley, Owen and Ginny, James, Max, Rose, Ava, Logan, and Amelia, thank you for being here."

I can't say any more, so I step down.

I'm not sure if it's possible to feel any emptier.

---

THE BEST THING about the wake is that I get to indulge in Owen's baking. I'm not really in the mood for being social, but it's the least I can do for both Mum and Dad.

I scan the room, smiling as I spot Rob and Amy. "Excuse me." I walk away.

"Corey," Rob says.

"Hey, Rob. Amy." I lean over and give Amy a kiss on the cheek.

She takes my hand and squeezes. "How are you holding up?"

"It's hard, but it wasn't exactly unexpected. At least she's not in pain anymore."

She nods, taking a look around. "Is Constance here?"

I frown. "Long story."

"Oh, shit," Rob says.

"We're not together anymore. Not by my choice, but there's nothing I can do about it."

Amy wraps her arms around my shoulder. "I'm sorry, Corey."

"Thanks, guys. I really appreciate you being here."

"You'll have to tell us all about it when you come over tomorrow for dinner," Amy says.

Rob rolls his eyes. "Hon, let him be. His mum just died; you are not interrogating him about his breakup."

"It's not an interrogation. More of an intense questioning." She winks at me, and I can't help but laugh.

"I don't know if I'll be any kind of company tomorrow. I'll give you a call when I'm ready." I press a kiss to the top of her head, and she sighs.

"As long as you're okay. Call us if you ever need anything. And I know everyone says it, but we really mean it."

"I know you do. And I promise I will. I just need a bit of time alone to process everything."

"Fair enough." Rob smiles. "Come on, Amy. Let's go grab some sausage rolls before they disappear."

"See ya later, you two."

They head toward the table loaded with food, and I take a deep breath. I'm going home tonight. I want to sleep in my own bed, and even if there are still traces of Constance there, it's where I need to be. It's time to move on.

"No Constance?"

I raise my gaze to see Tanya standing right in front of me. "No."

She licks her lips. "Where is she?"

"None of your business."

Her eyes widen. "I bet she went back to those weirdos. She did, didn't she?"

I suppress a sigh. "Like I said, none of your business."

"Shame. What are you doing after this?"

"What on earth are you talking about?" I raise an eyebrow when she rests her hand on my arm.

"Why don't you come back to my place? I know we've had our issues in the past, but maybe I can help take your mind off things. I'm so sorry about your mother."

I stare at her. Today of all days, this is not what I need. "Are you kidding me? I wouldn't fuck you with someone else's dick. How clear do I have to be?"

She recoils.

"Corey." Rob pulls my arm. "Let's get out of here."

I glare at Tanya. "So many times I've tried to tell you I'm not interested. That's still the case."

"I'll take care of this," Amy says.

I turn at the sound of Amy's voice, and bite down laughter at the angry look on her face.

The expression on her face is fierce, and I hold my hands up in surrender as she storms past me and frog-marches Tanya from the room.

"Well, that was fun." Rob says.

"It was certainly interesting." Letting out a sigh, I pat him on the back. "Thanks for being here. I know I already said that, but I really appreciate it."

He nods. "Anything for you, mate."

---

IF I THOUGHT it was hard to focus before Mum's death, now it's even harder. My mind's still on Constance, and my heart is broken, but I push forward through the worst week of my entire life.

After the wake and some time back at Dad's, we all head to the pub for dinner. I haven't had another drop to drink, turning to orange juice when I reach the bar. I'll knock that on the head before it turns into something I can't control.

I step in and sit at the kids' table. These guys always bring a smile to my face, no matter how down I am. Today's no exception. James joins us. He's turned up alone, and I'm not teasing him today of all days about this mysterious girl-friend. He'll tell us when he's ready.

There's a big age gap between them all. Max is fourteen now. I've loved this kid ever since he was a scrawny little baby, and it makes me so proud to see the man he's becom-ing. He takes looking after his younger sister and cousins very seriously.

I raise an eyebrow at Ava stealing a chicken nugget from Rose's plate. Rose frowns, and I grab Ava's hand. She looks at me with wide eyes.

"If you want more, I'll get you more. Don't steal from your cousin."

Ava gives me a mischievous grin, switches the nugget to her other hand, and sticks it in her mouth before I can stop her.

I'm torn between laughing and telling her off again.

"Come here, Rose." I hold my hand out behind Ava, and Rose pushes off her seat, walking around the table. I pull her into my arms, and plant a kiss on the top of her head.

"Say sorry." I focus my gaze back on Ava.

"Sorry, Rose." She reaches up and touches Rose's cheek.

"Everything okay?" Owen's eyes are full of concern. All this over a chicken nugget.

"Just your daughter stealing food off Rose's plate. Can you go to the bar and ask for another bowl of chicken nuggets?"

"Uhh, sure." Owen eyes up Ava, shaking his head. All she does is giggle.

"Corey," Adam calls.

Lily approaches, reaching for Rose. "Swap places? You'll want to see who's just arrived."

The hair on the back of my neck prickles at her serious tone, and I hand my niece over to her mother.

"All I'm going to say is be the bigger man," Lily says softly. "But know your brothers are right behind you if you want to start something."

I shoot her a confused glance, getting up and walking toward Adam. Before I reach him I see what, or rather who Lily was talking about.

*Ash Harris.*

I want to smack that smug smile off his face, and my hands fist before I know it. Adam lays a hand on my arm, and I nod.

"Ash." Drew's the one who speaks first, and he ushers Hayley behind him, creating a barrier between her and the interloper.

"Drew. Hayley."

A vein in my brother's neck pulses as the two men stare at each other. Harris would be an idiot to start something, but nothing would surprise me at this stage. Owen and James stand on my other side. The five of us, united, and staring down this prick.

"I just wanted to pass on my condolences. I never met your mother, but I know how painful it is to lose someone so close."

"Get the fuck out of here, Harris. We don't want your sympathy." My breathing accelerates at the thought of punching him.

He fixes his gaze on me. "Constance sends her regards. She regrets she can't invite you to her wedding."

Adam stands, stepping in front of me. "Corey told you to leave."

Ash opens his mouth as if to say something more, then obviously reconsiders as he closes it again. With a curt nod, he turns, and I hold my breath until he disappears outside.

"You okay?" Adam asks.

I nod, but I can't look at him. Anger rages inside me, but today I buried my mother, and there are more important things to think about, like my family.

When Constance first arrived, I held back on telling Graham despite knowing she could have a wealth of knowledge that would speed his investigation up.

Now, all I want is that bastard Harris taken down.

No matter what it takes.

**29**

---

CONSTANCE

*Three weeks ago*

THEY CAME for me on the fourth night Corey was away.

My head still aches from the blow to the head that knocked me out. Ash's sidekick, Jason, has long, angry marks on his face where I scratched him while fighting back before Liam issued the blow.

I never stood a chance.

When I wake, my brain feels like it's growing inside my head, pulsing in pain. There's a man sitting on the bed, and I turn my face to look at him. My eyes focus, and there he is—Ash Harris.

I let out a scream. My throat constricts. My mouth is so dry, and the sound goes nowhere.

He reaches down, brushing the hair from my face. "Finally awake."

"What are you doing?"

"Taking back what's mine."

"I'm not yours."

He narrows his eyes. "We had a deal. You broke it. I had to punish my delivery driver, who you sneaked out with."

"What are you talking about?"

"I spent a long time trying to work out how you managed to get away. And then I realised that night, I had a delivery go out. You hid in the truck, didn't you?"

"Are you asking me, or telling me? I want to leave."

Ash shakes his head. "You're not going anywhere this time. You'll fulfil the deal we had, or your parents will suffer."

"Leave them alone."

"No one makes a fool of me, Constance, and yet, that's exactly what you did."

"I don't want to be here."

He nods. "I know. But like I said, you owe me."

"I owe you nothing."

"Get off the bed. We're going for a little walk." He grabs my hand and pulls me to my feet.

"No." I lean back on the bed, and try to get away.

"Not even to see your precious parents?"

I swallow, hard. What if this is it? What if I never escape? If that's the case, I need to at least see my parents. Then, I'll know if they're okay.

"I'll come with you," I whisper.

"That's better. I don't want anyone thinking there's anything wrong, so you'll walk with me to their place. I'll leave you there for an hour to visit, and then I'll collect you. And you will be watched."

I nod.

"No smartarse comments for me?"

I fix my gaze on him. "You're not worth the effort."

Anger flares in his eyes, but I'm not backing down.

"Let's go," he says.

I take a step and the long skirts of the grey dress swish around my legs. My stomach rolls as I look down and take in the sight of it. Someone's dressed me when I was out cold.

When I meet Ash's cruel gaze, he laughs. "You needed to be dressed for the occasion."

I raise my hand to slap him, but he grabs my wrist.

"You were only wearing a shirt. It's not like you were wearing a lot to start with."

"You're a pig."

"And you need to pull your head in. I don't think your parents will stay safe if you misbehave."

I swallow down my anger, and follow him out the door. Four of his friends close in around me, and we walk as a group out of the main building and toward my parents' house.

The whole way, I keep my head up high and do my best to pretend nothing's wrong.

My parents' lives might depend on it.

***

"ARE YOU ALRIGHT?" Mum asks me for what seems to be the fiftieth time. I haven't answered her so far, and that's probably why she keeps asking. At least they had the decency to give us some space to talk.

"No." It's all I can manage. I'm trying to be strong while I figure out a way out of here again, but escaping won't be as easy this time around.

"This isn't right." She frowns.

"No shit, Mum. It's been not right here for years."

Her mouth falls open at my words. I was brought up not to swear, and I didn't as a general rule. Not until I fell in love with my potty-mouthed mountain man. Thinking of him in that way brings a smile to my face.

"It hasn't," Dad says.

"We all need to leave." I fix my gaze on my father, and he nods. "But not before I find out what Ash is up to. If I'm back here, that's the least I can do."

He sighs. "There's something not right with that young man."

"That's an understatement."

"Why did you come back?" Mum asks. "You were free, weren't you?"

I nod. "Ash and his goons found me and brought me back."

Tears well in her eyes.

"Not that I went far. I moved in next door."

Her eyebrows lift. "Next door?"

"I met someone. Fell in love. And then Ash dragged me back here. He's still carrying grudges for things that happened years ago." I sigh. "He's bitter toward me, and he worked out where I was."

Dad lays a hand on my shoulder. "Is he a good man? The one you love?"

I nod. "He's the best. But he's away working and won't know I'm gone for a couple more days."

"Do you think he'll try coming for you?"

"I don't know."

The Corey I know would come looking for me. But this place is dangerous, and there are already too many people here who I care about.

I don't know what to do.

## 30

## CONSTANCE

I LOSE TRACK OF TIME. Ash keeps me in this room day after day.

It doesn't help that I feel so ill all the time. I sleep so much, I don't know how many days have passed.

When the door opens, I roll my eyes and sit up, expecting to see Ash. My heart leaps at the sight of Julia.

"Constance," she says. A look of relief sweeps her face.

"Julia, what are you doing here?"

She grins. "Ash has had you locked down so insanely tight. No one was allowed in or out except for his select few. But I worked out how to get in."

I embrace her when she sits on the bed. "I'm so glad you did. I've been so alone in here."

"You were free. What happened?" Julia asks.

I let out a loud breath. "Ash brought me back."

"He found you?"

"I made it as far as next door. Fell in love with Corey

Campbell, the man who lives there, and that's where I stayed."

Her lips twitch in amusement. "I shouldn't smile, but that's so awesome. What's he like? I haven't met him, but I have met his brother, Drew, and he's gorgeous."

"I never got to meet Drew, but if he's anything like the rest of their family, they're all gorgeous. Especially Corey." I sigh.

"What does he want? Ash, I mean."

"He wants me to go through with what he originally had planned for me."

Her eyes widen. "No way."

I nod.

"We need to get you out of here."

I shake my head. "It won't work again. He'll make sure of it."

She stands up straight. "We'll see about that."

I flop backward onto the bed. "It'd help if I didn't feel so awful."

"What's wrong?"

"Tired, nauseous. Sometimes a bit dizzy."

She frowns.

"I'll be back in a minute."

I swear to god that this woman is Houdini, the way she slips out of the room the same way she slipped in— unnoticed.

My stomach rolls again, and I make a dash to the bathroom. I dry-heave, but nothing comes up. *What the hell has Ash done to me?*

"Here," Julia says, walking over to hand me a white stick. "Take the end off it and pee on it."

"What?"

"Either Ash has poisoned you, or you're pregnant. I know he's nuts, but I'd bet anything it's the latter."

I stare at her. "Pregnant? But he and that doctor of his made sure I got a contraceptive injection before I was due to do that little job of his."

Julia laughs. "Do you really think they have access to anything like that? That guy isn't a real doctor. I got the boys to check him out." She puffs her chest out proudly.

"The boys?"

"The undercover cops that are here. I'm assuming you know all about them given you've been living next door."

I nod. It's all coming together. "Kane and Jared."

"Yes."

"But why the subterfuge?"

"Ash likes to show everyone he's in control. I noticed that despite everyone getting these injections, there were still members of his little harem who got pregnant." She sighs. "Including me."

"That's screwed up."

"When it happens, he puts it down to how it was meant to be and how manly it makes him. He doesn't give a crap who he hurts." She nods at my hand. "Pee on the stick. I'll be outside."

I pull myself to my feet, and take a look at the test in my hand. Sighing, I pull the end off it, and do as Julia's told me to do.

The test sits by the basin. I wash my hands and take it back out to the bedroom.

"Well?" she asks.

"I haven't looked yet."

"Let's do it together."

*Two lines.*

"Two lines is …?" I ask, but I already know the answer.

"You're pregnant."

I gasp, slapping my hand over my mouth. *Corey.*

"He trusted me. I betrayed that trust."

Julia wraps her arms around my neck, and I fold into her. "No. You weren't to know. You were caught up in Ash's demented game. Ash wanted to show you he could exert control over you, but the truth is that you're in control. Don't let him win."

"What will he do if he finds out?"

She shrugs. "We need to get to the bottom of all this once and for all before that happens. If you're feeling well enough, let's go for a walk."

I clutch at my stomach. "I can't get caught. If he hurts me, he'll hurt my baby."

Shaking her head, she cups my face. "He won't catch us. I still have access to this building; I've found all of the ways out of it. It's too big a complex for him to guard the whole thing."

I stare at her. "Who are you and what did you do with Julia?"

She laughs. "What do you mean?"

"I mean, I remember when you came here. You were so meek and mild."

"Do you really want to know what happened?"

I nod.

"Ash happened."

Julia and I manage to sneak outside the house.

This place was once used for communal living, and there are plenty of interconnecting rooms. You just need to know which ones connect with which.

Turns out she's done a lot of exploring.

"Where are we going?"

"Most people are at dinner. It's still early, so we've got enough light to go and check out the bunkers. I think they're the key to whatever's going on, and you know them better than anyone else I know."

I swallow. "Isn't that what Jared was investigating when he disappeared?"

She nods. "Michael, too."

My mouth falls open. "No."

"Ingrid's been beside herself." She grimaces. "Ash offered to keep her company."

"Ugh. He's disgusting."

"That's what she said. And that's why she's currently shut away in her house as punishment."

"For what?"

Julia sighs. "Telling the truth. Anyway, we have to make this quick. If Ash finds out you're out of that room ..."

"He'll go after my parents."

She nods.

We make our way to the greenhouse without any trouble. The workers have long since packed up for the day and are in the food hall having dinner. I look across to the maize field. *Is the gap in the fence still there?*

"Constance."

I turn back to face Julia. "Maybe I could try and go through tonight?"

She shakes her head. "I wouldn't risk it. He tightened security at night since you left the first time. There's a much higher risk of getting caught." Julia grabs my hand. "We need to be fast. Once dinner's over in there, Ash will get a tray taken to your room."

"That's not a lot of time."

"Then, we need to get going."

I swallow and nod. "Come on."

Julia follows me down the concrete steps that lead to the outer door.

"I always thought this was just a storage room."

Shaking my head, I turn the handle, grunting when it doesn't open. "It's locked. It never used to be locked."

"I've got a key." From her cleavage, she pulls out a key on a long string.

"Where on earth did you get that from?"

"Ask me no questions and I won't tell you I cosied up to one of the Ash's friends."

"He knows you have it?"

She grimaces. "No. I stole it. He was dumb enough to have a label on it."

I bite down a laugh. "Let's get this done quickly."

She hands me the key and I unlock the door.

We step into the storage room, and I push the door shut before turning on the light.

Julia looks around. "This is just a storage room."

"That's what you're meant to think."

On the left-hand side of the room, is a board with tools hanging on nails. I find the edges of the board, sliding it sideways.

"Holy shit." She gasps.

There's a corridor. Soft lighting illuminates closed rooms on either side of it.

We used to bring torches down here, it was so dark.

"Come on," I say

We set off down the corridor, opening doors and looking for anything odd as we go. The corridor turns left and then right before forking. We go left first.

"How on earth can you find your way around this?" Julia asks.

"We used to play down here all the time as kids. Ash and I both know this place like the backs of our hands."

"Do you think we'll find anything down here?"

I shrug. "Who knows? These are all bedrooms. There's a storage room at this end."

We reach the end room, and I try the door handle.

"This is locked, too. Got any more magic keys?"

Julia shakes her head. "We could try this one again."

I shrug. "A lot of the locks inside are the same. Ash's father used to say it was easier to keep track of one key, and no one around here locked anything. You could give it a go."

She slides the key in, and her eyes widen. "Thanks, Ash's dad, for being lazy."

I chuckle, and she pushes open the door.

We gasp at the same time.

Sitting on the floor, their hands and feet bound together, are Jared and Michael.

"Michael?" I whisper.

Relief is written all over his face. "Constance. What are you doing here? And thank God you are."

"It's a long story." I look around for something to cut the ties holding the men's hands together.

"Jared." Julia runs to him. She cups his face, and the longing is clear in her eyes.

*When did that happen?*

"I'm sorry, Julia. I know you must have been worried." He presses his forehead to hers.

"Can you get up?" I ask.

He nods. His lips are cracked, although he seems to be in generally good condition.

"We need to get you somewhere safe.

Julia shakes her head. "We need to get him to Kane."

"That's the first place Ash will look. He knows they're friends."

"She's right," Jared says. "If I can find somewhere to hide until it gets dark, I'll go through the fence if the gap's still there tonight."

"Jared." Julia gasps.

"He can't stay here. As far as I know, the gap in the fence is still there. Ash seems to think I sneaked out with a delivery, and I didn't correct him."

Jared chuckles. "Ash thinks he's a lot smarter than he actually is."

I nod. "Even if anyone else notices it, no one will want to go and fix it. Ash and his men are the only ones who wanted the fence in the first place."

"We all need to go," Julia says.

*Corey.* I'm only surprised he hasn't turned up here yet. Not that I would know if he had. My stomach churns at the thought of him being somewhere within this complex.

"Is it just the two of you?"

Michael nods. "I brought Jared down here to check on a lead, but we got caught."

"Did you find out what Ash is doing?"

His expression tightens. "We need to get Jared out to his people as quickly as possible."

"Are you going to tell us?"

"Ash is bad, Con. Really bad. He's up to his eyeballs in illegal shit. You and Julia need to get out of here too. I'll help Jared."

"But—"

"Go, before you two are missed."

---

"Let's get Andrew and get out of here," Julia whispers.

I nod. We have to risk it. She sneaks back up the concrete steps, and looks around to see if anyone's watching.

We make it back to the house, and as we get back inside, I breathe a sigh of relief.

And then I see him. Waiting by the door to the room he's been holding me in, a small dark-haired boy in his arms.

"What are you two ladies up to?" Ash says. He chucks Andrew under the chin, and the little boy laughs.

"Just getting some fresh air," Julia says.

"And that involved breaking Constance out of a locked room?"

Her eyes dart between Andrew and me. "It's stuffy in there."

"Go back to your room, Julia. I'll deal with you later."

I turn my head, but his goons have us surrounded, and there's nowhere to run.

"And you can go back in there. Your special visitor's here

tomorrow, and I need to make sure you're safe and well looked after."

The men close in.

Fear makes my heart race. But I won't show him that.

"I made a promise, Constance, and when you left I had to break it. He picked you."

"He never even met me. You made the choice. I already know that."

Scott and Liam grab me by the arms, and pull me back to the room. They at least have the decency to be gentle when placing me on the bed.

"Scott Abernathy. Your mother would be so disappointed in you."

"Stop it," he says through gritted teeth.

But I can't. "Your father would kick your arse for treating me with so much disrespect. What's wrong with you?"

His tough-guy look cracks, and for a second I get a glimpse of the boy I grew up with before it hardens again.

He turns and leaves the room. I pick up a pillow and try to throw it at his head. It hits the wall with a soft thud and falls to the floor.

Ash closes the door behind him, and I finally let go of the tears of frustration.

There has to be a way out of this.

*Corey.*

## 31

## CONSTANCE

Tonight's the night.

My stomach rolls at the thought of what's coming. Ash has essentially sold me for the night before I'm married off. I could refuse, and I will, but I don't know if I'm strong enough to fight.

I miss Corey. Of all the people in my life, I thought he'd fight for me. But there's no knight in shining armour.

The light goes off.

I look up, and roll my eyes. It's still early in the day, but with this room sealed off, the only decent source of light has been the bulb that's just gone out. I look across to the alarm clock by the bed to check the time. The screen is blank.

Is the power out? We haven't had any power issues up here for years.

I sit up when the key turns in the lock, and Ash stands in the doorway.

"This is your fault."

"What are you talking about?"

He crosses the room in three large strides and grabs me by the hair, pulling my head back. "I asked you before, and I'll ask you again. What did you tell the police about this place?"

"Nothing. There was nothing to tell. All they know is that I didn't want the marriage you were forcing me into."

He growls, pushing me back with such force I fall backward onto the bed. "Sweet little Constance. At least you were sweet before you turned against me. But now you're my hostage, just like the rest of them. I'm sure *he'll* want you back."

*Hostage?*

He grabs me by the arm and pulls me from the bed, then drags me along behind him. I try to stand upright, but the wooden floor slips under my feet. His fingers dig into my flesh, but I can't get free, his grip is so tight. What the hell is going on?

Pulling me to my feet, he shoves me into the communal lounge. His harem is gathered there, and they all look at me with wide eyes. I seek out Julia, and sit beside her. Little Andrew wraps his arms around my neck, and I press a kiss to his head.

"What's this all about?" I whisper.

"The police are outside the building. They raided the bunker."

I let out a gasp. Jared and Michael must have escaped. It'll be over soon. It has to be.

*Corey.* He must be out there. Surely.

Ash stands beside the window. He plucks his phone from his pocket when it rings, and I hold my breath.

"I'll kill them all," he says.

Around me, panic starts to build. The hushed whispers give way to frantic calls to each other. These are women who have dedicated their lives to this man, in some cases for several years, and most of them haven't seen the other side of him yet.

"Get off my land."

I hate only hearing one side of the conversation. I'd love to know if it's Graham he's speaking to, and if they know I'm here.

Ash throws the phone across the room, and it hits the wall with a loud smack.

"Where are the other men?" I lean closer to Julia so she can hear me over the chatter around us.

"Only Ash was inside. I think the police got the others," Julia whispers.

"I hope so. If they're anywhere near here, we're in a lot of trouble."

She nods toward Ash. He looks out the window, a crazed look in his eyes. "We're already in a lot of trouble."

# 32

## COREY

I HAVEN'T HAD a drink since the day Mum died.

That doesn't mean I don't think about it.

How easy would it be just to drink my problems away … But I'm stronger than that. I have to be.

I'm on the couch in front of the television. It's the easiest place to be right now, and requires no effort.

I don't want to answer the door when someone hammers on it. "Who is it?"

"Graham."

I roll my eyes. I suppose I should go, because hopefully he's here to tell me their investigation's over and they're leaving my property. Cutting all ties to Constance for good can only help me move on with my life.

Making my way to the door, I glare at him. "What do you want?"

"I want you to come with me. Constance needs you."

He doesn't have to say anything more. I'm out the door before he can say anything else.

"The gate's open," he yells as I pull down the driveway in my truck.

Sure enough, the gates to the commune are wide open, and I swing between them. There are police cars everywhere. It's not a common sight around here. Graham has two constables as far as I know, so they must've brought in the big guns.

I park a little back from the row of black and white cars, and jump out. Seconds later, Graham pulls up beside me.

"In a hurry?" He narrows his eyes at me.

"You told me she needed help. Where is she?"

He places his hand on my arm. "Ash has her as a hostage. Along with his little harem."

I swallow. "So, what do you want me to do?"

"Nothing. I just thought it might be good for her if she knew you were here." He tilts his head. "Corey, I need to tell you—"

"What the hell is going on. Why haven't you got them out of there yet?" A ruddy-faced man is heading straight for Graham. Graham turns to face him.

"The negotiator's trying to get through. And we've got snipers in place. This is going to take some time."

The man turns to me. "My fiancé is in there."

"Sorry to hear that," I say, my gaze focusing on the building. My stomach aches with worry. Maybe Constance doesn't want to be with me, but I'll never stop caring.

And she can't deny what we had was special—what I want again.

"John Parsons."

I shift my gaze back to him. This is the man Constance ran from. He's short, and a lot older than her just as she described, and my anger builds at the memory of her stories about what he did to his first wife.

Looking around, I see the police are focused on the building. They don't need me causing a scene or anything that might put Constance in further danger.

I ignore the hand the man's holding out.

But I do have my eye on the cop standing in front of me. The one who's just put down the megaphone they must have been using to try and communicate.

I can't handle this anymore.

Knowing Constance is in there while these arseholes sit around watching the building is driving me crazy.

I take the two strides to the nearest car, grab the megaphone, and turn.

"What the …?" Graham says.

"Harris, you pussy. Come out here and face me."

"What are you doing?" Graham glares at me.

"Calling him out." I raise it to my lips again. "Face me like a man, Harris. Stop hiding behind the women."

"Who the hell is this?" An armed cop walks up to me.

"Corey, you can't—" Graham says.

I ignore Graham and turn to the officer. "My girlfriend's in there."

He holds up his palms. "I understand this is an emotional situation, but you need to step back."

From the right, another uniformed policeman approaches. "Sir, we can't get back through on the phone. He's not taking any more calls."

"Your plan's not working. Ash has those women in there,

and he's not coming out without a fight. He's far too arrogant for that."

The first officer turns to Graham. "Your call. What do you think?"

He fixes his gaze on me. "You think calling him out will work?"

"The guy's a dick. I had dealings with him when he erected that damn fence, and he's not one to give up." I lick my lips. "Look. I don't know much when it comes to all this psychological mumbo-jumbo you lot use, but I do know that Ash has a temper. He needs a target to take that out on, and not any of those women. Let me be your target."

Graham says nothing. I swear I can see the smoke being generated by his thought processes. He knows not everyone is going to survive this. We just need to make sure that if anyone dies, it's Ash.

"Try his phone again," Graham eventually says.

"You're wasting time," I say.

"Corey, I can't just hand this over to you. You would make a great police officer, but not today."

"And if he doesn't answer his phone? If he starts killing those women? When are you going to take action, Graham?"

John clears his throat, and I shoot him an irritable look. "For what it's worth, I think he's right." He points at me.

"Has he answered the phone?" Graham fixes his gaze on the cop who's trying to get through.

"No."

"Sir, he's moving." The sniper positioned behind the cop car speaks. Graham frowns, and I shrug.

"Is he in position?"

"Negative. He's by the window, but to one side. I can't get a clear shot."

Graham looks at me. "One more time. If it draws him out, I'll be a monkey's uncle, but what you did might just be working."

I grin, holding the megaphone up and facing the building once more. "Stop being a pussy, Harris. You had to try and drug Hayley to get her to want you, and even that didn't work."

*Hayley, almost lifeless in Kane's arms.* I'll never forgive Ash for that.

"Pussyyyyy." I take a breath. "Do you know what, Harris? I bet you had to drug all the women in your life to sleep with you. Who would want to have sex with a man who hides behind them at the first sign of trouble?"

There's so much more I want to say, but the last thing I want is for Ash to target Constance.

*Please don't hurt her.*

"Come on, Harris. You and me. Forget these guys." I drop the megaphone down and look at the building. *Please let her be okay.*

Graham glares at me. "That's enough. I told you to come here because I thought Constance might need all the emotional support she could get when she came out. Not to stir shit."

I shrug. "Stirring shit is what I'm good at."

Silence replaces our bitching. The seconds seem like hours with Constance trapped inside.

"I'm going in," I say.

"The hell you are. There are women and at least one child in there. Do you want to make things worse?"

John Parsons grabs me by the arm. "My fianceé is in there."

"Would you just shut the fuck up?" I yell, pulling away from his grip. This is really the man Constance chose over me?

Ignoring John and Graham, I storm past the police cars. There's yelling behind me, but I don't care. Constance is in danger.

"Ash Harris. Get your arse out here. I'm finishing this if no one else will."

Silence falls as I grow closer to the house. I'm sure any second I'll be tackled to the ground, but I'm not turning back to look.

She needs me.

**33**

---

CONSTANCE

ASH BECOMES MORE AGITATED as the moments go by. With each taunt from Corey, his pacing quickens.

"Who the hell does he think he is?" he asks.

*He's a real man.*

I swallow. "Ash. Do you think you should let us go? Maybe the police would go easy if you—"

Ash marches toward me, grabbing me by the hair and pulling me to my feet. "It's too late for that, Constance. You should have thought of that before bringing them here."

I lick my lips. "They were already here, Ash. You let them in a long time ago."

"What the fuck do you mean?"

"They knew you were up to something—they just didn't know what it was. The rest of them are here because they worked it all out."

A sob escapes his throat.

There's something so terribly wrong with him. It's more

than just him being caught out for whatever it was he was doing. He's turned into this lost little boy whose only way of dealing with this is to lash out at me.

"I'm sorry, Constance. You broke my heart."

"I was just a child, Ash. And I left because while I would have stayed here happily, you wanted to hurt me."

He lets out another sob. We're so much closer to the window, and I look out while I can. There are six police cars, and some other vehicles I don't recognise. But I do recognise Corey's black ute. My heart sings at the sight of it.

"He's what you want. Not me. Never me."

I take a deep breath and nod. "I love him."

In an instant, all my air is cut off. I scramble to catch a breath. Quiet, sad, reflective Ash is gone, replaced by the monster that's become so familiar.

"I only ever wanted two women: you and Hayley. And that Campbell family got in the way both times."

"Ash!" I gasp. His hands tighten around my throat.

"I waited. I thought I'd give you the opportunity to come to me. But you were always so busy with your mother. And then I realised you would have lived your life alone rather than be with me. That's why I wanted to hurt you. Why I still want to hurt you."

I fight to catch a breath, but his grip is tight, and I'm not strong enough to pull his hand away. None of the others help. They cower in the corner.

Julia stands. "Ash, let her go."

"I can't."

"Think of Andrew, Ash. He needs his father. He needs—"

Ash isn't even listening to her. He drags me to the front door. His grip loosens and I catch a breath, but his other hand digs into my hair as he grabs a handful to pull me along.

I get a brief reprieve from the scalp pain as he pulls open the door.

"If he wants you that badly, he can have you," he says. He only has one hand on my throat, but his grip is so tight, and I'm losing the fight.

Corey's standing not far from the house. His eyes widen as he meets mine.

"They're here to take me away, Constance. And if I'm going away, I'd better make the most of it now," Ash mutters.

He stops. Corey's metres away, and it's like time is frozen for just a moment. Ash's grip tightens again and I flail, fighting for breath.

"Let her go, Harris."

Ash shakes his head. "Screw you. You took Hayley away from me, so I'm taking Constance away from you."

Corey takes a step toward us.

"Don't come any closer," Ash says.

My vision blurs as I struggle to get any air. I scratch at Ash's hand, anything to try loosen his grip.

"He's got a gun," someone yells in the distance, and I hear the click beside me.

Corey's right there, and I can't tell him again that I love him. My chest aches at the effort to breathe.

"Hold on, sweetness."

I'm Corey's. Till the end. For such a short time he was mine.

The story goes that before you die, your life flashes before your eyes. Mine doesn't. But I wrap myself in Corey's love, and say one last prayer in my head for my baby.

*I'm so sorry.*

Blackness closes in, and I make one last effort to get air—anything—into my lungs.

*It hurts.*

And then it doesn't.

# 34

## COREY

My head swims.

I was so ready to get in there and fight him until he pulled out a handgun. Then I knew all bets were off.

She falls to the ground as he lets go of her, and I run. I run to the woman I'm in love with.

I shoot a glance at Ash as I get to her. He lies on the ground, his eyes forever staring into nothing. There's blood all over the ground around him, showing the sniper's done their job.

I'll be forever grateful to whoever they are.

"Constance," I yell. Her eyes are closed, but she's taking deep breaths. If Ash Harris wasn't already dead, I'd kill him.

I bend beside her, cupping her cheek as her eyes flicker open. "Corey?"

"I'm here, sweetness."

Footsteps behind us tell me we're not alone. An older man drops to the ground beside her. "Thank God."

"Dad?"

She pushes herself up, and he pulls her into his arms. Cradling her, he meets my gaze. "Thank you."

For a moment, I watch as she sobs in her father's arms.

"Constance."

I bristle at the sound of the guy who approached me. Her fiancé.

Her face is buried in her father's chest, and I can't see her reaction to John Parsons. But I'm feeling like the odd one out.

I back away. That reunion is for family—for Con and her dad and the man she's going to marry.

It's not for me.

"What the hell were you doing?" Graham yells when I reach him.

"Isn't this what you wanted?"

"Well, it's not exactly orthodox, but no one could accuse you of being that."

"I'll take that as a compliment."

I turn back to look. My view of her is obscured by the crowd gathering around her. The weight that had been crushing my heart lifts at the knowledge Constance is okay. But I can't watch this. I can't watch her with *him*.

I turn again.

"Aren't you sticking around? Isn't she who you wanted to save?" Graham asks.

"She left. And I'm leaving now."

I try and sound like I don't care, but inside I'm miserable. She made her choice, and it wasn't me.

Striding toward my ute, I slap it in reverse once I'm in, and turn around to leave. For a moment, I close my eyes. The past few years, I've watched my brothers fall in love. First Adam reuniting with Lily, then Drew finding Hayley. And Owen, the least likely of us all to settle down—I was sure he'd be the last one to get a happy-every-after.

The only single brothers left are myself and James, and for a brief time, I thought I'd found the one. Even James seems to have found someone.

"Corey. Wait. You need to—"

I change gear, ignoring Graham, and head toward the big gate, turning left and driving the short distance home. I slam the door once I get out of the ute, then stalk toward the house.

*Constance.*

Everything makes me think of her.

Maybe I should have kicked her out at the start and left her to stand on her own two feet. She would have found her way, I wouldn't be in this painful position.

The crushing heartache becomes unbearable, and I throw myself on the couch to mourn what was, if it was ever anything.

About ten minutes later, there's a hammering on the door. No doubt Graham wants to give me a piece of his mind over the way I acted back there. I guess I owe him the courtesy.

Instead, I find myself looking into those grey eyes I know so well. The ones that haunt me at night when I'm alone.

I can't help it. Reaching for her face, I run my thumb across her lower lip. She closes her eyes.

Constance flings her arms around my waist, and for a moment, I flail before resting my hands on her shoulders.

She buries her face in my chest and I close my eyes. At least for a short time I can pretend everything is okay.

"You left," she whispers.

"You were all safe. I waited to see you reunited with your fiancé."

She smacks her palm against my chest. "It's you I want."

"You left." I echo her words back at her. Reaching down, I grasp her chin and pull her gaze up to meet mine. My heart aches to see the bruising on that perfect neck. At least it'll fade.

"Has a doctor looked at that?"

"There was a paramedic with the police. I'm fine."

"Why are you here, Con?"

"I didn't leave you. Ash took me."

"When I came back, you were gone. That's all I know. You ripped my heart out, and all I've been able to think about was you being with that piece of shit. Choosing him over me."

She shakes her head. "I never chose him over you. You. I choose you."

I'm not arguing semantics with her. I bend to claim her mouth.

I chose her that night she stood in the rain.

My heart knows that, even if my head didn't at first.

She's home.

---

"Are your parents expecting you back?" I ask as I pour hot water into the cups.

She shakes her head as she picks up the mug of coffee. "I told them where I was going. They know I'm safe with you.

Besides …" She runs an index finger up my chest. "Nothing was going to keep me from you once I got out."

I smile, and follow her back out to the living room.

She sits on the couch, placing her coffee on the table, and I sit beside her and do the same.

"I didn't choose to go back." She lets out an exasperated sigh. "When Jared went missing, they didn't get much out of him, but they got enough to find out I was here."

"Ash was in my house?"

She nods. "With two of his men. I didn't want to go. Graham told me Ash threatened my parents trying to find out where I was, but I still didn't want to go back. I never would have left if …"

I cover her mouth with mine, and the rest of her sentence disappears down my throat. I'd trusted Graham and his lot to protect her, and even they didn't know she'd been taken. The guilt over believing she'd voluntarily left me gnaws at my stomach.

"I'm sorry." I press my forehead to hers. "When I came back to find you gone, it broke me. I should have known—"

"I understand," she whispers. "It's okay. It's all over now, and we're together. Isn't that all that matters?"

"I've missed you so much."

"I've missed you."

I sit up, scanning her expression. It's full of uncertainty, and that's the last thing I want her to feel. "I love you."

Her lips part as she gazes at me.

"I should have told you that day when I left for work, and I don't know why I didn't. The whole week, I wished I could get phone reception to call and tell you."

Her chest shakes as her eyes fill with tears. "I love you, too."

Reaching up, I cup her cheek. "That's settled, then."

She smiles, even with tears running down her face. "I guess it is."

"I'll tell you something else."

She sniffs. "What's that?"

"Fuck the coffee. I'm about to strip that dress off you. And this time it's going in the fire."

Constance laughs loudly, and I reach behind her, peeling the buttons open one by one.

"You think I'm joking, right?"

She shakes her head. "There's one thing I do know about you, Corey Campbell, and that is that you don't joke about things like that."

"Never when it comes to you."

The fabric of the dress tears a little as I tug the sleeves down her arms, but I don't care. This dress needs burning, and I need to be inside the woman who wears it.

I grasp her forearms and pull her to her feet. The fire's back in her eyes. Ash might have taken my girl, but he didn't break her.

She laughs when I grip the fabric and tear it down the middle to her stomach. The rest of it falls to the floor, and she steps out and into my arms.

"Let's get rid of this before we do anything else." I pick the dress up and grab her hand, leading her toward the fireplace.

She shivers. "Corey, I'm standing here in my underwear."

"Let me get this fire lit and that'll be gone too."

The fire's set, and I light the kindling. It doesn't take long to pick up, and I throw a log on, and the dress with it.

I pull Constance into my arms as the flames flicker around the fabric. Shifting my gaze to her, I have a surge of emotion. I thought I'd lost her, but now here she is, and I'm never letting her go again.

"Corey." She sighs as she rests her head on my chest.

I plant a kiss in her hair. "Let's get you out of that underwear."

She laughs, and I scoop her into my arms and gently lower her to the rug. Her eyes are full of love, and I kneel beside her.

"I love you." I cup her cheek, and she closes her eyes.

"Come and show me."

She lets out a contented sigh as I pull my T-shirt over my head. My heart's on fire looking at her. Without a doubt, she's it for me. She was from the moment I laid eyes on her.

I've found my one.

Positioning myself between her legs, I kiss her thighs.

"There's something I need to tell you," she whispers.

"I'm about to eat your pussy, and lord knows I've missed doing that. Can it wait?"

She laughs softly. "Corey, I'm pregnant."

My heart stops. I pull myself up until I'm level with her. She's got the smallest of smiles on her face, but how can this be good news? "Are you telling me that piece of shit touched you?"

She shakes her head. "No, it's—"

I growl. "Whose is it? I'll rip their fucking heads off."

"It's you. I've only been with you."

My heart starts again as our gazes are locked. All I see is love in her eyes. "But—"

"I thought I was safe. The needle was a placebo. It was just another way for Ash to control us."

I pull her face to mine, my lips massaging hers as I stroke her back.

She pulls away. "We're having a baby, Corey. Or maybe I am if you don't want me with that."

"I want you. Just give me a moment."

She bursts into tears, and I pull her into my arms. It's easy to forget she's not streetwise, that despite everything she's been exposed to, she's still led a sheltered life.

"I know, sweetness. It's over now. It'll be you and me and our baby."

"Corey. I thought I'd never be with you again." She sobs, and I hold her tighter.

"I love you. And I'm not letting you go that easily." Pulling back, I look into her teary eyes. "I'm sorry for not keeping you safe. I swear I'll never make that mistake again."

She nods, and I close my eyes. This is it. I've got her back.

And we're having a baby.

---

IT DOESN'T TAKE LONG for us to end up back in bed. And it's where I'll keep her for days if I have any say in it.

*I'm going to be a father.*

Having a child is something I've always thought about, but in an abstract way. It's something other people do, and I watch from afar. Now it's really happening to me, and it's with the only person I could imagine doing it with.

All I see is Constance and our baby.

"What are you thinking about?" she asks, snuggling into my chest.

"How I came so close to losing everything." I palm her cheek, hooking my fingers into her hair. "You, the baby. The things that matter most to me. I'd never felt so lost."

"You were all I thought about when Ash had me. I thought I'd die without being able to tell you how I felt one more time."

I sigh, running a finger down her neck. "I'm so angry he did this to you. I wanted to nail the bastard, and then he pulled that gun, and—"

She runs her nails down my chest, and my body responds. I can't take back what Ash did, but I can do my best to make her forget he ever existed. "I knew you were there. In what I thought might be my final moments, I drew comfort in that. Maybe you hadn't said it, but I knew you loved me."

I plant a kiss on the top of her head. "Always."

"And now, we can look forward to our baby coming. You don't think what Ash did could have hurt it, do you?" She looks up at me, her eyes so full of fear.

"We'll go and see Doc Paton. And then I guess the next step is to talk to Margaret. She's the midwife around here."

"The only other person who knows is Julia, back home. She's the one who told me to take a test. Our parents are going to be so excited."

I suck in a breath. Of course, she doesn't know what happened while she was away. I doubt Ash told her.

"Umm, Mum died."

For a moment she says nothing, but the sorrow written

all over her face makes me wish I didn't have to tell her. Tears well in her eyes. "When?"

"We buried her a week ago."

She clings to me, her hot tears spilling onto my neck. "I'm so sorry I wasn't here for you."

"It wasn't your fault."

"I hate him."

My heart aches at her pain. "If he wasn't dead, I'd kick his arse for everything he's done. And then I'd kick his arse for laying a hand on you. And then, I'd kick his arse again for daring to breathe the same air as you." I run my finger down her cheek. "I love you so much. There is nothing that will ever keep us apart again."

"I love you, too." She gives me a small smile.

"We have to put the past behind us, sweetness. You and me." I run my hand across her stomach. "And this little one. We have to focus on the baby and make a new life."

She nods. "I know. I wish I'd been here, though."

"I was a mess without you. Ask my brothers. They'll probably tell you what a dick I made of myself."

Laughing, she plants a kiss on my chest. "I'm sorry."

"It's not your fault. I even went through the fence one night."

"You did?"

"Kane stopped me. I wanted to tear the place down looking for you, but they said you'd gone back voluntarily. I didn't know any different, and I didn't want to put you at further risk by making a scene."

"Oh, Corey." All the emotion is clear in her voice. "When you didn't come, I thought maybe you thought I was a mistake."

I shake my head. "I've made a lot of mistakes in my life, sweetness. You could never be one of them." Pausing, I let out a contented sigh. "Come here and let me love you one more time before we go to sleep."

"Only one?"

Shrugging, I lower my mouth to hers. "We'll see."

---

It's dark when I wake in the morning. It's always dark.

The only bit of light in the room is the woman in my arms.

I've got her back for good.

My heart is full right now. It's so far from where I was a week ago, and it's all because of her.

Slipping my arm out from underneath her, I climb out of bed and pull the curtains. Morning sun floods the room.

"What are you doing?" She laughs, rubbing her eyes. "You love this room being dark."

"Not anymore. We'll go for a drive to Carlstown and buy some new curtains. Something that is closer to my mood." I turn. "I've been in the dark for long enough."

She smiles at me as I climb back into bed and pull her back into my arms. I take a deep breath, inhaling the familiar soapy scent of her. "I spent far too long moping around over something that wasn't mine to want. Now, I have a family of my own to care for, and I feel whole."

Fixing her gaze on me, Constance plants her hand on my chest. "We are whole."

"Our kid is going to have the best upbringing. We can

give him or her everything, Con." I suck in a breath. "If you wanted, we could move closer to town, too."

"Why would I want that?"

I shrug. "More convenient."

"And have our child miss out on this place? There's no way we're moving." She says it so matter-of-factly, it makes me smile.

"Good. I didn't really want to move." I laugh. "And now the investigation's over, no more having the police on my land."

"It's just us now." Her eyes shine with happiness.

I nod. "It's just us."

## 35

## CONSTANCE

I NEVER THOUGHT I'd be back here again.

My parents still being here is a draw, and I have two very important things left to do. I need to introduce them to Corey, and give them the news that they're going to be grandparents.

Corey squeezes my hand as I turn the handle and open their front door.

"Hello," I call.

"Hello, love." Mum beams from her spot in the living room, and I walk over to her, bending and wrapping my arms around her shoulders.

"Mum, I'd like you to meet Corey. Corey, this is my mum."

Corey nods. "It's very nice to meet you, Mrs Shaw."

"Please. Call me Jackie."

He smiles, shaking the hand she holds out. "Then, it's nice to meet you, Jackie."

"Constance." Dad appears in the doorway, and I run to him. He pulls me into a tight hug. "Oh, my sweetheart. It's so good to see you."

"Dad, this is Corey."

Dad lets me go, and walks toward Corey, his hand extended. "Peter Shaw."

"Corey Campbell."

The two men I love most in the word shake hands.

"Take a seat, you two. I'll make some coffee," Dad says. I take Corey's hand and lead him to the couch.

"I'm glad you came to see us, Constance. We were worried when you ran off like that, but Senior Sergeant Taylor told us that you'd be safe." Mum shifts her gaze to Corey. "And thank you so much. You put yourself at risk for our daughter."

Corey squeezes my hand. "I just wanted her to be safe."

I swallow. "I had to make sure things were good with Corey. He didn't know Ash had brought me back."

My mother's eyes grow sad. "That man had a lot to answer for. It's a shame he'll never have to face the consequences of his actions."

"No, but he'll never be a threat to any of you again," Corey says. "That's all that matters."

"Drugs." Dad stands in the doorway, two mugs in his hands. "The whole time, and right under our noses."

I stare at him. "What do you mean?"

He places the coffee cups on the table and goes back to the kitchen for the sugar bowl and milk.

"The bunkers. Ash had quite the methamphetamine factory going on."

My heart sinks. The men closest to him must have known about it.

Dad hands Mum her coffee and sits in a chair opposite us. "Scott and a couple of Ash's other guys knew. Michael and the rest had no idea. They thought he was stockpiling food because he was so paranoid."

"That piece-of-shit was …" Corey stops himself. "Sorry."

Dad nods. "It's okay. He was a piece-of-shit."

"The police are questioning everyone, but Ash wasn't stupid. He used his father's paranoia to his own means. Robert meant the bunker and tunnels to be used for our survival, not for Ash's money-making."

I widen my eyes. "Did they get Ash's associate? The one he wanted me to—"

"He's been arrested, too. You and Julia deserve so much of the credit, sweetheart. If you hadn't freed Michael and Jared, the truth would still be buried under those glasshouses."

Corey slips his arm around my shoulders, and I lean on him, relief flooding through me.

A smile plays on Dad's lips. "It's funny how things work out. Julia wouldn't know that bunker like you. Without your help, she might not have found either of them."

Tears well in my eyes. "So, all those years of being disobedient paid off?"

He chuckles. "You were always such a wild one."

"What happens now? Do you all have to leave here?" Corey asks.

Dad shrugs. "I'm not sure. A lot of us contributed to the land, and it was in a trust controlled by Robert, and then Ash. What happens to it now, I'm not sure."

"Well, I don't have a big house, but if you and Jackie need somewhere to live, it's open to you."

I wrap my arm around Corey's waist and bury my face in his chest. "Thank you."

"Family's family, sweetness. I can't help everyone, but we'll make it work if your parents need it."

"Thank you, Corey. Hopefully it won't take long to unravel this mess, and we can work out where to go from there." Dad shifts his gaze to me. "I'm assuming you're not coming back now."

I sit up. "About that." I flick a glance at Corey. "There's something I need to tell you."

Mum leans forward. Uncertainty crosses her face.

"I'm pregnant. You two are going to be grandparents. I'm not exactly sure how far along I am, but—"

"Does this mean there's a marriage on the horizon?" Dad asks.

Mum smiles.

I have to stop myself from rolling my eyes.

"Dad, I—"

"Soon," Corey says. "My brother's about to marry his partner, and they've been through so much to get to this point. I wouldn't want to take anything away from them."

I stare at Corey. We haven't even discussed this, so I know he's winging it. But he's given my dad exactly the answer he wanted to hear.

"I'm not trying to apply any pressure. All we want is for Constance to be happy. She's been through enough lately."

"Agreed," Corey says. I loop my arm in Corey's and finally get his attention. He plants a kiss on the top of my head.

"Constance will be well taken care of. You can count on it. I'm just so relieved she's safe and back with me."

A smile spreads across Dad's face. "I'm relieved she's found someone who truly loves her. Ash abused our trust, and by the time we all realised just how bad things were, it was too late."

Tears prick my eyes.

"I'm so sorry, Constance," Dad says. "If I was a younger man …"

I nod. "I know, Dad. It's not your fault. Ash took advantage of the power his father gave him, and we were all caught up in that."

"You know in the old days, you would never have been matched with someone like John Parsons. And you would have had a choice if you disliked the other person that much."

I sigh. "I know that, too."

"I'm sorry we didn't see the warning signs."

Shaking my head, I reach for Dad's hand. "You weren't to know. And this is your home."

"I'll always regret what you nearly went through."

I smile. "We're all safe now." I pause. "What will happen with Mum's care?"

Dad smiles. "If we can stay here, there are going to be some big changes. The whole community were up talking for half the night."

My heart thuds. "So you'll all be okay?"

"The one thing that is true is that we're self-sufficient."

"What does that have to do with Mum's care?"

"I'm retiring, Constance. I talked with the police last night, and I'm old enough to claim a pension. It's not a huge amount of money, but I'll be able to be with your mother and take care of her."

Tears roll down my cheeks. "I'm not far away if you need help."

"Sweetheart, you'll have more than enough on your plate."

Corey's grip tightens around my waist, and I snuggle in against him.

The end of Ash has meant the start of something good—something that should always have been.

———

I HEAR Julia before I see her.

"Andrew." Her voice carries in the air, followed by her laughter.

As Corey and I draw closer, I see Andrew. He's running around in the sunshine, and it makes me smile. Julia sits with Jared. His arm's around her waist, and that just makes my smile grow.

"Hello," I say.

She looks up, gasps, and leaps to her feet. "Constance."

In an instant, I'm in her arms, and she's holding onto me for dear life. "I see you're doing okay." I nod. "Jared."

"Oh, no. His real name is Taylor."

"Of course." I grin. "You were undercover."

"Not anymore. I'm sticking around." He laughs.

"You're leaving the force?" Corey asks.

Jared, or rather, Taylor, nods. "Julia and I are going to give it a go now everything is settling down."

"The whole thing is crazy, huh?" Julia lets me go. "I knew

Ash was up to something, but even I had no idea how big it was."

She squats, beckoning Andrew to her. The little boy runs straight into her arms, and she scoops him up.

"I'd like you to meet Andrew." She faces Corey. "I named him after your brother. He probably saved both our lives."

"I hope Drew doesn't know. He's got a big enough ego already." Corey laughs. He reaches out, tickling Andrew under the chin. "Maybe you should rename him Corey now."

Julia laughs. "I'm so thankful for your family. He and Hayley were so good to me. I can't thank either of them enough."

"I'll be sure to mention you to them next time I see them."

"Maybe they can come and visit?"

He nods. "Maybe. They've got children of their own. Twins. They're about 9 months old now."

Her eyes widen. "That must keep them busy. I have enough trouble with one two-year-old."

Corey laughs.

She shifts her gaze to me. "So, I guess you're not coming back?"

"I'll be right next door."

Taylor stands, moving behind Julia and wrapping his arms around her waist. I guess I'm not the only one to get a happy ending.

THE CAR JOURNEY home might be short, but it's silent. Until we pull into our driveway.

"Why did you lie to my dad?" I ask.

"What?"

"About us getting married."

Corey flicks a glance at me. "I told him the truth."

"Since when?"

"I'm not in the habit of lying to people, Con. You know how I feel about you." He pulls to a stop in the driveway.

My heart swells. *He meant it.*

Corey captures my wrist and brings it to his lips. "Every word I said was true. It's you and me, sweetness. Even before the baby. It always was."

Tears prick my eyes. "We haven't discussed it."

"I know, but this is it. We *are* getting married. First, it's Adam and Lily's time to shine. They earned it."

"And that's it." I don't mean to sound whiney, but I'm disappointed he's made a decision without even asking me.

His expression softens. "If you're angry because I didn't propose first, I will—when the time is right and we're both ready for it."

I pout.

"Come here, my walking bunch of hormones." He pulls me into his arms as much as he can, thanks to the gearstick between us. "Let's go inside and I can show you just how happy you make me."

"Promise?"

"I promise to give you the whole world. We can build our life together, Constance, and you'd better believe that includes me putting a ring on your finger. We'll give our children everything."

*Children.*

*Plural.*

I raise my face to meet his. "I'm sorry."

"For what?"

"Doubting you."

He shakes his head. "There's nothing to be sorry about. We're together, and that's all that matters from now on."

His kiss tells me everything I need to know—he loves me.

## 36

### OWEN

GINNY TAKES the news that Corey and Constance are having a baby hard.

It's not fair.

If anyone was a natural at this mother stuff, it's her. When I see them together, I am watching a mother and daughter. She's the one Ava turns to when she needs comforting, and when she can't sleep. I don't envy them that as my relationship with Ava is just as close.

I know it's Ginny's body that won't co-operate, but I feel like a failure. My girl bravely battles on and holds her head up high when I know she wants to curl up and cry. Because sometimes she does just that.

I wish I could take her pain away.

Neither of us know what will happen now she's had the surgery, and I'd try over and over again if it would give her what she wanted. But I don't know how she'll cope if we lose another one.

It's a Saturday afternoon, and Ginny and Ava are at home watching a movie. I'm over seeing *Moana* for the four hundredth time, so I've excused myself and made my way down the road to the pub. It's been a long time since I've been here alone. With Ava and then Ginny moving in, all my evenings have been with them.

I haven't missed this place, but it's nice to be alone with my thoughts.

My phone buzzes with a text from Adam, responding to the one I sent inviting him here an hour ago.

*Lily's visiting Constance. I'm at home with the kids. Come around here if you want.*

My second beer sits in front of me, and the car's at home, given that it's not a long walk.

*I'm just going to finish this and go home I think. Ava's movie's probably finished by now.*

*Moana? Haha*

*How did you guess?*

*Mate, Rose loves the music. I've seen it a million times.*

I smile. I'm glad to know that at least one of my brothers is going through a Disney obsession too.

"Owen?"

I look up. A blonde woman is heading straight for me, and I take a deep breath. Occasionally, someone from my past turns up somewhere, and when they do I'm always glad if Ginny's not with me. All it does is hurt her.

"It's Michelle."

"Oh." *Shit.* Her brother and I were friends through high school. Michelle used to follow me around with big puppy eyes, but there were two reasons why we never hooked up. One was that she was three years younger than me, which is a huge amount when you're fourteen. And the other thing was that she was Brian's sister. That made her a no-go zone as far as I was concerned.

"Hey, mate." Brian's right behind her, and I smile at him.

"Hi."

"Mich has just moved back from Wellington, so we thought we'd come down to have a welcome home drink."

I nod. "Fair enough."

"It feels like we haven't seen each other forever," she says, nudging my arm.

"You've been gone five years." Brian laughs. "I'll get the beers."

"I'm not staying," I say.

"Just the one? I haven't seen you down here for ages." Brian says.

"Okay. Just the one. Then I have to go."

"Why? Got a hot date?" Michelle laughs.

"Something like that."

We sit in awkward silence for a minute.

A beer appears in front of me, and I nod toward Brian. "Thanks, mate."

"No problem. How've you been?"

"Good. Really good. Life's a bit of a rollercoaster, but I think we're on the right track now."

Brian looks over at Michelle. "Owen found out a little while ago that he had a daughter."

She smiles. "Why am I not surprised?"

Her comment irritates me, even though I know it's not meant in a nasty way.

Michelle leans in closer, hooking her arm around my

shoulders. I try and shrug her off, but she doesn't get the message.

Her brother's not so slow. "How's Ginny?" Brian asks.

"She's good. Her and Ava are watching *Moana,* and I'm a bit over it. I'll be heading home once I finish this drink."

"Mich, why don't you go and play pool? I'm sure someone will turn up to play against you." His tone is resigned, like he knows she's not going away. Maybe it's time to stop being subtle.

"Owen?"

I turn to see Ginny, hand in hand with Ava, staring at me. She shifts her gaze to Michelle, and if looks could kill, Michelle would be about twenty feet under.

"Babe, I was just saying to Brian that I'm going after this beer." I hop off the bar stool, shaking free from Michelle's arm.

"Oh, you were." Her tone is flat.

"I don't know if you know Michelle, Brian's little sister? She's just moved back to town."

Ginny's expression stays tight, but she nods toward Michelle.

"Let's go grab a booth and order some food." I take Ava by the hand and slip my other arm around Ginny's waist and guide them toward an empty booth.

From out of nowhere, Mary Cuthbert appears. "Ava."

Ava's eyes widen, and she giggles as Mary sweeps her into her arms.

"Are you here for dinner? Me too," Mary says. She looks between Ginny and me. "Can I steal this little one? You two can have a nice quiet dinner, and Ava can sit at my noisy table."

She jerks her head toward the table behind her, and I smile at the sight of Joe, her husband, surrounded by their four grandchildren.

"Family night out?" I ask.

"Something like that. We've got a full house this weekend." She jiggles Ava. "One more for dinner won't make a difference."

"Do you want to go?" Ginny asks.

Ava nods.

"Go on then. We'll just be here." I shift my gaze to Mary. "Put her dinner on my tab."

They disappear, and I take a big breath before slipping into the booth beside Ginny.

"You're not going to invite your friend, Michelle, to join us?"

"Why would I do that?"

Ginny shrugs. "I don't know. She seems pretty friendly."

"She's always been touchy-feely. I've never been there, though, and I don't plan on ever going there."

Ginny looks tired. Has she looked that way for a while? God, I love this woman, and the hell she's been through these past few months has worn her down.

"I love *you*," I say. Gripping her chin, I pull her face toward me and kiss her softly. "I know things are tough right now, but you know my love for you will never change."

She snuggles in against me. "I keep thinking maybe I should offer you an out."

"I don't want one. I've got everything I need." I plant a kiss on her forehead. "I'll order us some food. What do you want?"

She picks up the menu waiting on the table, studying it for a moment.

"The fish and chips are usually good."

I grin. "Good choice. We can recreate our first meal together."

She laughs, and it's music to my ears. I have no idea what I'd do without my Ginny.

---

SHE'S QUIET DURING DINNER, and more than once I catch her watching Michelle. Michelle and Brian are still sitting at the bar, and I just wish they'd go home or something.

I pick up an onion ring and smile.

Ginny looks up as I slide out of the booth. I grab her hand to pull her with me.

"What are you doing?" Her laugh is half-hearted.

When I step out, I turn, dropping to one knee.

"Owen." She casts her gaze around. No one's paying much attention to us. They're all eating and drinking.

"Virginia Helen Robinson, will you do me the very great honour of becoming my wife?" I slide the onion ring onto her ring finger as her expression grows emotional.

"Why are you doing this?" she croaks.

"I want you. I'd be lost without you, Gin. I want us to get married, and for you to adopt Ava."

"Adopt Ava?" Tears slide down her cheeks.

"We should make it official."

She slips her arms around my neck. "I love that idea. And I love you. Owen Campbell, I would very much like to accept."

I stand, pulling her to her feet and kiss her.

She laughs and snuggles into my chest. "Can we get a real ring?"

"We'll go shopping tomorrow. Maybe Ava can pick something out."

She raises her head. "You know that means I'll end up with a *Paw Patrol* watch or something."

I chuckle. "Maybe you can get one of those *and* a ring."

"Owen." I turn at the sound of Mary's voice. "Ava's got something to ask you."

I raise my eyebrows and look down at my daughter. "Do you?"

She nods, and I let go of Ginny, squatting in front of her.

Ava leans closer. "Daddy, can I go for a sleepover?"

"I can't see why not. Should we ask Ginny?"

She fixes her blue eyes on Ginny. "Mummy, can I go for a sleepover?"

Ginny nods. "That's a great idea, sweet pea. We're going for a drive to Carlstown tomorrow, but if you want to stay with Mary tonight, it's fine with me."

"The kids are all getting on so well. My youngest *moko* is the same age as Ava, and the two of them have really hit it off," Mary says. "Besides, I saw what just happened." She winks, and we laugh.

"You're the only one who did, I think." I grin. "Ava's only ever had sleepovers at Adam's place. We'll pop home and grab some things for her."

Mary shakes her head. "Don't worry about it. We've got plenty. I'll drop her off in the morning."

I grin. "Are you sure?" Leaning in, I murmur, "She wears a pull-up to sleep."

"So does Kiana. We'll be fine. Enjoy your night."

I scoop Ava up into my arms and plant a kiss on her cheek. She giggles and reaches for Ginny. Ginny pecks her on the cheek, too.

"Love you. Have fun." Ginny shifts her gaze to Mary. "Please call us any time if she needs picking up. Have you got the bakery number? It's forwarded to the house at night."

Mary nods. "I do, and I will."

As she walks away, I slide my arm around Ginny. "That was an unexpected bonus."

"I'll miss her."

"So will I, but we get to celebrate. Just the two of us."

She widens her eyes. "Whatever will we do?"

I grin. "Oh, I have plenty of ideas."

---

I'm shattered.

Ginny and I have had a lot of sex since we got together, but last night was like running a marathon. I might work out, but I'm not made for this.

It makes me laugh when I think of my reputation prior to being with Ginny. No woman ever put as many demands on me as Ginny did, but oh, how I loved giving in to them.

When I roll over, I smile at the sight of her.

She's lying on her stomach, her auburn hair all over the damn place. I can't see her face as it's buried underneath all that hair.

"Ginny," I whisper.

"What?" she mumbles. "I'm tired. You wore me out last night."

Laughing, I plant a kiss in her hair. "How about I make breakfast?"

"That sounds like a good idea. Gotta prove you're husband material somehow." She chuckles, and I land my hands on her waist, tickling her.

She shrieks. "Owen!" Ginny rolls over and onto her back. The love she has for me is written all over her face, and it makes me smile. This makes up for the tough times.

"Oh, so you're still going to marry me?"

Ginny runs her fingers through my hair. "Maybe. If you're lucky."

She's so beautiful, her long hair spread out over the pillow. Her eyes still show signs of her recent tiredness, but she's happy. Seeing her like this warms my heart.

"I'm already lucky. I have the best girlfriend—"

"Fiancée." She grins.

"Fiancée. I stand corrected." I laugh. "Ava's going to be so excited when she finds out we're getting married."

Ginny's eyes widen. "We can look for little flower girl dresses. Ohhh, Owen, she's going to look gorgeous."

"So will you. Let's not wait too long." I peck her on the lips. "I'll go and make some breakfast."

As I reach the living room, there's a knock on the door, followed by a giggle I'd know anywhere. I pull open the door to see Ava grinning up at me.

"Not today, thank you." I push the door as if to close it.

"Daddy …" She laughs.

"One Ava, returned home safe and sound," Mary says.

"Thanks, Mary. I hope she wasn't too much trouble."

Ava scoots around me and heads up the hallway.

"No manners. I hope she said thank you."

Mary nods. "She's lovely. She has better manners than my lot. Any time you want a night off, just let me know. Ava's always welcome at my place."

"Thank you so much. We really appreciate it."

"It's never a problem. See you soon, and congratulations, you two."

I smile as I close the door. "Shit."

"What is it?" Ginny asks from the hallway.

"We're going to have to make a few phone calls today. As much as I love Mary, news of our engagement will be all over the place by lunchtime."

She laughs. "I'll just call my mum. She'll spread the word on my side."

"Have you told Ava?"

"Not yet. She's literally just walked in the door. I thought we could do it together?"

Ginny leads Ava into the living room.

"Come and sit down, sweet pea," I say.

We all sit on the couch. For a moment, I'm distracted by the fact that Ginny's dressed in one of my T-shirts, her long bare legs stretching out in front of her, and …

"Owen?" Ginny sounds amused.

"Sorry. Ava, do you want to go for a drive to Carlstown today?"

Ava nods.

I take a breath. "We're going to find Ginny a very special ring."

"A ring?" Ava's eyebrows knit.

"Well, Daddy and Ginny are getting married."

Her mouth forms a perfect *O* as she stares at me. "Can we have a wedding?"

I nod. "It might take a little while because we've got our new house coming too, but we can have a wedding. And there's something else."

Ginny looks at me, confused.

"I'm going to make it so that Ginny is your mummy. I know you already call her that, but we'll make it all official."

Tears appear in Ginny's eyes. Ava says nothing.

"Ava?"

"Ginny is my mummy. And then I have my other mummy."

I nod. "Just like you have two daddies."

She beams as if she's the smartest kid on the planet.

And that's because she is.

---

"Breakfast's ready."

Ava leaps onto one of the chairs, and I shake my head. "Are you hungry, by any chance?"

"I am," Ginny says. "Starving after last night. All that exercise made me hungry."

I chuckle. "Bacon and eggs, coming right up."

I place a plate in front of each of them and sit down with my own. Ginny's eyelids flutter.

"Are you okay?" I ask.

The colour disappears from her face, and she slaps her hand across her mouth. "I can't eat that."

"My cooking's not that bad," I joke.

"No, it's just …" She gags, and stands, running from the room toward the bathroom.

Ava and I look at each other. "Mummy's sick?"

I nod. "Looks like it."

Leaving Ava at the table to eat her breakfast, I walk to the hallway. "Gin, are you okay?"

"I'll be fine." Her voice wobbles.

"Let me know if you need anything."

Still worried, I sit at the table. Ginny's been through more than enough these past few months.

"I love bacon." Ava stabs a piece with her fork.

"So do I. Is this your second breakfast today?"

She nods. "We hobbits today, Daddy."

"Well, you are, sweet pea." I laugh. She learned that from me a long time ago. I'm so proud of how smart my girl is, and how good her memory is. Except for when she uses it against me. "Owen, can you come in here?" Ginny's voice shakes as she calls me from the bathroom.

I run.

She's standing in the centre of the room, tears streaming down her face. In her hand is a pregnancy test. My heart lurches at the sight of it. Despite our promises to each other not to stress, every month is agonising no matter which way it goes.

"Hey, hey, it's okay. We knew this could take time. Do you know what I think? I think we should just relax and forget about it. Just be together and if we make a baby, we make a baby." I don't know what to say about what will happen if she suffers another miscarriage. I'm not sure she can take it again.

She shakes her head. "No. I'm not crying because I'm not pregnant. We did it." Ginny raises her hand to show me the white stick, and for a second it's so close to my face it's fuzzy, but sure enough, there are two stripes.

"We did it?"

Ginny nods. "I don't know if it'll stick, but we did it again. And now I've had the surgery there's a better chance."

"I know. Let's just take it slowly and see how we go." Inside, I'm screaming with joy.

"Daddy?" Ava sticks her head around the door and frowns. "Why are you crying, Mummy?"

Whenever Ava calls Ginny that, it just makes her cry harder. Now is no exception.

"She's just really happy about something." I hold my arms open, and Ava leaps into them. I stand with her in my grasp. "Give her a hug."

Ava stretches across and wraps her arms around Ginny's neck. "I love you."

"I love you, too," Ginny whispers.

"Don't cry, Mummy."

"I always cry when you call me that."

Ava's mouth falls open.

"It's okay, though. I love you calling me Mummy."

Ava clings to Ginny, and I'm reluctant to let her go the whole way into Ginny's arms. Ginny will be doing as little as possible if I have anything to do with it.

"How about we all go and sit down on the couch together?"

Ava nods, letting go of Ginny, but not taking her eyes off her. Those two are so close that every up and down Ginny goes through, Ava's right along with her.

When we get to the couch, Ava crawls onto Ginny's lap and those arms go back around Ginny's neck.

"I'm fine, baby," Ginny whispers, hugging Ava tight.

"I don't like you crying."

"You know what? I'm just so happy to have you and your dad in my life. I love us being a family."

I extend my arm, and Ginny snuggles into me, Ava in tow. More than anything, I wish I could capture this feeling in a bottle and hold onto it forever.

———

IT TAKES HALF the morning to call around the family with the engagement news. In the afternoon we drive to Carlstown where Ava picks out the perfect ring, and a *Paw Patrol* watch.

The whole day, I watch Ginny.

Every so often, she stops and places her hand on her stomach, and a small smile appears on her face. I love seeing that smile, but the thought of something going wrong terrifies me. If she loses this baby, it will kill her inside.

By the time she joins me in bed, she's looking relaxed and happy. Long may that last.

I open my arms to her, and she nestles in.

"No sex tonight?" she asks.

"I think you took every last drop out of me last night. My balls need to recover."

She laughs. "I'll leave your balls alone tonight, then."

"They might like it if you …" I don't finish my sentence because the bemused look on her face tells me she's going nowhere near them.

"Ava took the news well."

"She loves us. She had her whole life turned upside down, and between us we've turned it the right way up." I kiss Ginny on the forehead.

"I love her, Owen. I'll be a good mother to her. No matter what else happens."

"I already know that. You're a good mother now." I pause. "I'll always be sorry that she doesn't have her biological mother in her life, but she's happy. Can you imagine how excited she'll be when she finds out she's going to be a big sister?"

Ginny grins. "I can't wait to tell her."

I place my hand on her stomach. "This one just needs to keep safe a few more weeks and we can tell her. Or you can. I want to see the look on her face when she realises."

Ginny's eyes are so full of life, and love. "Me too."

## 37

### COREY

CONSTANCE FITS back in as if she hasn't left.

She might not ever have met Mum, but Dad adores her, and the rest of the family think she's great—and she is.

I spent last night working, and this time Constance stayed at Adam's—not that I'm worried about Ash's friends—the ones who were in on his scheme have been arrested. It'll take a while for everything to settle next door, but the fence is already being taken down and most of the people there are staying. For some of them, that life is all they've known.

Right now, I'm just anxious to get back to Constance.

I sigh as I pull into Adam's driveway. Lucky greets me at the gate. I scratch his head as we walk toward the house.

Kicking off my boots, I turn the handle and push the front door. "Hello."

I grin at the sound of little footsteps running toward me, and I stand still as a statue until I feel a small hand grabbing at my pants. I look down to see my little blonde angel, Rose, looking up at me.

"Oh, hello."

"Orey."

"What's that? Can you say Corey?"

She giggles, and I bend, scooping her into my arms. "Are you my welcome party?" I make my way into the kitchen as Rose snuggles herself into my neck.

"She found you, then." Lily laughs, holding her arms open for Rose to go into.

Rose abandons me for her mother, and I shake my head as I let go of her. "Traitor."

I sense her before I see her. Despite all that girly stuff she bought with Lily, Constance still shares my shower gel, and I'd know that scent anywhere.

"We'll leave you to it. See you in the living room," Lily says.

Constance wraps her arms around my waist and takes a deep breath against my chest.

"Hey, beautiful. Did you miss me?"

She raises her face, and I find myself lost in her for a moment.

"I'm so glad you're back. I've enjoyed being here, but I just want to be at home with you."

"Feeling's mutual." I bend, sweeping my tongue across her lips before kissing her. She lets out a whimper when I deepen the kiss. I want to take her home and bury myself inside her for a week. "I'll go say hello, and then we can get out of here."

"I'm not sure it's going to be that easy." She laughs. Taking my hand in hers, she leads me into the living room where we sit on the couch.

"We made Constance a Facebook account," Max announces this proudly, his chest all puffed out.

"Did you now?"

Constance laughs. "Max insisted. Now I'm Facebook friends with most of the family."

"Bud, we can't get internet at home. When's she going to use it?" I poke my tongue at him.

"Ash had internet," Constance says.

"Yeah, he probably paid a fortune for satellite. It's possible, but it's pricey." I drape my arm over her shoulders and plant a kiss on the top of her head. "I don't know if it's in my price range, sweetness. Even mobile data is patchy, and not cheap."

"It's okay. I can just look at it when I come to visit these guys." She turns her face up and kisses my cheek. "You are so growing that beard back once the wedding is done. This stubble isn't enough."

"Agreed." Lily laughs, and I roll my eyes at her.

"You two ganging up on me."

"Of course." Lily walks toward us. "Do you two want to stay for dinner?"

"We could do. If you have enough to feed us," I say.

"Adam got a lamb roast big enough to feed half of Copper Creek for fixing a tractor. I think we can cope." She laughs. "Besides, I've got some baby clothes you two can have if you want to go through them. I should have got them out last night, but I only just thought about it."

Constance reaches for one of my hands and squeezes it. "Thank you, Lily."

"Aren't you guys going to have more?" I ask.

She shrugs. "Maybe another one. I think we both just want to get through this wedding in one piece."

I nod. "That's fair enough. Maybe if we borrow the baby stuff, we'll be giving it back to you next year."

Lily laughs. "We'll see."

Constance leans against me, and I bury my face in her hair.

As much as I love my family, I can't wait to be alone with her.

***

AS AMAZING AS DINNER WAS, getting home with Constance is even better. I'm looking forward to sinking into a warm soft bed with her in it.

"Corey," Constance calls from the bathroom, and when I get there, what I see makes me catch my breath.

She's so far from that modestly dressed woman who arrived on my doorstep. Standing naked, she turns side on to the mirror and runs her hand over her stomach.

"What *are* you doing?" I laugh.

"Is there a bump? Do you see a bump?"

"What I see is my naked girlfriend who I've been away from for a full twenty-four hours. I can't see anything else because the blood is nowhere near my brain right now."

She grins, sauntering toward me and taking my hand. I chuckle as I run my hand over her stomach.

"There's a small bump. Are you happy now?"

She nods.

"And now we're going to bed because I am not standing

here watching you touch yourself without having some of the fun for myself."

Constance wraps her arms around my neck, pressing her naked body against me.

"That's not helping." I chuckle, bending to reach her mouth.

"I missed you," she murmurs.

"I missed you, too. Is this what every reunion's going to be like? You prancing around naked?"

"Are you complaining?"

I shake my head. "Never."

I slide my hands down her sides, and she jumps. I catch her as she wraps her legs around my waist.

"Let's go to bed," she says.

"You're so naughty, Ms Shaw."

"I was lonely last night."

I laugh. "Shall we go and fix that, then?"

"Yes, please."

I place her gently on the mattress, and strip off my clothes. What I need is a shower, but I need her more. Always her.

When I climb into bed, she straddles my hips, rubbing herself against me.

"Hey. Don't I get to play first?"

"You can play later. I know what I want." She lifts up a little before lowering herself onto my erect cock.

"Someone's already wet."

Constance leans over. "Someone's been missing you."

She surrounds me, and it takes me back to that first night we were together—the first night she was mine. I can't pretend it means nothing to know I'm the only man who's ever been inside her. She was mine from the start, and she always will be.

"I love you," I whisper.

Constance leans over, her mouth closing in on mine. I have no idea what I'm going to do when I have to camp out for multiple nights. My need for her will be off the charts.

"Did I tell you how much I missed you?" she mumbles against my mouth.

"I'm pretty sure you can feel how much I missed you."

She grins as she pushes herself up. I suck in a breath when she rocks her hips.

Constance raises a finger to her lips and gives me a thoughtful look. "I think so. I might have to try that again to check."

"I didn't come home so you could torture me." I laugh.

She shivers as I run my hands up her back, and her hips rock against me again. "I'm just making the most of it."

"God, you drive me crazy, lady."

She laughs. "As long as you always come home to me."

"Always." I twist my lips into a sly smile. "As long as I always get a welcome home like this."

Constance looks at me with so much love, it takes my breath away. "Always."

# 38

## COREY

ONCE UPON A TIME I thought this day might kill me.

I guess it was inevitable from the moment Adam and Lily first saw each other that they'd marry. After twelve years apart and two children, nothing's going to get in the way of them being together.

I couldn't be happier for them. They decided to delay the wedding until the spring. It meant all the bad things were behind us. Mum's death and everything Constance went through battered the family a bit, but today we're together and nothing is going to go wrong.

And, in the absence of Lily's father, I'm the one giving away the bride.

She takes a deep breath.

"Are you ready?" I ask.

"I've been ready for years."

I lean over, pressing a kiss to her forehead. "I know you have. Adam's a lucky man. Don't you ever forget that."

Tears well in her eyes. "I'm the lucky one. Not only do I have Adam, but I have all of you as my family."

"We're getting pretty good at this family stuff."

She smiles, and her whole face lights up. "We really are. All of us." Lily wraps her arms around me. "Thank you."

"What for?"

"For today. For always being there when I've needed you. Max and I couldn't have got by all those years without you being around to take care of us."

I shake my head. "Lily, you took care of you."

"Once, you asked us to move in with you. And over the years there were times I almost wished I'd said yes."

"Almost?"

She raises her head. "You're going to make an amazing father, Corey. I know this because you've always been so good with Max. Because you love him."

I nod.

"And now you're with the right woman, and I am so happy that you two are together and you're having a baby."

I smile. "She is the right woman."

"I knew it when I first saw you two together."

My smile grows. "We weren't even 'together' together then."

"No, but there was a real connection between you. Besides, I've never seen you devastated over a woman. Not to the extent you were when you thought she'd gone back." She pats me on the chest. "That, my friend, is true love."

It's a small gathering, with family and close friends attending. After all this time Lily and Adam wanted something small and intimate. I think they would have been happy with no one else there. It's all about making the commitment to one another.

I wink at Lily as I pass her hand into Adam's. He'll take good care of her, and he'll love her for the rest of their days.

I thought this would leave behind a hole, but my heart's full of love instead.

I turn to take my seat, my eyes going straight to the woman whose smile is just for me. Lacing my fingers with hers, I pull Constance's hand to my lips and plant a kiss on it. Her eyes are full of so much love, and I lean over and peck her lips.

"*Love you,*" she mouths.

"Love you too," I whisper

I slip my arm around her shoulders, and she leans against me as we watch my brother and the woman he loves exchange vows. I place my hand on her baby bump. She's five months pregnant now, and I love it.

"I promise to always love you and be there for you. Every single day for the rest of our lives." Adam grips Lily's hands. "I've loved you from the moment I laid eyes on you. I never stopped, and I swear to you I never will."

Constance squeezes my hand in hers, and I press my lips to the top of her head.

"Through the good and the bad, I promise to love you always. And you know we've had more than enough of the bad. I only want the good for us from now on." Lily's eyes are full of tears as she says the words.

I'm so proud of her. Of both of them.

We all seem to be getting our happy endings.

---

"So, you ready to give up that secret?" I nudge James.

He chuckles. "Not yet. Maybe next year."

"It must be pretty big."

Shrugging, he reaches for another beer. "I promise I'll tell you one day."

"You'd better. This family's suffered enough because of secrets."

His mouth falls open. "I would never hurt anyone. You told me you lied to Graham Taylor over Constance being at your place at first."

I nod. "That's right. But, dude—"

"Did you ever stop and think that maybe I'm not talking about my love life to protect someone too?"

"I was just going to say that I'm just giving you shit. I worry about you, little brother. But if you tell me that you're safe, then you can keep your secret."

He lets out a loud breath. "I'm sorry. Just on edge a little. I hate that Mum missed this."

I grasp his shoulder. "I know. She did her best to meddle in their lives, but they beat all the odds. I think at the end, she appreciated that. I'm just glad she got to know Max and Rose. Along with her other grandkids."

"I'm sorry she'll miss meeting your baby. She was always so proud of you."

I chuckle. "Not always. We had our moments."

"We all had our moments with her." Drew walks up behind us. "Some pretty recently."

James pulls away. "I'm gonna go see how Dad's going."

As he walks away, I spot Constance heading toward me. She stops just before she reaches us and lets out a big yawn.

"Have you had enough, sweetness? We can get out of here."

She shakes her head. "I'm fine. We can stay as long as you want."

"Nope. If you need to rest, then we're going home. Go get your stuff."

"Okay." She presses a kiss to my cheek. "You take such good care of me."

"I like taking care of you."

Drew shakes his head as she walks away. "You are so pussy-whipped."

"Look who's talking." I laugh.

"True. I guess we're both in the same boat now. Mind you, so are Adam and Owen. James must be next."

"James has something going on he's not talking about."

Drew's eyebrows rise. "Really?"

"Dude. You see more of him than I do. How can you *not* know that?"

He shrugs.

"Did you two want another drink?" Hayley walks toward us with two beers in her hands.

"I won't say no," Drew says.

"I know you won't." She hands him one. "Corey?"

"Where are the twins?"

"Ginny and Constance have one each with them. I think they're practicing."

"Constance was on her way to get her things."

Hayley grins. "Well, I might have distracted her."

"Do you want to take one of them with you? If Ginny takes the other one, we'll get a night alone." Drew slips his arm around his wife's waist.

"No, you can look after your own children. I have plans for tonight." I waggle my eyebrows.

"I don't want to know." Hayley laughs. "Today's been such a good day. I'm glad it all went well."

"It can't have gone worse than the last time." Drew pulls away from her as Hayley elbows him in the ribs. "Ouch."

"I'm going to go and rescue my lady from your baby and get her home. I'm sure she's exhausted," I say.

Drew hooks his arm around Hayley's shoulders. "I'm sure that's why you want to get her home."

I grin. "See you two tomorrow?"

"We'll be here for lunch. Maybe dinner, too, if history is anything to go by," Drew says.

"Make the most of it while they have all the food."

Lily's over-catered a little, considering it's family and close friends. Tomorrow's going to be like the days after Christmas with us grazing on leftovers all day.

I walk over toward Constance. Lily's beside her as they both fuss over the baby. Getting out of here might take some time.

Lily stands as I approach. "You're going home?"

I nod. "Time to get this one to bed. So she can sleep, for a change."

Constance blushes, and I laugh while Lily punches me in the arm. I smile at my sister-in-law. "I hope you guys get some time alone."

Lily nods. "Max and Rose are having a sleepover at

Owen's place with Ava. They're all camping in the living room."

I laugh. "That'll be fun."

"They're pretty good. Max is taking the book he's reading so he can escape from the girls."

"Wise move." I grab her hand and squeeze. "Congratulations. Today was amazing."

"Thank you. Both of you. Having you here made it even better. See you tomorrow?"

"Wouldn't miss it for the world, Mrs Campbell." I lean over and peck her on the cheek.

Lily lets out a loud breath, reaching over to take Amelia from Constance. "That'll take a bit of getting used to."

"You waited long enough for it."

She grins. "It was worth the wait."

"Thank you for letting me give you away."

Her eyes light up with happiness. "Thank you for being there for me."

"Always. You know that."

She nods. "I know."

I plant a kiss on top of Amelia's head. She kicks and squeals.

"Look at what you started." Lily frowns.

"I'm leaving now."

"You'll have your own to deal with shortly, Corey Campbell."

I grin because I really can't wait.

# CHAPTER 39
## CONSTANCE

I wake, surrounded by Corey. His body envelops me, and while my bladder screams, I'm not sure I can get out from underneath him. Since I've been pregnant, he's been even more protective than normal.

I wriggle out of his grasp and make it to the edge of the bed before a large hand lands on my waist and pulls me back toward him.

"Where do you think you're going?" He plants a kiss on my neck, and I laugh.

"I really need to pee."

He sighs. "I suppose I could let you go for a few minutes. But you'd better come straight back."

"Promise." I make my way through our home to the bathroom. The fire's died down from last night, and I might be naked, but I'm still warm from the memory of Corey loving me on the rug in front of the flames.

Even though I'm pregnant, nothing's killed the need we

have for each other. And our favourite place in this house has to be the spot right in front of the fireplace.

He's still been working away from home, sometimes for days at a time, but from now until after the baby's here he's grounded.

When I jump back into bed, his arms wrap around me in a bear hug. "You were gone way too long," he says, nuzzling my cheek.

"Sorry." I laugh.

"Let's just hibernate for a while. We'll stay here like this."

"The baby might have other ideas."

He places his hand gently on my baby bump. "Stay in there as long as you can. I need to have my wicked way with your mother so many more times before you're born."

"How many more times?" I stare at him.

He chuckles, returning to nuzzle my neck. To a lot of people, Corey is gruff and mean-looking. He doesn't suffer fools, and he's not afraid to speak his mind. I know he's all marshmallow inside.

He'll be a wonderful father.

"I know you don't want to get out of bed, but we have somewhere to be."

He sighs. "I know. I'll be in trouble if I stay here any longer. Lily will kill us if we're late."

I place my hand on his chest. "I'm sure we have enough time for you to have your wicked way with me."

Waggling his eyebrows, he plants kisses on my breasts before disappearing under the covers.

Life couldn't be any better.

"It's about time, you two." Lily looks up from the table. "We thought we'd do the barbecue for lunch and then leftovers for dinner. Just so we're not eating the same things three meals in a row."

"Good thinking." I loop my arm around Corey's waist.

"Well, with you and Ginny being pregnant too, I wanted to make sure we had freshly cooked food. No cold meat for you two."

"Thank you," I reply.

Corey pulls me in against him tight and plants a kiss on the top of my head. "Thanks for looking out for my girl."

I sigh with contentment, and Lily's eyebrows rise. She grins at me.

"Babe, is everything ready to go?" Adam places his hands on Lily's shoulders, and she tilts her head back to look at him. He bends to give her a kiss. "Barbecue's ready."

"The meat's on the middle shelf. There are plain steaks and some in the marinade you like."

"I'll give you hand." Corey pecks me on the head and follows his brother.

"Sit down, Constance. Take the weight off your feet," Lily says.

I sit at the table opposite her. "Where's everyone else?"

"Owen and Ginny aren't here yet. Hayley has a headache and is lying down in my room. Drew took the twins for a walk with Max and Rose."

"Nice and quiet for you, then."

She laughs. "It won't last. Did you enjoy yourself yesterday?"

"It was beautiful. I was tired, but just getting out of bed makes me tired these days."

Lily nods. "I was like that with Rose. It passed, but for a while it felt like it was going to go on forever. You'll have your baby before you know it."

"I can't wait."

Corey walks back into the kitchen, opens the fridge and grabs a big plate of meat. He shoots a wink at me, and all I can do is smile as he walks back out.

"Must be your turn next," Lily says. "Getting married, I mean."

I sigh. "One day."

"I'll make your dress."

"You'd do that for me?"

She smiles. "Of course I would. I know exactly what it's going to look like."

Laughing, I cock my head. "Do I get a say in any of this?"

"Nope."

After dinner, we make our way out to the ute. It's been a long, wonderful day with family—and they are my family now.

But there's nothing like going home.

I yawn as we reach the turn-off for the mountain, and glance sideways at Corey as he makes a left turn instead of right.

"Where are we going?"

He chuckles. "I've got a surprise for you."

The road turns to gravel, and I nearly fall asleep as we slowly make our way towards our mystery destination.

He nudges my arm. "Stay awake. You'll love this. I promise."

I stifle a yawn and nod.

We turn down a driveway which seems as long as the road was, but after what seems like forever, I see a farmhouse in the distance.

Corey pulls up outside the house and walks around the truck to help me out.

"What is this place?"

"You'll see." He knocks on the door, and a grey-haired man opens it.

"Dennis Neill?"

"That's me. You must be Corey Campbell."

Corey nods. "This is my partner, Constance."

Dennis nods. "Nice to meet the two of you. It's already dark out there, so I assume you just want to get down to business."

"Yes, please."

We step back as Dennis walks down out the front door and towards a large shed.

I nudge Corey's arm as we follow. "Business?"

He laughs. "I told you. Just you wait and see."

Inside the shed, there's a row of cages. The first one contains the skinniest sheep I think I've ever seen. I can't take my eyes from it.

Dennis stops at the third cage. "Here we go."

In the corner of the cage is a small dog. He's black and brown, a Huntaway puppy.

"A puppy?" I ask.

Corey nods. "He's a rescue dog. Dennis takes in rescue

animals from around here. They're usually neglected cows or sheep, but I heard that he had a special case."

Dennis clears his throat. "This little one was abandoned. But someone's hit him or something. He wavers between growling and cowering."

My heart melts at the thought. "Can I go in?"

"Sure." He opens the cage door, and I step through. Corey stands behind me.

"Hey, boy," I say softly, taking slow steps toward the dog.

A snarl comes from his throat.

When I reach him, I squat. The dog whimpers as I reach my hand out. I turn my hand palm up, and the sounds stop.

"It's okay," I whisper. I reach under his chin.

"Careful," Corey says.

"It's okay. You're not going to hurt me, are you?" My hand makes contact with the dog, and in response, he pulls back. "It'll just take some time to get him used to us."

"So, you're keen on taking him?" Dennis says.

"Yes." I look back over my shoulder toward Dennis and Corey.

Corey smiles.

I turn back when the warm, wet tongue of the puppy hits my hand. "Oh, look at you."

"He's a friendly wee thing while you're at his level," Dennis says.

"He's perfect." I reach out, scratching the top of his head.

"I'll go get the carrier out of the back of the ute."

I stand, turning to face Corey. "You've got it with you?"

He grins. "I know you. And this guy needs a loving home with someone who will understand him. I had to be ready to take him with us."

I fling my arms around his neck. "Thank you. I know this must be hard," I whisper.

"It's time for me to move on with my life. And if you bond with him the way I think you will, he'll protect you when I'm not around."

Tears roll down my cheeks at his thoughtfulness. We could have gone and got a puppy from a breeder, but he wanted to help this poor, abused little animal.

He kisses my temple. "I'll be back in a minute."

I nod as he lets me go.

"He likes you." Dennis nods toward the puppy, and I turn to see he's taken a tentative step toward me.

Just like that.

The puppy and I have a lot in common. He's acting how I did when I first arrived at Corey's place. I barked and snarled because I was scared, and I didn't know if I could trust him.

"We'll be fine. Won't we?" I say.

I place a hand on my stomach.

Our little family just grew.

We put the pet carrier in the bedroom for the night. There's no point in disrupting the puppy too much, and he seems happy enough with some food.

Corey takes him out to the back yard to go to the toilet before bed, but we place down extra towels on the base of the cage to take care of any mess. The most important thing is that the puppy feels safe and wanted.

"What are we going to call him?" I ask.

Corey shrugs. "I didn't even think about that."

"I think we should call him Cassius."

Corey looks at me quizzically. "Why?"

"He was one of Caesar's assassins. Along with Brutus."

Corey's face lights up. "That's warped, but I love it." He wraps his arms around my waist. "I also love living with a walking encyclopaedia. You're just full of useful trivia."

I laugh. "Well, growing up, I didn't have all the distractions of TV or a boyfriend."

"I think I like the 'no boyfriend' distraction the best." He nuzzles my neck and I sigh.

"Besides, Cassius starts with C, and that seems to be the trend in our family. Maybe we need to look at baby names beginning with C."

Corey laughs. "I think that's taking it a bit too far."

"He or she might feel left out if we don't."

Corey shakes his head. "Let's go to bed and get some sleep."

I look down at the puppy. Corey left the cage door open, but Cassius seems content to curl up in there.

"He'll be fine for the night. It won't take him long to be part of the furniture around here."

"I just hate that he was hurt."

Corey grasps my chin and pulls my gaze to his. "We've all been hurt, Con. But we're alive and together, and that's all that matters."

When he pulls me into his arms, I feel safe.

He's right.

Being alive and together *is* all that matters.

# ALSO BY WENDY SMITH

Coming Home

Doctor's Orders

Baker's Dozen

Hunter's Mark

Teacher's Pet

A Very Campbell Christmas

Fall and Rise Duet

Falling

Rising

Fall and Rise - The Complete Duet

The Aeon Series

Game On

Build a Nerd

Bar None

Coming soon Love on Site

Hollywood Kiwis Series

Common Ground

Even Ground

Under Ground

Rocky Ground

Coming soon Solid Ground

Stand alones

For the Love of Chloe

Coming soon Only Ever You

The Friends Duet

Loving Rowan

Three Days

The Forever Series

Something Real

The Right One

Unexpected

Chances Series

Another Chance

Taking Chances

Lifetime Series

In a Lifetime

In an Instant

In a Heartbeat

In the End

At the Start

# ABOUT THE AUTHOR

Wendy Smith published as Ariadne Wayne for three years before deciding she didn't want to be someone else all the time. Heavily influenced by stories in the media, she decided to try something new, and the Copper Creek series was born. With lots of love and a touch of darkness, her stories will twist their way into your heart.

*Find me online*
www.authorwendysmith.com
wendy@authorwendysmith.com

www.ingramcontent.com/pod-product-compliance
Lightning Source LLC
Chambersburg PA
CBHW022308310726
48973CB00001B/262